# Arresting Beauty

Heather Cooper grew up in a small village in northern Lancashire, and was educated at Lancaster Girls' Grammar School and the University of Durham. She also studied at the London College of Printing, and subsequently worked at the Westerham Press, Faber & Faber, and Eel Pie Publishing.

In 1981 Heather moved to the Isle of Wight, where her son and daughter were born. While living on the Island she has worked for the National Trust, in local government, and later in the NHS.

Heather's first novel, *Stealing Roses*, was published in 2019 by Allison and Busby. *Stealing Roses* and its sequel, *A Shape in the Moonlight*, have also been published in Germany by Goldmann. She contributed to *A Love Letter to Europe* published in 2019 by Coronet.

She now lives in Cowes with her partner.

# Arresting Beauty

Heather Cooper

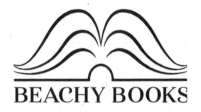

BEACHY BOOKS

First published by
Beachy Books in 2023
(an imprint of Beachy Books Limited)
www.beachybooks.com

1

A CIP catalogue record for this book is available from the
British Library.

ISBN: 978-1-913894-15-3

Also available in
Hardback ISBN: 978-1-913894-16-0
eBook ISBN: 978-1913894-17-7

Printed and Bound by
CPI Group (UK) Ltd, Croydon, CR0 4YY
Set in Sabon

*For Joshua and Rosalind*

# Acknowledgments

First—my undying admiration and thanks go to Dr Brian Hinton and the Julia Margaret Cameron Trust, the band of volunteers and enthusiasts who saved Dimbola from demolition and turned it into the inspiring museum and arts centre it is today.

Grateful thanks to my agent, Sarah Such, and to my publisher, Philip Bell, for their support and enthusiasm; to my friends and family; and as always to Terence for his unfailing encouragement and endless patience.

I would also like to thank my friend Kevin Hemmings, the descendant of William Hemmings, for his permission to imagine a character for his ancestor.

The following books have been invaluable in my research for this novel: *Immortal Faces* by Brian Hinton; *From Life* by Victoria C Olsen; *Julia Margaret Cameron* by Helmut Gernsheim; *Tennyson, The Unquiet Heart* by Robert Bernard Martin; *Julia Margaret Cameron* by Amanda Hopkinson; *Tennyson, to strive, to seek, to find* by John Batchelor.

*Arresting Beauty* is, however, a work of fiction, and any mistakes are my own.

# ARRESTING BEAUTY

*'I longed to arrest all beauty that came before me, and at
length the longing has been satisfied.'*

Julia Margaret Cameron in *Annals of My Glass House*

It's my wedding day, and Julia is taking my photograph.

The glass plate will be blank, at first. A transparent surface.
Even when the developing solution is poured over it, nothing
will change for a while. Then the faintest outline will start to
appear—a blur, a smudge—then a shoulder, a face, a hand. The
image of a ghost, with its white gown made dark and its dark
hair made white.

It is only when the printing is done, though, that the true
picture emerges. I thought it magical, at first, before I understood the process; and even then I always found it strangely
moving to see the faces of people I knew captured forever. The
line of a jaw, the set of the mouth, the gaze. A tangle of curls.
Light gleaming in eyes that one day would close forever. That
light will gleam still, on a rectangle of stiff paper, in shades of
dull brown, a hundred years hence. People will look into those

eyes. They might even look into my own eyes. I wonder what they will see.


Julia thought, when she took me in—rescued me, as she would put it—that I was a blank plate, on which she would develop something beautiful. I was a project, an enthusiasm, one among so many. She overflows with enthusiasms, with benevolence of a particular kind; she will be generous to you whether you wish it or not. I think even her closest friends find this peculiarly oppressive. 'Take this!' she cries, pressing on them things she has decided that they will like. 'Take this seed cake, this embroidered shawl, this piano! take this hideous plant, this volume of unintelligible poetry! take this life, because I have decided that it is exactly what you need, what you most desire!'

How could she know what life I most desired? How could I know myself? I was a child. I was ten years old. But I was not a blank sheet of glass; nor was I a clean page, waiting to be written upon. I was already there. It is just that she could not see me.

# 1

*You're a quick study, Mary Ryan.*

Mammy always said that. *You're a quick study.* Oh, she was
pleased with me when she realised how fast I learned! She didn't
even have to tell me what to do, for I had already listened and
observed her doing the things that meant we had something to
eat, and made the difference between sleeping under a hedge and
finding a bed. It's hard, though, for a woman, even a young and
pretty woman, to stay looking lovely when she has nothing to
eat but black bread and she drinks gin as though it were mother's
milk. Her looks were fading fast, even then, under a layer of grime
and weariness. But I'd seen how she bent her head and then lifted
her dark soulful eyes, and how the rich people were occasionally
moved by that look. I tried it out myself, and it worked.

I learned very quickly some subtle variations on this theme. For
a respectable middle-class woman, walking home from church,
perhaps, with her milk-faced daughters by her side, it was important not to be too Irish. If I changed my voice, sounded as though I
too was a respectable English girl—and I could do it, easy enough,
I was, as Mammy said, a quick study—if I looked modest, sweet,
gentle, they might think: there but for the grace of God. My state
was close enough to theirs for them to feel a little shudder of fear,
and a few pennies was a cheap enough offering to their vengeful
god. *And now abideth faith, hope, and charity, these three; but*

*the greatest of these is charity.* You could almost hear the words forming on their prim lips as they extended their fastidious little hands and dropped the coin into my grubby upturned palm.

The gentry, though; they were a different matter. They had no fear that they might ever find themselves sleeping in a ditch. We were a different race from them, altogether, on two counts: Irish, yes, but more significantly, poor. With them, the act had to be different. I had watched my mother often enough. Look at the woman first, then the man; dip your head, look up through your eyelashes. Twist a dark curl in your fingers as you gaze at them. You can be as Irish as you like, but whisper your words, make your voice a little low, let it come from the back of your throat. When they meet your eyes, let yourself smile, just a little, as though your smile was only for them. I could not have explained in words why I did all this, child that I was, but I knew it worked. Not every time, but more often than not. A man with his wife would bring out a coin, murmuring something about the deserving poor, and she would nod, and they would walk on as I scampered back to Mammy; but a man alone might give me silver, or even a sovereign. I would curtsey, peep up at him, smile again. If he put a finger under my chin, or tweaked my curls, I bore it, though I stepped away as soon as I could—still smiling, smiling, of course, lest he change his mind—but if he did more, if he placed a hand on my arm or on the back of my neck, Mammy was out from behind the trees like a jack rabbit, pulling me away, calling blessings on his head for a honest Christian gentleman, until the sovereign and I were safely out of reach.


When I saw Julia, I was flummoxed for a moment. I was used to knowing straight away how to categorise the people who strolled on Putney Heath. Clothes, voices, the way they walked, the way they looked about them. But this woman—well, she certainly sounded like the grandest of the grand; you could hear her voice a hundred yards off, it carried so. The gentry always speak as though they are shouting. It's so the servants can hear them from the next room, I suppose. Or the foreigners. But when she got closer, I was confused, for although she sounded so la-di-da I saw she looked like a washerwoman, short and dumpy and all fusty trailing shawls, and her dress, a sort of deep crimson with a faint stripe, was bit grubby round the hem, and with odd fringes tacked on here and there in a random fashion. Then I thought: perhaps she's an actress. That's good; actresses are not often wealthy, but they can be sentimental, given to warm impulsive gestures. That could include giving money to little Irish girls with big dark pleading eyes. The man at her side—much older than her, her father, perhaps—now he looked kind, with his crumpled face and soft eyes and his long snowy beard. She was talking away to the old man, gesturing so that her shawls were slipping off her shoulders. It seemed like a certainty.

Mammy gave me a hard pinch on my arm, the pinch she always gave me when we saw a likely-looking one, the pinch that meant *go on, Mary, off you go,* and I trotted forward, smoothing my ragged skirt, pushing my hair behind my shoulders, standing at the side of the path so that I was not obstructing them but they could not fail to see me. I put my head on one side, parted my lips, lowered my eyelids.

'Spare a coin,' I said, 'sweet lady, a coin?'

She stopped, mid-sentence. A shawl fell onto the muddy grass beside me, a patterned shawl of reds and golds, and I stooped to pick it up. I had never felt such a thing against my skin before; it was like holding the down of thistles, it weighed nothing and yet I could have wrapped my chilled shoulders in it and never felt cold again. When she reached for it I wanted to cling to it, but of course I could not. I smiled up at her, calculating that now she must give me something, for I had performed a service, and surely a shilling at least would come my way for that? The feel of the shawl had made me revise my first thoughts; she must be a toff after all, to have such a thing.

The old man was rootling in the pockets of his coat, and brought out a handful of change; it was coppers, I could see, but better than nothing. He tipped them into my hand, and I bobbed, and thanked him, and began to turn away.

'Wait!' she shouted, and she clutched at my arm. What now? Was she going to take the money back, while lecturing the poor old fellow on the inadvisability of giving to beggars, for it only encourages the poor and means they will never learn to shift for themselves? (I have heard that one often enough.) I sighed and began to draw the coins from my pocket, for I knew there was no point in running. They make a fuss, the crushers come, there are accusations and it ends with a night in a cell, and I tell you that even at ten years old I would rather have slept in a ditch than in a stinking freezing cage. Next thing Mammy was by my side, whining that we had not meant any offence, we had nothing to eat, and if the lovely lady and the kind gentleman could just see their way to helping a poor widow and her little child there would be blessings for them in heaven ... 'Beauty!' shouted the woman. 'Beauty! Look, my love, look!' (*My love?* Not her father, then. He must be twenty years older than she, but perhaps he is rich, I thought.) 'Look at this face; did you ever see such an angel?'

He nodded benignly. I tried to step back, but her fingers were gripping my arm quite painfully.

'Very pretty, indeed,' he said vaguely. 'Now, my dear, shall we get on? Tea will be on the table, I dare say, by now—'

She ignored him, and Mammy started up again. Yes, she had indeed been blessed with a beautiful little angel, and the lady was goodness itself to say so ... Mammy's words were, for once, quite lost, however.

'I must have this child! Yes, yes; look at her, those eyes! Oh, exquisite! You, my good woman, you are her mother, I suppose? Now let us talk; yes, you poor thing, you have fallen on hard times, I see, but beauty must not waste its sweetness on the desert air, and this child is a pearl from the dark unfathomed caves of ocean if ever I saw one ...'

Mammy had clearly met her match in terms of the gift of the gab she always claimed for herself, but she rallied now. She and Julia began to talk at each other, arms waving, eyes flashing, their voices trilling out over the heath so that other people strolling about turned to stare. There was nothing I could do, and at last I lost interest in following their discussion, or argument, or whatever it had turned into, and went to sit down upon a fallen log nearby. I pulled up some daisies and began to tear the petals off one by one. Eventually the old man, who had been standing helplessly by, his occasional bleat quite lost in the torrent of words, came to sit next to me on the log. It was quite peaceful, sitting there in silence, while the two women blathered on. I suppose he felt, after a while, that he should say something, and he asked me my name.

'Mary,' I said.

Silence fell again. I thought I should ask his.

'Charles.'

He got out a pipe and began to stuff it with tobacco. I went back to the daisies. I wondered if I would get anything to eat today, and my stomach growled at the thought. He fished a humbug from a waistcoat pocket, and offered it to me. It was a little furry, and with a few flakes of tobacco stuck to it, but beggars can't be choosers. They really can't. I took the humbug, and began to suck it very, very slowly, in case that was all I was to get. Still they talked, on and on, and I had let the last sweet sliver of hard sugar dissolve in my mouth by the time they turned and beckoned. We both got up, the old man and I, like two obedient servants and walked over to them. Mammy had a gleam in her eye like I had not seen for a long time.

'Now, Mary,' she said, 'this sainted lady is to take us in, and I am to work for her, and you will learn to be a maid in a grand house! Now what do you say to that?'

At least someone asked me what I thought, even if it were a purely rhetorical question. No one asked the old man, I noticed.

## 2

Of course before we were properly sure of our new and surprising good fortune, Mammy had to get a Character, for even Julia now and then took the trouble to make sure her servants were not likely to murder the entire household in their beds or run off with the silver. I could not see how Mammy was going to get one at all, seeing that she had not been in a position before, but she said that our priest would give her one, and to my surprise he did, not that we had ever been regulars at Mass, but then he was a forgiving sort which was his job after all.

The arrangement was, it seemed, that Mammy was to be a sort of assistant to the cook, cleaning vegetables, getting the water, scrubbing the table and the floor, lighting the stove, plucking the fowl, while I was to wear a white apron and learn from the parlourmaid so that in time I might graduate to being a parlourmaid myself. First, though, the order was that we must both take a bath, and there was a screen put up and the kitchen filled with steam as we poured the cans of hot water into the tub which had been dragged out and set in front of the fire. Mammy grumbled bitterly under her breath but she was still in a daze at our good fortune, so she went along with it. She got in first so by the time it was my turn the water was not so clean as it might have been, but I still liked the sinking into the warmth and the smell of the hard green soap. Mammy poured jugs of water through my hair until my head felt light and afterwards I let it dry before the fire, combing it out with my fingers, and it felt fine and silky, the dark strands curling down over my face and the fire giving them a touch of copper. All the time the cook was clattering about the other end of the kitchen and I could tell she was not happy at the intrusion into her domain. You would think she might be glad of two pairs of helping hands but she was muttering about Irish beggars and tinkers in a voice loud enough for us to hear quite clearly, so I think she wasn't as pleased as she might have been.

There was a bed placed in the corner of the kitchen, a real bed, with a sheet and a blanket, and underneath it a littler bed on wheels that drew out. The big bed was for Mammy and the little one for me. That first night I lay there and listened to the noises of this new place. I could hear Mammy snoring—that was quite usual—but there was no one else there, apart from the scratching and scrabbling of the mice and the rustle of the black beetles. No one groaned or cried or cursed. I thought of the bed I had slept in last night, if you could call it a bed, for it was just a heap of rags in the corner of an upstairs room in a lodging house, with a dozen other bodies all squeezed into the same room. There, Mammy had managed to get a place by the wall so no one would tread on us in the night, but it was under the window and the glass was broken so a cold draught always blew steadily on my shoulders, for Mammy would have the blanket and I couldn't get it off her.

I thought of that room and that bed, and of the things I had hidden in a corner beneath the rags, under a rotten floorboard. Somehow in the flurry of our new fortunes I had not managed to get them to bring with me, and now I turned them over in my mind. There was my doll (I had found her, thrown on a midden, her face cracked and one arm missing); a piece of dark blue velvet

18

I had once picked from a thorn; a white pebble with veins like marble. Most importantly, though, there were my books—my alphabet with pictures, and my book of rhymes. My father had taught me to read, and the books had been a gift to me from him, the only things I had. Now I hardly remembered him, but I wanted the books. I sat up, and Mammy stirred.

'What are you up to, Mary?' She was groggy, half-asleep.

'I'm going to get my things from the lodging,' I said.

'Don't be daft. There's nothing there.'

'I had a shilling,' I said. 'I left it under the bed.'

She was awake now.

'A shilling?' She thought for a moment. 'No, Mary, it's not worth going back for a shilling. That witch of a landlady will get you and we'll have to pay the rent, which we don't have, so we'd be worse off, now wouldn't we?'

'I won't let her catch me. It's the middle of the night.'

'Even so. Go back to sleep, now.'

I didn't want to go back to sleep. I wanted my things.

'There was bottle of the hard stuff, Mammy, with plenty left in,' I said.

I saw her eyes open wider, the red gleam of the kitchen stove in them. She liked gin well enough, and it was cheap; but the whiskey was what she liked best of all.

'There was. That's true. Get on then, but don't be getting caught.'

She was asleep again before I'd slid the bolt on the back door, and then I was out into the basement and up onto the street. I knew my way well enough, and it wasn't far across the corner of the heath and into the dark street behind the inn. There were no bolts on the doors of the lodging house. No one there had anything worth stealing. So I was in the back and up to the room, quiet as I could be, though no one there would have cared

19

or noticed, they were all sleeping like the dead or snuffling and groaning in some dark world of their own. Someone else was in our place under the window now, and I thought that after all I wouldn't be able to get to my hidden treasures; but then I saw it was only Billy.

Billy Hemmings, two years older than I, and my friend. He had been at the lodging house when we moved in, a month ago, and he had been the one to show us the best place to sleep, to tell me which of the men to keep away from, and where the landlady sometimes kept a bit of a pie or a piece of cheese you could get without being noticed. Billy was only there for a while, for he had grand schemes. He was going to travel to America and make his fortune, but for now he was making his plans, that was all. I whispered in his ear to wake him.

'Move over, will you, Billy. I need my things, and Mammy's bottle of whiskey.'

He was instantly awake.

'Where are you off to, then, Mary Ryan?' He was whispering too, so as not to wake the snoring heaps of animal that lay around the room.

'We've got a place. Mammy is to work in a big house, and I'm to be a maid when I've learned.'

'Are you now?' He sat up and let me reach for the doll and the books and my little purse with the pebble and the velvet and the shilling. 'Where is that, then?'

I told him.

'Are they hiring, then?'

'I don't know. Where's the whiskey, Billy?'

'Here.' He produced the bottle from his heap of rags.

'There's a lot less than there was.'

'I may have had a mouthful to keep the cold out, Mary. Your Mammy wouldn't grudge me, would she?'

'I won't tell her, in case she does. But we're not coming back here in any case. Not ever.'

Oh, it gave me such a warm feeling to say that. The truckle bed in the kitchen was already calling me. But I was sad to say goodbye to Billy. Suddenly I had an idea.

'Come tomorrow and if they are hiring maybe they'll take you too.'

He mulled this over. I took a sip of the hard stuff myself, while I waited.

'I don't know,' he said at last. 'I have plans. I haven't time to waste. Besides, I've not trained as a butler or some such. Not that I couldn't, if I wanted.'

The idea of twelve-year-old Billy as a butler struck me as not altogether likely. He was clever, of course, but still—

'You could be—' I tried to think of stories I had once heard from my father, of castles and kings and romances. 'You could be a page.'

'A what?'

'A page. They are boys who work for queens. They—they carry things, and wear nice clothes.'

'I could do that, right enough.'

'Well, you know where the house is, Ashburton, that great place with the fancy windows. Come tomorrow, Billy. The mistress is a bit crazy, but I think she's a good heart.'

'I might,' he said airily. 'And then again I might not.'

I would have started to try to persuade him, but just then an old boot sailed through the air towards us together with a curse and an instruction to shut our mouths, so we did, and I tiptoed out again with my treasures clutched in my old shawl. Back in the truckle bed, I tucked the books and the other things right under Mammy's bed where they could not be seen. She did not wake, and I was asleep soon enough myself, and before I knew it the morning had come, the first morning of my new life.

# 3

There was bread and milk for breakfast, soft bread, milk that was fresh. I ate as much as I thought I would be allowed and no more. Then it was into a dark dress and a white apron and I set off to follow Eliza the parlourmaid about, carrying a duster, trying to do as she did and smooth the lovely shiny furniture down, which was hard as every table and chair was piled with books and papers and letters; and then there were mirrors with curly-sided frames and endless ornaments, vases and carved elephants and figures with too many arms, and I was in terror lest I broke something, but Eliza was kind and showed me how to steady them with one hand and dust them with the other, and she said the odd speck hardly mattered for the mistress here was not too hard on things like that. There was so much to look at, what with the elephants and the silk cushions and the pictures everywhere, and all the time I was feeling not like myself at all, with my skin and hair all clean and the touch of the new dress—an old one of Eliza's and much too big for me—and the apron was starched so it made little creaking noises when I moved. It was all so new that I was tired by the middle of the morning, as tired as though it was evening, but Eliza took me back to the kitchen for a cup of tea and she begged the cook for a buttered muffin and shared it with me, so I was made up, and beginning to think we had fallen on our feet for sure.

Mammy, though, did not look as happy as I thought she would. The cook was called Mrs Lyle and she came from the far north-east of England and already she had a cross way of looking at Mammy and she was slamming the cups and pans about which sounded angry without her having to say a word. The truth was, I knew, that Mammy thought she was too good to be a servant, even though we had been reduced to begging, for in Limerick she had been the daughter of a farmer, a tenant farmer, it's true, but a hard-working man, and when she had married my father from the farm next door that was a step up, for he had been to school and could read and do the accounts. They were set for a steady life in that rich country, with the soft rain on the green fields, and they had a house they were making into a fine home, the house where I was born. They had whitened the walls and got curtains for the windows, Mammy said, they had a grand field of potatoes and a pig, and they were talking of a house cow too. Much good my father's book-learning did him, however, for the Famine took all that away, and my mother blamed the English for that all her life; the food had all gone across the sea, she said, even when Irish folk were dying for want of bread.

Well, the landlord cleared them out. There was nothing for them in Ireland, nothing for anyone except the rich, so they took me—I was just a little child then—and they travelled on the boat to England, where they had heard that my father could get a job working on the railway. Mammy said that he held me up over the ship's rail so I could see the last of Ireland as we sailed away. We got to Liverpool and then to London, and he did get work, carving out the new iron roads that were branching off in every direction. We lived in a poor way but we had food, food better than a black rotting potato at least. I don't recall much of that time, but I know we would sit by a little fire in the evenings and my father would read to me from the handful of books he

24

had brought from Ireland, and he would tell me tales of the old country, of the Little People and the Banshee, pots of gold and faerie cats. I cannot recall his face now, but I can hear his voice, now and then, deep and warm, and I can feel the hard muscle of his arm around me as I leant against him. I wish that I had a photograph of him; but photography was hardly heard of then, and certainly not for the likes of us.

Julia could have made a portrait of my father, if she had ever known him. She likes photographing the peasantry, as she calls them. She might have dressed him up as an Irish chieftain, perhaps, or a mighty hunter. Julia could have made James Ryan into Finn MacCool, for sure.


I call her Julia, in my thoughts; but I have never called her that to her face. Naturally not. For a while I called her nothing at all, for I still had not worked out which voice and manner would work best for this strange woman, this fairy godmother, this witch, who had plucked Mammy and me from the gutters of Putney and installed us in a real house, a grand one, where we could sleep in the warm dark kitchen and eat three times a day, so whenever I saw her I just kept quiet and bobbed my head, which seemed safest. Then Eliza told me that *Madam* was the proper address, and that I might shorten it to *Ma'am*, and I began to use that, and for years that is what I called her. But her friends and family call her Julia, or Aunt Julia, or Mama, or (out of her hearing) *that impossible woman*. Now I call her Mrs Cameron. The words still feel strange in my mouth.

That first day, though, I was still silent and wary. I had got through the morning, and Eliza was showing me how to set the table for luncheon, putting the heavy silver forks and knives in the right places and folding the big starched napkins just so, when the doorbell chimed. It was Eliza's job to answer it, so off she went leaving me in the dining room, but it opened off the hall so I could hear what was happening, and floating out clear as a bell came Billy Hemmings's voice. My heart lifted when I heard it, for I had thought he might have decided to go to America after all and that I would never see him again, so I sidled up to the door and listened. He was giving Eliza a bit of soft talk, and although he was only a lad he was already tall, and he had the dark hair and blue eyes that made Mammy say that Billy might have been from Ireland himself, with his handsome looks and his way of talking so smooth, so Eliza did not shoo him away as I feared she might, and at last she said she would get the mistress. I don't think Billy was from Ireland at all; he had told me he came from Roehampton, but he said perhaps his ancestors might have been kings of Ireland and for all I knew he was right.

When Eliza came back into the room she did not scold me for standing by the door listening instead of dusting, she just winked and stood next to me so we could both hear Billy talking. I peeped through the crack between the door and its hinges, and I could just see Julia—today she was wearing a purple dress which looked like it had been made from old curtains. I wondered what Billy would make of her. There were some respectful good mornings and politeness, and then he told her that he had come to see if she needed a page, and at that I blushed because I had only said he might be a page in a fanciful way, not dreaming he would actually use the idea, and I thought she would laugh at him and send him away; but she did not, she gave one of her shrieks like she was always doing when she was struck with a new and wonderful idea, which to be fair was about twenty times a day but her enthusiasms never seemed diminished by their frequency.

'A page!' she cried. 'Young man, you must have been sent by Providence, for how else could it be that my wants were divined before I knew them myself?' (Hearing this, I felt rather important, for since it was I who had brought Billy to her door, this surely put me on a level with Providence.) 'Of course I must have a page—for my own grandpapa, you see, was a page, a page at the French court—he danced once with the Queen of France—yes, these very hands, you see, have touched the hands that touched the hands of Marie Antoinette—' and after a great deal more exclaiming and explaining and delighting in whose hands had touched whose, she asked him if he could supply a Character, and bold as brass he said that Mrs Ryan would give him a Character, as though my mother was a respectable source of a reference. Julia, however, seemed to see nothing strange in this, and the long and the short of it was that Billy Hemmings was instantly hired to be a page to the Camerons, and a tiny room up in the attic that had been hitherto full of trunks and boxes was cleared for him to sleep in. The consequence was that the trunks stayed in the attic corridor all the time the Camerons lived in Putney, and Mrs. Lyle the cook and Hilda the lady's maid grumbled about the trunks every day even though they very quickly took to Billy, and somehow I felt they blamed Mammy and me because if we hadn't already been sleeping in the kitchen Billy might have slept there, so it was our fault really, as most things seemed to be in the eyes of Mrs Lyle and Hilda. I didn't argue with them over the trunks, however, for more than anything I wanted Billy to stay; while Billy was in the house I had a friend, and that was far more important than the black looks from the cook or Hilda's way of sniffing whenever she caught sight of me, as though something nasty had gone up that long nose of hers. Mammy didn't see things quite the same way, however; she didn't like the way Mrs Lyle and Hilda were with her, and she was very ready to answer back when there was a sly comment or a cross word, and often even before the cross word was uttered she was ready to get her retaliation in first, for she had always a fiery way with her; and I believe that was the beginning of why things went the way they did, and why as Julia grew larger in my life Mammy grew smaller and at last she disappeared altogether.

# 4

Julia had some children. There were older ones, a daughter who was married, and sons who were grown, or nearly grown, away at school or university, but the youngest, Charlie and Hal, lived at home and had a tutor who came in every day. Charlie was my age, and Hal three years younger. The tutor gave them lessons in a parlour at the back of the house, and I was interested to hear what was going on, so I persuaded Eliza to let me do the dusting and sweeping in that parlour every morning. I was supposed to do it first thing, before the lessons started, but I managed to find reasons to go back into the room while the lessons were happening. The tutor never noticed me, for servants are invisible to some people and he was one of them. I was just a rustling and a scraping in the grate, or a shadow by the wall. Hal and Charlie noticed me, though, and they used to make faces and I would make a face back, and I might say mine were a lot scarier than theirs and I made them laugh so that they got a sharp rap from a ruler once or twice.

Every time I got into their lessons I listened hard because I was greedy to know what it was they were studying. I had read my own books a thousand times, and I had managed to get a few of the books that always lay around Julia's house and read them too when I though no one would find me out, but I had to do it secretly, and I felt quite bitter when I realised that these spoilt boys were allowed to just sit in a lovely room and have someone to read to them and tell them and show them so many extraordinary things, maps of distant countries with great rivers and mountains and cities, histories of people who lived centuries ago and spoke in languages whose letters even looked different, stories of mythical creatures with three heads and goddesses who walked the earth. I held all the words that tutor spoke in my head, as though I was a bowl full to the brim with some precious liquor, and I kept them there until I was back in my truckle bed at night and then I rehearsed them over to myself so that I would not forget them. Now and then the boys would leave their lesson books about and I would get to look into them and sometimes I borrowed them when no one was looking and I could see where they had gone wrong. Once I got a pencil too and corrected all Charlie's mistakes for him but I don't think he even noticed.

Of course I was caught in the end. I had gone into the school-room parlour after the day's lessons were over because I had been told to get the curtains down for washing. It was hard because I had to stand on a stepladder and take every one of the brass hooks out of its curtain ring while holding up the rest of the thick dusty velvet with my other arm and trying not to overbalance. After a while my arms were aching so badly that they were trembling and my knees were shaking too and the dust had got up my nose and into my throat, and I thought I would just take five minutes to sit down and look at one of the books on the tutor's desk. It was a book of poems he had been reading to the boys that morning and I wanted to find out more about it, and I took the book and sat on the floor and started reading and those words took me away to somewhere else. They were more than words—they were music and pictures too, full of colours and sounds and feelings, and they thrilled me as though I had opened a window and breathed something new that was better than ordinary air. *Silver, snarling trumpets*, I read—*the tiger-moth's deep-damasked wings—rose-bloom—soft amethyst—the poppied warmth of sleep*—and I liked those words so much that I must have begun to say them out loud. *Candied apple, lucent syrups*, I was murmuring, *from silken Samarkand to cedared Lebanon*, when all at once there was a shriek (of course) and Julia was standing over me with her hands on her wide hips and her square face looming over me.

Instantly I thought I had ruined everything, that I had brought disaster back upon Mammy and myself. I thought I had wrecked our new safe warm lives, that we would be thrown out back onto Putney Heath and be cold for ever and always hungry. I stared up at Julia with panic racing through my blood and wondered what I could say or do to make her give us another chance. I scrambled to my feet and I began to say that I was sorry, that I would never read another book, that I would work late into the evenings and get the curtains down and wash them myself, but she wasn't listening.

'Oh, Mary!' she cried, flapping her shawls about, 'you can read, you have a feeling for words, for poetry, I can hear it! Now leave those curtains and read to me, read the verses you have just spoken, read on!'

I sank back to the floor again, not sure if I was abandoned or saved, and I read as well as I could all about St Agnes' moon and Porphyro like a throbbing star and his Madeline with her voluptuous accents. I dare say my voice wobbled a bit to begin with, but after a while I almost forgot everything but the magic of those words. Julia sat down on one of the schoolroom chairs and listened, she really listened to me, reciting the words silently with her mouth as I went on, giving little sighs and gasps now and then, and at the end of the poem she said that I was a wonder and that I must have lessons with her boys every day. I should

31

have books of my own and paper and pencils and learn poetry and Latin and mathematics and all about the world.

It was too much to take in. I thought perhaps I should kneel or curtsey but then I was already sitting on the floor so instead I just clasped my hands together and bowed my head as though I was in church, and for that moment I actually believed Julia might be a saint.

I was to do lessons in the morning and then do my work as the under-parlourmaid in the afternoons. Julia didn't seem to think there would be anything odd in this, but everyone else did. Charlie and Henry minded least, perhaps, although they protested a bit and said that girls didn't learn things like mathematics and why did their mama not just let me have lessons in sewing? At that Julia got almost cross with them and said that she did not want to hear that sort of talk because women were as good as men and often better, so the boys had to bite their lips though they both made faces at me for that.

Mammy was half-pleased, I think, and half-cross. *My little girl is a good as these fine folk any day,* she said to Mrs Lyle, *as clever as a bagful of monkeys, so she is;* but when we were alone she told me not to get ideas above my station. *That was my undoing, Mary,* she said. *I thought I was something grand and that sort of thinking only leads to disappointment. You'll do better knowing your place in this world.* Hilda sniffed harder than ever whenever she looked at me; Mrs Lyle clattered the pans about in a pointed manner whenever I was in the kitchen; Eliza, who had always been so nice to me, got a bit sulky, and said that she wasn't planning to be in service for long because she had a young man and they would be married soon, so she for one wouldn't be needing fancy book-learning. Even Billy teased me a bit, making exaggerated bows whenever he saw me and pressing his face against the window of the schoolroom parlour when the tutor wasn't looking to try to make me laugh; and I was dead on my feet half the time, because of having to do the parlour-maiding in the afternoons as well as trying to read all my lessons over by the kitchen firelight at night when Mammy was asleep.

So all in all it wasn't the unmixed blessing that Julia thought it, to give me a chance to be educated. Nevertheless I held onto it fast and ignored the looks and comments as well as I could, for I had found new worlds in the books and the maps and the ideas I first discovered in that back parlour in the house in Putney, and I still have those worlds and I shall always have them whatever else befalls me.

## 5

I think that Mr Cameron truly was a saint. Not a saint like Saint Sebastian who was shot full of arrows, or the blessed Saint Thomas à Becket hacked to death before the altar (even though Mr Cameron did look like Moses or even the Almighty himself with that long white beard) but a saint nonetheless for I never saw him cross whatever Julia did. She invited constant streams of people to luncheon and tea and dinner, to poetry recitals and amateur dramatics and musical evenings, although I quickly saw that Mr Cameron would have preferred a quiet life. She pressed gifts on everyone she knew, quite indiscriminately, whether the recipient was likely to want them or not, seizing random possessions from the house to distribute as largesse, not caring if she might be giving away something her poor husband might actually have liked to keep, like his books or his pipes or mementoes from his travels. She lectured their friends and acquaintances, she dictated to them and bullied them and said things that were at the best candid and often frankly caustic. Yet even when she had been at her most outrageous, with her mad dresses and her screams and her enthusiasms and her remarks of the most personal kind, the only thing I ever heard him say was *I do not think it quite answers Julia to throw a bombshell into the lap of society*. Even then all she did was give one of her shrieks and tousle his beard and laugh and then announce that she had invited sixteen people to dine that evening, all of whom were artists and geniuses and simply divine and that she was going to serve them all with mock turtle soup and roast veal and calves' foot jelly so as to use both ends of the animal as well as the bits in between and then she would make them listen to her reading very long poems written by one of her many friends who was a Great Poet.

Saint though he might have been, however, Mr Cameron stood firm against his wife on one point; he was determined to go away. It seemed that all the money they had, the money for the house and the furniture and the curtains and the servants and the carriage and the horses and the clothes and the books and all the lovely lovely food that they seemed to take for granted, came because Mr Cameron grew coffee in Ceylon and he was not happy in Putney and he wanted to go back to his coffee. He told me about Ceylon, when he was poorly and had taken to his bed as he often did, to get a bit of peace I should think, and it was my job as under-parlourmaid, as I now was, to take him the food and medicine that Julia insisted he must have six or seven times a day whenever he was ill (beef tea with arrow-root, gravy soup, creosote zinc, mulligatawny, quinine, curry, poached eggs, gum arabic, and great quantities of port wine).

'It's beautiful there, Mary,' he said. 'The coffee trees have red berries and dark glossy leaves, and before that there are creamy flowers that smell like incense. There are birds that call among the trees, birds with emerald feathers or scarlet or turquoise. The sunsets are all red and gold and the hills are blue.'

I closed my eyes for a moment so that I might see this better, being careful, though, not to spill the gravy soup and the port wine that I was carrying on a silver tray.

'I would like to see that,' I said. 'Is it far?'

'Far, far away,' he said. 'Many days and weeks on board a ship. I may die before I return there.' He looked mournful. 'It is my spiritual home, you see, my true home, and my wish has always been to be buried there.'

Of course at that age I thought it very likely that he might die at any moment, for he seemed to me as old as Methuselah, and I thought it very sad that he was not to be buried where he wanted to be.

'You could be taken there after you die,' I said helpfully. 'In a coffin on the ship, and then you could be buried there after all. Or if you live, you could take a coffin with you, in case you were to die on the way.'

He nodded thoughtfully.

'That's an idea, Mary,' he said. 'Now take the nasty soup away, there's a good girl, but leave me the port wine.'

He did recover from that illness, and as soon as he was well, he began to say again that he must go back to Ceylon. There had been a letter saying that the coffee crop was faring badly, and he had made up his mind. I thought he would never be allowed, for Julia wept and wailed and lamented but it was no use, for beneath the saintliness of Mr Cameron was just a little bit of hard steel and at last he packed up and went. Well, it was Julia who packed for him—trunks and trunks full of flannel waistcoats and handkerchiefs and special mixtures for his health—and she did truly miss him when he went away, for she hated to be alone, and being in a house full of servants and children did not count in her eyes. As soon as he was away she started to fasten upon her friends with still greater fervour, sending them presents and making them come to visit and showering them with such ferocious affection that they mostly gave in through sheer exhaustion. After a few months, though, she decided that she could not bear the loneliness any longer, and to make it all worse the friends she loved most, her Great Poet Mr Tennyson and his rather delicate wife, were also living over the sea. They were not as far though as her husband, and she went off to visit them for a week or so, giving us all a bit of space to breathe; but when she came back it was all shrieks and excitement again and even more so this time, for she had hit upon a plan to follow them and live near them. She had already seen a cottage there which she would buy, where life would be lived in purity and simplicity, and she sprang this news upon the household and then within weeks we were all packing up and preparing to move. For a while Mammy and I thought we were heading back to the old country but we had misheard, for Julia had not said Ireland but The Island, which turned out to be the Isle of Wight.

As the day grew nearer when we would leave Putney I became excited, for it seemed like a great adventure to be going somewhere over the seas with Mammy and Billy. Mammy, though, was not excited, she was downcast and morose, and began to say that she would not go to wherever this Island was, for she had had enough of Hilda and Mrs Lyle and their grumbling and flouncing; and she even began to say that she missed the old lodging house where people were a bit more convivial of an evening and she had been able to have a quiet drink without people making *tut-tut-tut* noises just because a woman took a nip of the hard stuff to keep her spirits up. They drank enough upstairs, she pointed out, so why was it so wrong for the servants to follow the example of their so-called betters?

'We were well enough as we were, Mary,' she said to me, the night before the great removal, as we lay in our narrow beds in the warm dark kitchen with the black beetles rustling over the floor. 'Here it's do this and don't do that and know your place and the need to be grateful all the time.'

'We have enough to eat, Mammy, here, and somewhere to sleep. And clean clothes. And baths.'

'We're servants, though, Mary. Nothing but servants, and a servant is next door to a slave. Is it worth it?'

I thought it was, on balance; but it seemed that Mammy did not, for when I woke the next morning she had gone. There was no note, for she could not write, but she had left a red hair-ribbon for me, at the end of my bed, and I supposed that was a sort of goodbye, even though I knew she had stolen it from Hilda and I could not wear it for that reason. I was in a dilemma now, for in the bustle of departure no one seemed to notice that Mammy was missing, or if they did they didn't care, and I was afraid that if I said anything I might be left behind as well. I managed to find Billy and ask him what he thought I should do.

'Don't say anything, Mary,' he said. 'Once we get to this Island they won't be able to send you back. After all, your Ma knows where we're going, and when she wants to join you she will. She won't be long, Mary, she's probably just saying goodbye to old friends, or she needs a bit of time to herself.'

'That will be it,' I said, 'she will come and find me when she's ready, won't she?'

'She will, of course; and until then I'll look after you.'

I felt better when Billy said this, for although he was only two years older than I he seemed to know a good deal more about the world, and anyway he was still saying that one day soon he would be going to America to make his fortune, and I rather hoped that when that day came he might take me with him.

38

It must have been a sight to see when the entire household set off in a carriage and various hired traps for the railway station. Julia did not believe in travelling light, and there were trunks of dresses and shawls and cloaks, hat boxes and shoe boxes, crates of books, leather cases for jewels, and bags full of lace and feathers and artificial flowers and scarves and all the other frills and furbelows she liked to ornament herself and her friends and her house with; and that was just for her. Her boys had plenty of clothes and toys and books of their own, and the upper servants had a fair amount themselves. The furniture and the china and the linen all went separately by carrier but there was plenty to take with us, including the bits that had somehow been overlooked but that Julia decided at the last minute she could not do without so were shoved into paper packages and tied with string or thrust into old laundry bags and hung on the side of the traps. We must have looked like a gypsy caravan, and interested groups of people gathered in the streets to look at us. I kept turning back to see if perhaps Mammy had changed her mind and decided to come with us after all, but there was no sign of her. Billy noticed, I think, for he tried to distract me by talking about the trains. He claimed he had once travelled on one, whereas I had only seen the plumes of steam in the distance and heard the thunder and the screech of them. When at last we arrived at the station I had never seen so many people all in one place and my neck began to hurt from looking up at the great high roof all made of iron and glass; and then I saw the locomotive itself, a beautiful enormous dark red machine with shining black wheels, and the strong steel pistons, and the steam coming from its chimney in white puffs with a noise as though it were a dragon breathing.

There was a deal of kerfuffle with finding enough porters to load all the baggage off the traps and into the guard's van, with Julia shouting orders and causing a scene when a case was dropped and a swathe of embroidered shawls fell onto the platform but at last it was done. Julia and the boys were travelling first class, of course, and Hilda got to travel with them. Lady's maids think they are next door to a lady themselves and I don't mean one step along the landing. It annoyed me, seeing Hilda stick her long nose up in the air as she hurried after Julia carrying the jewel cases and looking so important. Still, our third-class carriage was exciting enough, with the step so high up I had to scramble to get in, and its wooden seats and a leather strap to pull the windows up and down; and there was roaring from the engine, and shouts and clattering from the platform, and then a long piercing whistle, and at last the whole train gave a tremble and a jolt and we began to move, slowly at first, with a cloud of white steam all about us and coming in the windows to make us cough, and then we moved faster and the steam rose and cleared and we were leaving the station and I could see the backs of rows and rows of houses and feel the thudding of the wheels beneath us, and then we were dashing, speeding, flying, with the houses and fields streaming away in a blur behind.

And so I made my first railway journey, and I loved it, and I have loved the railway ever since. It will always mean something magical to me, to enter a railway station and smell the coal and the smoke, to stand on the long platform and see the huge locomotives waiting like mythical creatures that have been tamed to do our bidding, to climb that high step up into a carriage and find a seat, to hear the whistle blow, to feel the first shudder as the train begins to move, and to look through the window at the world rushing by and see the long shining rails stretching out ahead of me, taking me away, taking me to somewhere new.

# 6

I had no memory of the sea; none that I could bring to mind. I was looking out of the carriage window for all the many miles of that journey, at the fields and the trees, the towns and villages, at all the stations and the coming and going of the people on every platform; but what I was looking for most of all was the sea. We had changed trains at Brockenhurst and after that the country was rather flat and full of gorse blossom and tall trees, and before I knew it the train was slowing and I was out on the platform and there was a smell of salt and tar and a breeze coming from up ahead, and there it was, the sea, rather grey that day, a dull grey like pewter with little waves chopping at the dockside. We got ourselves and all the luggage off the train, every porter in Lymington, I think, struggling with it while Julia flapped on gaily ahead, her shawls flying out behind her as she marched up the gangplank of the steamer boat which was to take us to this Island she was so crazy about. The boat looked a bit small in my view to be taking a crowd of passengers plus all those trunks and cases across a wide chilly expanse of water, although I said nothing, but once we were on deck I held the rail very tight. It was cold and greasy beneath my hands but I did not let go, and when the boat began to roll and dip I held even tighter.

'This is an adventure, eh, Mary Ryan?' said Billy. He looked pretty much at ease, although I noticed he was holding on to the rail too. I was glad Billy was there, but I wished at that moment that Mammy had been with us too.

*When we left the old country, your father held you up over the ship's rail so you could see the last of Ireland*, said my mother's voice in my ear. I liked to hear her voice even though she wasn't there. I imagined my father's hands around my waist, lifting me up, and I wished I could remember that last look.

'It is indeed, Billy,' I said. 'And good practice for America, I should say, crossing the sea on a ship and trying out a new place.'

Billy agreed that it was, and then we both turned towards the front of the steamer and set our faces forward to watch the long misty strip of land getting closer.


This island was a very different place from Putney. I stepped off the steamer, my legs a little wobbly now because of the rolling about on the water, onto the stone harbour wall of a town so small it was barely a village, despite having a castle and a church. The whole place could have got itself lost in the back streets of London and no one would have noticed. There was the usual drama of getting the family and the servants and everything else into the transport which was one half-respectable fly and a couple of farm carts which did not normally see service as a baggage train for a strange bohemian lady and her entourage and were hung about with straw and worse. Still at last we were loaded up and off we set, over a bridge and up a hill, and everything looked wild and untamed, with only a few low cottages set about here and there, no proper streets or gaslights, and hardly any people either, and by then night was falling for we had travelled all day and I felt a shiver of fear at being in this dark strange country and I wished again that Mammy were here. I leant my shoulder against Billy's and that gave me a bit of comfort and I wondered if he were feeling frightened too but being Billy he just winked at me and whistled a bit of a tune to keep our spirits up. It seemed a long journey that first evening, which I laugh at now for it was only over the hill from Yarmouth to Freshwater which is hardly any distance at all.

By the time we reached the place where we were all to live it was too dark to see much at all, and I was tired beyond anything and hardly able to keep my eyes open. There was a house which looked more than a cottage to me, despite what Julia had said about living a life of simplicity, and I had to help lug boxes and bags from the carts and carry them into the house which felt cold and damp as though no one had lived there for a good long time and everywhere smelled of fish. At last someone shooed me up some stairs and then up more steps, narrow rickety ones, and into an attic room and I lay down just as I was on the dusty wooden floor and slept.


The sun was what woke me the next morning. There was a little window in the slope of the roof and through it came a beam of light with dust swirling in it like motes of gold. I got to my feet, stiff and cold from my night on the floor, and went to look out. I could see fields sloping down towards a bay, a curve of shingle and tall rocks rising from the water, and the waves coming in, white foam on the crest of each that broke as it reached the shore; and the sea was dark blue and bits of light were glittering on it so that I was almost dazzled as I looked. I gazed and gazed at the sight, and I thought that as soon as I could I would get down to that bay and take off my shoes and put my feet in the blue shining sea and feel the rush of the waves.

Of course in that moment there came the first sounds of the household waking and pretty soon there was a shout for me and

I was to get to the kitchen and take hot water upstairs for the family to wash, and after that it was the usual treadmill of the servants' day, made strange by the fact that we were all somewhere new. Billy, whose lodging was over the stables at the back of the house, was sent out to purchase carbolic soap and vinegar and new dusters and we were all set to clean the house up while Julia dashed about shrieking about the beauty of the place though if it had been she who had been scrubbing the fish-smelling floors and hoicking the thick black cobwebs down from the corners and sweeping the soot and the feathers of dead birds from every fireplace she might have been a little less enthusiastic. This went on for days while she drove us all mad changing her mind about where the furniture was to go and putting things on tables that had still to be moved and unpacking books and trinkets before there was a space for them to go. I worked as hard as I could, we all did, and at last the house began to look more like a place you could live in and less like a shabby warehouse that had been hit by a train.

It was a pretty house, really. It was called Sunnyside and that was a good name, I thought, for the sun seemed to be shining there more often than not. It had tall pointed gables and was draped with ivy and roses so there was something of the fairytale about it. Like something in a story, too, there was another house just like it standing next door as though perhaps Hansel had lived in one and Gretel in the other. The two houses stood looking down towards the bay, with high green hills rising up all around it and along from the bay there were white cliffs and more hills. There was a large building which was a hotel over at the foot of the western slope, and more houses along the lane from ours, and a straggle of cottages round about, and a row of shops, and an inn or two. Behind the houses were gardens and then woods, and all in all it was a bonny place to live, peaceful and open, and always with the sea shining just down the road. Billy grumbled that it was too quiet, and I did know what he meant; at night there was no noise at all but the distant murmur of the sea and the melancholy call of owls. He said he missed the sounds of London, the rattle of wheels on cobbles and the shouts of people turning out of the public houses and the odd brawl in the street, but I found I could do without those well enough.

Billy had taken very swiftly to his place in the Cameron household. Being Billy he had somehow managed to turn his role into the sort of thing he liked best while still making people believe he was working hard. Julia liked to call him her page, and he had a nice suit of clothes and a pair of shoes with silver buckles so that he looked the part, and he had got very good at opening the door to visitors and bowing politely and carrying things about for Julia, but that was hardly a full-time job. So when he wasn't doing that he would go to the stables; he liked horses, and he was good with them, he could whisper to them and soothe them and he got very quick at harnessing a carriage horse and then pretty soon he was driving the trap for Julia whenever she wanted to be taken about. The joy of this arrangement was that when he wasn't in the house charming Julia and her guests they all thought he was working with the horses, and when he wasn't in the stables the head groom thought he must be working in the house, so half the time I should say he was doing a spot of fishing down by the bay, or talking to the pretty girls in the village, or was up on the downs lying on the grass gazing up at the sky and smoking tobacco that one of Julia's visitors had carelessly left about for him to find.

I envied Billy his times of freedom and sometimes I could not help thinking he was a good deal luckier than I, but I did not tell him that because I was so glad to have him there. I missed Mammy, and this new place was strange and a long way from wherever she might be now; and although Mrs Lyle and Hilda had travelled down to this Island, Eliza had not come with us, for she was to be married to her young man and did not fancy the journey in any case, and she had been the only one of the servants in Putney who had been kind to me, and things did not look much more promising here. (I did not count Billy; he was always kind, always my friend, and in any case I never thought of Billy as a servant, somehow.) You might think that this feeling would have made me more anxious to be accepted by the other servants, and might have made me try to please them and get into their good books, but it did not. Instead I grew more determined to stand on my own two feet and not to try to be part of their closed little world; and I had only been on the Island for a short while when I decided to change the way I spoke.

I had learned fast enough, when Mammy and I were walking Putney Heath, that I could switch my voice from very Irish to a little bit Irish to hardly Irish at all, depending on which was likely to be most profitable at the time. When we went to live with Julia I had settled for a little bit Irish, and maybe I had begun to pick up a bit of the London sound from Billy. But when we got to the Isle of Wight new servants were hired; a parlourmaid called Louisa, to replace Eliza, and a gardener and a kitchen maid, and they were all from Freshwater where Julia's house was. They tended to stare at me and ask where I was from with my strange way of talking, and I might have asked the same of them, because to me they sounded foreign with the way they stretched out their o's and a's and said their words in a slow burr. I kept my mouth shut for a while, and thought about this, for I needed to show them that I was not a wicked Irish tinker which is what Mrs Lyle was quite likely to tell them all if I let her.

I could have mimicked any of their accents easy enough if I'd wanted; but I didn't want. One morning I got up and I decided that I wouldn't be Irish any more, nor would I be London, and I certainly would not be Freshwater. So I started to speak just as Hal and Charlie did, as Julia did, as all the gentry did. It wasn't hard. *You're a quick study, Mary Ryan,* said Mammy invisibly in my ear.

The funny thing was that while all the other servants remarked on the change, Julia and her family never noticed at all. I suppose I was just talking in their language now, the easiest language for them to understand, and I sounded normal, whereas to the the others I sounded foreign again. I came in for a bit of teasing, some mild and some spiteful. *Aren't you afternoonified now?* said Billy. *Ooh, Lady Muck,* said Hilda. But I stuck to it and after a while it became so natural that I didn't think about it at all, and I supposed that everyone else got used to it soon enough.

# 7

It soon transpired that Julia, being Julia, wasn't content with doing anything as ordinary as just buying a house and living in it. From the first day she had her eye on the house next door. It was lived in by a nice old fisherman called Mr Long, who had built both houses and when he'd sold Sunnyside to Julia he had moved into the other one. She started on at him to sell that one to her as well, and after a while like everyone else she'd ever met she wore him down and then she had two matching houses. To tell the truth it had been a little crowded in Sunnyside and having the new house did mean there was more room all round although of course for us servants there was also more to clean and more fires to light and when it was raining, as it did now and then even on the Isle of Wight, we had to scamper through the weather from one house to another. Julia said she was going to build a bit in the middle to connect the two houses and eventually she did, a tower with a glorious high window looking out to sea; but for now it was two houses, built just the same but with the rooms laid out the other way about as though someone had held up a looking glass and you could step through into a perfect mirror image of the house you had just left.

\* \* \*

As soon as she'd got poor Mr Long to move out and had the next door house, she was in her element because now she had lots of room to invite her friends. I say friends but I am not sure everyone who came to stay or dine was actually a friend; sometimes I thought they were just taking advantage of Julia and her generous hospitable nature but then again sometimes I thought that Julia was taking advantage of them too, for what she wanted was to surround herself with anyone whom she believed to possess genius or beauty and sometimes her guests certainly had to sing for their supper so perhaps it evened out.

She called the new house Dimbola Lodge. Dimbola, it seemed, was the name of the Camerons' coffee estate in Ceylon. From the moment she got the keys to it there came a procession of people, some seeming very happy to be there and enjoying the sun and the food and the garden and others frankly looking a little hunted as though they had had one too many in a public inn and had woken to find they had taken the Queen's shilling unawares.

Dimbola Lodge was, I could see, a magical place to visit. Julia's guests were welcome to stay in bed until noon if they wished, or to rise with the dawn. On summer nights Julia might lead a party down to the bay to watch the moonlight on the water, or up onto the downs with lanterns and music. There were long luncheons and late suppers, impromptu dances, theatricals and play readings, picnics and excursions, unexpected visitors who turned up and were welcomed with screams of delight and then stayed on for dinner and then for a night and then for a month. Julia would decide on dinner at midnight served on the lawn, or suddenly require hampers of food packed for a carriage ride along the coast. Her guests might come in with soaking clothes after wading into the sea and take hot baths in the middle of the day, or choose to take champagne and cake in the garden at breakfast time.

49

Of course all this daring informality took a good deal of work behind the scenes. Invisible, unnoticed, we servants cooked and cleaned and washed and ironed, carried trays laden with food and drink, cleared everything away, swept and tidied and scrubbed and sluiced, so that every morning the guests would wake up to a fresh day, their chamber pots emptied, hot water and tea brought to their rooms, their clothes brushed and pressed and hung up, their shoes cleaned, their breakfast served, their coffees and luncheons and teas and dinners appearing all over again, day after day. Just like magic, they must have thought. If they thought of it at all.

As the months went by there were some guests who were there on a regular basis, so that I got to know who they were and what they liked for breakfast and how fussy they were about having their bedrooms tidied or whether they would notice dust along the top of the pictures. Some were Julia's family—she had sisters, quite a few, in fact I believe there were seven sisters altogether including Julia. They had been the Miss Pattles before they married. The tutor in London had taught Charlie and Hal and me about the seven sisters in the mythology of ancient Greece, who were transformed into stars and were called the Pleiades, which was very suitable because they were quite starry, these Pattle sisters, and those I met were extremely beautiful women, which surprised me when I first saw them because to tell the truth Julia was not at all beautiful, in fact plain is the kindest word I can find, but it is to her credit that she did not seem to mind her sisters' loveliness and they seemed all to be very close, as though they formed a sort of club which no one else could join, and they seemed to like the same things. They all dressed in flowing robes and exclaimed constantly about beauty and art and made extravagant gestures both literally and figuratively speaking, and they brought husbands and children with them to stay now and then. Of course the Tennysons and their two young sons came to dine as often as Julia could entice or command them; and there were other poets, and artists and writers and scientists—during my first year at Dimbola I recall Mr Darwin, who had sailed across the world and written a book which explained how we all came to be here at all; Mr Lear, who was shy and anxious and wrote verses; a Great Painter whom Julia and her sisters all called Signor (they were very fond of nicknames); and Sir Henry Taylor who worked at the Colonial Office but also wrote poetry and had a big white fluffy beard very nearly as impressive as Mr Cameron's. Sir Henry was a particular favourite of Julia's; she had known him for a long time and he had been a victim of the relentless present-giving for years, but I do think he genuinely liked Julia for he came back to Dimbola many times. She thought him a genius and never failed to tell him so which might have encouraged him; but Mr Tennyson once said in my hearing that Henry Taylor had a smile like a fish and after I had heard that I could never quite put it out of my mind.

Life at Freshwater settled, as life always settles, into a pattern, and I must say that after the first strangeness of living so far from London and of missing Mammy and everyone talking so oddly I began to like it. I shared the attic room with Louisa the new parlourmaid, and although she was a few years older than me we got along well enough. I had my own bed and my own clothes, a wooden box under my bed to keep my belongings in, I had a Sunday dress in pale blue cotton that I bought with my own wages, and we could take a hot bath every week. Gradually Louisa became a friend; she stood up for me against Hilda, whom she disliked almost as much as I did; and she softened my feelings towards Mrs Lyle, whom she thought kindly enough under a brusque manner, and when I began to take a different view and spoke more politely to Mrs Lyle she seemed to soften a little towards me too.

There was another way in which Louisa was a good friend to me, as well; being older than me she told me what to expect as I grew into a woman. It was something Mammy had not got around to telling me, and I was mightily grateful for that or I should have imagined I had a terrible disease and was mysteriously bleeding to death. Louisa showed me how to use rags to cope with the monthlies, and brought me gin in hot water when I got painful cramps. I imagine she stole the gin from the cabinet in the dining room, which was another point in her favour as far as I was concerned, since it showed she valued me enough to take a risk. It was what Mammy would have done, after all.

The winter in Freshwater that year was chill and grey, and there were storms that lit the sky while vast waves rolled and crashed against the rocks. But spring came early, and soon the elm trees all were in leaf, and there was hawthorn blossom like cream in the hedgerows, and always the blue-green sea sounding at the end of the road. The days lengthened and when I had an afternoon off or I was not too tired in the hour before bed I could walk up onto the high downs, and I would take off my shoes and feel the smooth sheep-cropped grass beneath my toes and the breeze fresh and cool after the labours of the day; or I would go down to the beach and dip my hot feet into the little waves that curled over the smooth white pebbles.

The household being what it was—that is, Julia's domain—our roles as servants were not always as clearly defined as they might have been in another house, so that the work was doled out in something of a random fashion. Sometimes I would be told to take on kitchen work or lady's maid duties if Mrs Lyle or Hilda fancied a bit of a rest and I didn't mind that, it meant a change from always parlour-maiding, although I noticed they never took any of my tasks. Louisa, though, would always be fair about the work and we would share it, turn and turn about. One afternoon Louisa and I were serving tea in the drawing room when Hilda came in, looking both annoyed and sly.

'There's the Irish tinker at the kitchen door, Ma'am,' said Hilda. 'Shall I send her away?'

Julia, as always, was entertaining. There was a gentleman called Mr Dodgson there who was a friend of the Tennysons—he was a rather buttoned-up man who took photographs and was something extremely clever at Oxford—and Mr Tennyson himself, and a few of Julia's glamorous nephews and nieces. I could tell Julia did not want her gathering to be interrupted and she waved at Hilda to go away but the woman stood her ground.

'I tried to tell her to go, Ma'am, but she says she will see you. She says you have her daughter and she wants her back.'

I had been just about to pour the tea for Louisa to hand round, and now I let a china cup clatter into its saucer and the hot tea spilled onto my hand. I gave a little cry of pain and the whole room turned. I felt a hot flush of shame wash over me, shame at being looked at, shame at having Hilda come in and say what she had said, shame because now all these people knew that it was me who was the daughter of an Irish tinker, for Hilda was staring straight at me with a little air of triumph as she spoke her words. At the same time I wished I might just run out of the room and into Mammy's arms, for she had come for me at last, just as Billy had said she would, my own Mammy, and we would be reunited and I would never lose her again.

53

Julia made a big play of rearranging her various shawls about her, while the guests all raised their well-bred eyebrows and exchanged glances.

'I will speak to—to the lady later, Hilda,' she said at last. 'Please offer her some refreshment in the kitchen. That will be all.'

Hilda gave her usual sniff and stalked out. Louisa took the tea things from me and started handing them round, and conversation resumed among the guests, and when every guest had been served with a cup of tea and offered Genoa cake and caviare sandwiches, and then had their cups refilled, Louisa and I bobbed and backed out of the room. I leant against the wall for a moment, biting my lip, trying to stop the shaking that had somehow taken me, and Louisa put her arm about my shoulders. She said nothing, but I could see the curiosity written large upon her face.

There in the kitchen was my mother. She was sitting in the chair Mrs Lyle usually used, with a drink of tea before her. Mrs Lyle and Hilda both stood with their arms folded watching her, and all in all I was not surprised that they were staring. Mammy was a sight to see. She was wearing a plaid dress with a big patterned shawl over the top and a feathered bonnet which was set askew and the skirt of her dress was too short and showed a pair of hefty boots beneath it, boots which looked like a man's, and her ankles were clearly visible and she was not wearing stockings. I suppose that is what she had always looked like, but I had got used to dressing in clean clothes and taking care of my appearance and I had begun to forget my former days. It did occur to me that had Julia spent a few months on the road she might have looked much the same as Mammy, but Julia could probably have got away with that sort of thing if she had wished. For Irish beggar women it is quite a different story.

I saw they had given Mammy a chipped cup but nevertheless she was looking pretty smug. When I came in she stood up and opened her arms and I walked blindly into them.

'There, there, my girl,' she said. 'Your Mammy's come back for you. No need to take on.'

I did not want to cry in front of the others.

'Shall we walk into the garden, Mammy?' I said, my voice muffled in her shoulder. She finished her tea and without meeting anyone's eye I led her outside.

'Oh, Mammy,' I said, and then the tears did come, properly, and she held me close while I sobbed and gulped and clung to her. At last I stopped, and we went to sit on the wooden bench beneath the Judas tree.

'You look well, Mary,' she said. 'I'm thinking you're growing into a beauty, as I always knew you would.'

I was pleased to hear her say that. She herself, alas, had not improved in looks, her face roughened by the weather and her hair with some grey streaks in it and all of her none too clean.

'It's a fine place to live, here, with the sea and the hills and all the interesting people who come and go,' I said. 'You'll like it, so you will.'

'I don't know that I would,' she said. 'It's by way of being on the quiet side, for my taste.'

'You will like it, soon,' I assured her. 'Just give it a month or so.'

'A month or so? I wasn't thinking I would be living here, Mary.'

'Mrs Cameron will give you your job back,' I said eagerly, 'sure she will, and we will be together again.'

'What I was thinking of,' said Mammy, 'was staying a night or two, just for a bit of a rest, then we can be off. We can make a proper living, you and I, two handsome women together.'

I could hardly take this idea in.

'On the road again, Mammy? But here, it's grand—a bed, food—Billy, Louisa—'

'Who? No, the freedom's what I'd miss, Mary, and with you by my side we won't want for much.' She stroked my hair. 'Look at you, my bonny girl, you'll make our fortune, so you will.'

'No, Mammy,' I said, panicked, 'no, I can't go back to the old life. Stay here, stay with me, you will like it soon, I know—'

'Well, living here, you need to know your place, that's what I'm saying.'

'I do,' I said, 'I do know my place, Mammy.'

She said nothing more. I leaned against her and we sat quietly in the sunshine, with the birds singing all about us and the first roses beginning to come out, and I began to be certain that this place would work its magic on her as it had on me. Julia would employ her again, and perhaps some day Mammy and I would live together here in a little cottage close to the sea, cosy and clean, with a garden, a garden with roses in it, and perhaps a cat.

I was called in to go and clear the tea things and then to wash up. Later Julia came to the kitchen and asked me where my mother was, and then she went outside and through the window I could see her talking to Mammy in the garden. There was smiling and nodding and when I saw that I almost laughed out loud with sheer delight. Of course Julia would persuade Mammy to stay; Julia could persuade anyone to do anything. And when they came in I was overjoyed, for Julia said firmly to the others that Mrs Ryan was to have a bed made up for her in the kitchen that night until the terms of her employment had been quite discussed, and when I went to bed that night I thought I had never been happier. I had shown Mammy the room where I slept, with my own bed, and my Sunday dress, so that she could see how comfortable our lives were to be; and (despite the hostility you could almost touch emanating from both Hilda and Mrs Lyle) Mammy had been regaled with a good supper and a pint of ale, on Julia's instructions, so by bed-time she was looking very pleased with the whole set-up.

I fell straight to sleep, but in the grey hour before dawn I became aware of Mammy shaking me into wakefulness. She was kneeling by my bed, gesturing me to be quiet, while Louisa slept on.

'Are you sure, Mary, that you want to stay here?' she said, her voice soft and low.

'Of course, Mammy,' I whispered. 'Now you're here, I do.'

'They treat you well, do they, my girl?'

'They do, Mammy. They will treat you well too,' I reassured her. 'The work is hard, sometimes, but you won't mind that.' I was doubtful of this last statement but I repeated it to convince myself. 'You won't mind the work, Mammy, I know.'

She gave a little sigh.

'Well, back to sleep, now, Mary. You need your rest.' She kissed me and I went back to sleep for a while, but it was an uneasy slumber, and I woke as the sun was coming up. I thought I'd go down and see how Mammy had slept, so I dressed hurriedly and tiptoed out and down the back stairs. The kitchen was empty, and when I went out into the garden there was no one there but Mr Cameron, who as he often did in the early mornings was wandering about the lawn in his dressing gown.

'Hello, Mary,' he said. 'Dabbling in the dew, eh?'

'Yes, sir,' I said. 'Have you seen my mother, at all?'

'Mother? Your mother?'

'My mother, yes.'

'Woman with a hat and boots? Feathers, and so on?'

'Yes.'

'Went off about an hour ago. Down the road. She asked me if I had any tobacco, so I gave her some. And a sovereign. She said she needed money for the fare.'

'The fare to where?' I asked him. 'Did she say?'

'Well, for the ferry, I think. Not sure after that.'

I stood still for a moment, and then I went and sat down on the bench where yesterday I had leaned against my mother's shoulder and had those ridiculous thoughts. After a while Julia came out too, carrying her cup of tea, and I stayed there dully while Mr Cameron explained to Julia what had happened. She came over to me then and sat with me for a while, stirring her tea thoughtfully from time to time, while I swallowed again and again in an effort to prevent tears from beginning because if I started to cry I thought I might never stop. After a while she patted my hand briskly, and cleared her throat as though trying to think what to say, while her husband ambled about in circles casting an anxious glance at us from time to time.

'What happened to your father, Mary?' said Julia at last.

It seems odd, now I think of it, that she had never asked me this before.

'My father went away. He left my mother and me to shift for ourselves. He was called James Ryan,' I added, as though this were somehow relevant. It felt important to speak his name, to give him an identity, for he was hardly anything but a shadow to me now.

'James. My father too had that name.'

Julia fell silent again, and after a while she drifted off to stare at the rose-beds, leaving me with Mr Cameron. I hesitated, wondering if I should go or stay, but he seemed on the verge of saying something so I waited.

'She doesn't talk of her father, Mary,' he said at last. 'Biggest liar in India, James Pattle. She was attached to him, though.'

'Naturally, sir,' I said, uncertainly. 'Was she—was she very young when he died?'

'Young? No, no. Thirty or so, I suppose. Died in India. They sent him back in a coffin-full of brandy, pickled. To preserve him.'

'I see.'

'Storm at sea, though. Coffin lid burst off and up he rose out of the cask. Julia's mother happened to be present. Never the same afterwards, poor lady.'

'I would imagine not,' I said, with a shudder.

'The lesson there, Mary, is to get your coffin lid nailed on tight,' said Mr Cameron, nodding to himself, and he wandered off back towards the house, his dressing gown belt trailing behind him through the dew like the tail of a big gentle animal. After that I tried not to think of Mammy too much. When I found my thoughts turning towards her I resolutely closed my mind; and although I still heard her voice now and then in my head I did my best to disregard it.

# 8

One of the first things Julia did when we had all settled into the new houses was to have a gap in the back wall of the garden knocked through and a wooden door fitted. I thought at first this was just so she could walk easily in the woods behind the house, but I soon realised that there was a more definite purpose. The estate of the Great Poet, Mr Tennyson, who had been the reason that we had all ended up here in the first place, lay behind that wall. Julia had cunningly chosen to live right bang next to him—not exactly next door as it would have been in London, shoulder to shoulder on a long grey street, for the Great Poet's house was half a mile away through the woods, but close enough for her to be going back and forth whenever the mood took her which was pretty much constantly. She loved to take them presents, of course, as she was always doing for all her friends, but with the Tennysons she surpassed herself. Poor Mrs Tennyson suffered most I think because while the Great Poet could be grumpy or reclusive and everyone just said it was the Artistic Temperament his wife was more correct and felt she must be polite and grateful and what she must have felt when she received some of the things Julia forced on her I can only imagine. Billy was sometimes sent to carry things to them and he always regaled me with stories of them afterwards, so I got a fair idea of the presents, and legs of mutton and jars of preserves are one thing but there were others which must have made Mrs Tennyson shudder or groan or both. He had to deliver a dozen rolls of wallpaper of the most virulent bright blue with a separate frieze of naked people cavorting to go round the top, and he was once sent with what was practically a whole grove of young trees which required planting immediately. Then there were old dusty catalogues and pictures and prints which anyone else would have thrown out with the rubbish, and odd garments, shawls and robes and wraps, mostly hideous and often slightly grubby, trinkets from India, a pair of guinea fowl, baskets of quinces going brown at the edges, huge vases, a hatstand ... on and on it went, this stream of gifts, so generously meant, so thoughtless, so patronising. Mrs Tennyson always wrote a thank-you note straightaway, naturally, for she was that sort of lady and I liked her good manners, and sometimes Billy was asked to wait while she wrote, and I think she must have had to grit her teeth very hard sometimes to write *thank you dear Julia how very kind* so often for things she must have wished she had never received. I think she tried to get her own back once for she sent Julia a jacket, a rather ornate thing with beads, and perhaps she thought that might even things up but no, for Julia wrote to say she was not worthy and sent it straight back, which was frankly rude, so poor Mrs T got nowhere after all.

I was intrigued by that green-painted door into the Tennyson estate. My life at Dimbola Lodge (for by now we had dropped Sunnyside, and called the whole establishment Dimbola Lodge as being more glamorous) had settled into a pattern of lessons in the mornings and working in the afternoons. Julia had dispensed with the London tutor, or he with her, as he had expressed him-self unwilling to venture to the Isle of Wight, and she had got a

61

lady governess called Miss Berthold who came from Prussia and was perfectly willing to travel a little. I liked Miss Berthold and unlike the old tutor who had always turned his nose up at having to teach a female who was also a servant she seemed to think it was quite usual to have a girl for lessons and she never made me feel like a servant either, just like a real person who wanted to learn things. Charlie and Hal had got used to my being in the schoolroom too by then and the mornings were the happiest times of my days. During the lessons I forgot everything else, forgot I had ever been a beggar and that I was still a servant, and as long as I was puzzling over sums and learning poems and following great rivers in the atlas and conjugating verbs and forming my letters in elegant script I became just me, Mary Ryan, like the boys were just Charlie Cameron and Hal Cameron and didn't have labels slapped on them to confine them in a box for the rest of their lives.

When the lessons had ended, however, I had to step back through the invisible wall into my real life, tie my white apron round my waist, and became a servant again.

I needed a way to escape. I don't mean to escape from Dimbola Lodge; I regarded it as my home, now, for London was fading from my mind. Sometimes Mammy came into my dreams and said she would come to live here too, before very long, and when that happened I would awake with tears on my cheeks and it would take me a while to shake off the sadness; but I was safe here, with a room and a bed and enough to eat, and the joy of my books and lessons, and I had the sea and the hills and I had Billy. But what I longed for most of all was some time to myself, to read, to be alone. After the lessons ended I was supposed to go straight to the kitchen for the servant's luncheon; then it was straight to work, dusting and drawing water and sweeping, laying fires and carrying coal, curtseying and saying *yes ma'am no ma'am* and fetching tea trays and clearing up, setting tables and polishing glasses. It went on until after the family's dinner, when you might get a half-hour to sit down but that would be back in the kitchen with all the others, eating the left-overs from upstairs, hot and tired and ready to drop and then the younger servants were all sent to bed and I suppose by then we were ready for it.

It wasn't that I was ungrateful for what I had. I reminded myself now and then that if it hadn't been for Julia I might still have been begging on Putney Heath. But I wanted just a bit of space, like Billy had managed to find, and soon I found a way to get it.

I made a plan. I announced to all the other servants that Mrs Cameron had told me to spend two hours every afternoon mending her clothes. She had said, I explained, trying to look a bit sorrowful as though it were a penance, that I was to go to her dressing room every day with my sewing basket and start going through her clothes and mending everything, the moth-eaten shawls, the fraying lace mantillas, the velvet dresses with loose braid hanging off them. I was to do this every afternoon from two o'clock till four and I was not to be disturbed. Hilda looked at me very suspiciously when I said this for it should have been a lady's maid's job to do that, but I happened to know that Hilda hated sewing (she liked to curl hair and arrange Julia's perfume bottles and fold up her clothes, but all in all I believe being a lady's maid to Julia Cameron must have been a sinecure as servants' posts go) and so she was not likely to argue with me about it.

I thought this idea had a flash of genius. Everyone was used to Julia's having sudden eccentric ideas. Everyone could see that her clothes needed attention, and that Hilda was rather grand for a lady's maid and probably too dignified to mend clothes. And if Julia had said I was not to be disturbed they would not disturb me, and they would hardly question her about it. The only flaw in my plan that I could see was that people might notice that her clothes were not getting any smarter or neater but, I reasoned, they might put that down to my bad sewing or to her tearing things again as soon as they were mended. So I started every afternoon by going up the wide polished front staircase as though I was heading for the dressing room. I carried a little work basket and I looked purposeful. If any of the family saw me of course they thought nothing at all, for why should they? As far as the gentry are concerned servants are just part of the background, like the chairs or the pictures on the wall. We don't make much noise, we don't get in the way. We know our place. We just scuttle about like the black beetles in the kitchen and are supposed to be grateful not to be trodden on.

It worked like a dream. I had been given leave to read any books I liked from the schoolroom and even from Mr Cameron's library, and every day when no one was looking I popped a book into my work basket and at two o'clock off I went, modest yet brisk like the very best servants, up the stairs and along the passage and then I changed my quick firm footsteps into a silent glide and I flitted past Julia's bedroom door and tiptoed down the narrow back stair, the servants' stair, and through the garden door and I was free. If by chance any of the other servants saw me going out and questioned me I just said I had been sent on an errand, which I did not care to specify.

Of course then I needed somewhere to be alone with my books. I took Billy into my confidence, and he was impressed with my plan and promised to back me up if he should ever be questioned. Better still he suggested an indoor place where I would not be found, which was in the stable, up a ladder to the loft where the hay for the horses was kept. I made a kind of nest among the sweet-smelling hay and even kept some of the books there for a while if I thought no one would miss them, although I had to stop that when the mice started nibbling them. Oh, the happy afternoons I had there, up in that hayloft, snug and safe with the light falling through the window or the rain pattering on the slates, and the horses shuffling and snuffling peacefully below me. I could be lost in my books, certain that no one would find me and that for two whole delicious hours no one would tell me what to do or where to go. Or what to be.

When the weather was fine, though, I liked to read outside. I had to be careful, but there were a couple of places that seemed safe—beneath a laurel bush, up against the house wall, where the dark leaves hid me from sight and made a dry space; or tucked behind the fowl-house, in the corner of the garden wall, screened by an ancient rusting wheelbarrow. Often, though, tiresomely, there were people in the garden and when that happened I feared I should be caught so mostly I stuck to the stable.

One day in late June the garden was full of people. There were always visitors and this time it was two of Julia's beautiful sisters and three of her nieces and her friend Sir Henry Taylor so there was no chance of reading peacefully out of doors without being caught, and it was hot in the loft, dusty and dry, while outside the day was all blue and gold and full of bees and roses and so lovely that I did not want to be indoors, and it occurred to me that I might escape through that gate in the garden wall and get into the Tennysons' park instead and be among the cool green trees.

I had to wait a while until the party in the garden were all distracted, but it wasn't long before Julia was in the middle of making them all rehearse for a play she had written, and trying to stop them laughing because apparently it was a tragedy and they should have been crying instead, which only made them laugh more, so there was enough noise to cover the tiny bat-squeak of the gate's hinges as I pushed it open, and a maid with dark hair in a black dress is no more than shadow in the corner of people's eyes. I only intended to get into the bit of woodland the other side of the wall, not to go anywhere near the Tennysons' house itself, but once through I thought at least I might walk a bit, since it was such a fine summer's day and it was so cool among the trees. I was in a bit of a daze, I suppose, finding myself suddenly in another place, a place I certainly should not have been, nervous but exhilarated. I had been learning some poetry by heart and I thought that for once instead of reading I would say the lines out loud to myself, and see how much I had remembered. The poem I was learning was called *Ode to a Nightingale* and the words seemed made for the moment, because there I actually was in a melodious plot of beechen green and shadows numberless, fading away into the forest dim, following the verdurous glooms and winding mossy ways. All of summer seemed to be around me and I was lost in it, free and happy and feeling the words of the poem like honey on my tongue.

In that sweet dreaming state of mind I found that I had got to the edge of the woods, and there in front of me was a great sweep of velvet grass and at a distance was the back of a house, with arched windows and turrets like a small castle. I wanted very much to get closer to it and see more, but that would have meant crossing the lawns and being out in the open, so I just stood for a while looking at it. There seemed to be nobody about, just wood pigeons murmuring above me in the elms, and I saw that there was a tree standing alone, not far from me, with low branches that I might quite easily climb to get a better view of the house. It was only a few yards from the edge of the wood so after taking a deep breath I ran towards it and hauled myself up through the boughs until I was properly hidden among the leaves. There was a broad branch that I could get astride, and I got quite comfortable, and now I was able to survey the world below, the handsome house with ivy draped about its walls, the signs of its invisible occupants (two hobby horses lying on their side on the grass, a wicker chair set just below my tree) and the roll of the hills beyond. There with the leaves rustling all about me I pretended to myself that I was an eagle looking down upon the land below from a great height, and I wished I could stay there for the rest of the day but I knew that soon I should have to climb down and find my way back through the woods.

Just as I decided that I had stayed out long enough, however, I saw the Great Poet himself come out of a small door and start to walk over towards me. I thought he must have seen me and I was already trying to concoct some story in my head to justify why I had trespassed into his garden and climbed his tree, but he just came and sat in the wicker chair and drew out a big crumpled notebook and then he started to speak. For a horrible moment I thought he was addressing me, but I quickly realised he was speaking words he had written. I was trembling in case he looked up and saw me but after a while it seemed clear that he was quite wrapped up in his poem and had not noticed me at all. I supposed he was practising for the next time he decided to read to his friends.

It seemed like a sort of blessing, that hot afternoon, to be there, all unseen in my leafy bower, listening to poetry read by the man who had written it. His words floated up to me, his voice rather deep and all on one note, the doves still keeping up their throaty music all around me as he read. I tried to follow the story the poem seemed to be telling, but I could not, at least not exactly, although in my view poems do not always need to be perfectly understood to stay ringing in one's mind for ever. There was something dreadful going on in this one, horror and madness and death, but there was music too and I closed my eyes so that I could see the pictures in my mind that the words made for me, the gloss of satin and the glimmer of pearls, the ruby-budded lime, the red rose and the violets. That was my undoing for with my eyes tight shut and the colours and the scents and the sounds of the poem beating in my ears I swayed and lost my balance and fell ungracefully from my branch and landed right at the feet of Mr Tennyson.

# 9

I wasn't hurt, just scratched, but the breath had been knocked right out of me so I couldn't run, I couldn't even speak. I just lay in a tangled heap there on the grass, wheezing and gasping and thinking that now everything would unravel. The Great Poet said nothing for a while, just looked at me.

'Now,' he said at last, 'who have we here?'

By now I had managed to get a bit of breath back.

'Mary Ryan, sir,' I said, still coughing and choking. 'Mrs Cameron's parlourmaid.' I'd promoted myself from under-parlourmaid, hoping it sounded a bit less dispensable.

'Ah,' he said, nodding. 'Julia's maid, eh? Did she send you here, to keep an eye on me?'

I thought for a moment of going along with that idea. He would swallow the story, probably, he was used to Julia and her wild notions. But it wouldn't wash, really, for long. He was bound to tell her that one of her maids had fallen out of a tree onto his lawn and nearly squashed him and then I would be undone.

'No,' I said, struggling to my feet. 'I came in of my own accord, and then I climbed the tree to see your house, and then when you started reading the poem I closed my eyes to listen and then I fell.'

He didn't look as though he thought that particularly odd.

'And what did you think of the poem, Mary Ryan?' he asked.

'I liked it,' I said, truthfully, 'especially the bit where he is waiting in the garden for the girl, and there are spices and musk, and he thinks he will hear her steps above him even when he is dead because he loves her so much.'

At this he looked pleased.

'Well, you are an intelligent girl,' he said. He looked at me with more interest. 'Queen lily and rose in one, eh?'

'Although I'm not sure I understood it all perfectly, sir,' I added. I thought I should be scrupulous on this point.

He sighed.

'That's what people often say, but it is only because they have not paid sufficient attention. Listen again.'

And with that he went right back to the beginning and read the whole thing through, while I sat on the grass at his feet, and it took a long, long time. I knew I should go back or I would be found out, but I could not leave, somehow, for although there was much that I did not care for and some lines that sounded not like poetry at all, still every now and then among the strange anguished rambling lines there would come a verse which was so full of richness and beauty that like the poor man in the poem I felt my heart start and tremble just to hear it.

By the time he got to the end I was stiff and cold and the sun was sinking towards the western hill. I thanked him and told him I must go back, and I bobbed a curtsey and set off at a run back through the wood to the green gate and into Julia's garden.


Of course I was caught. I was caught by Julia herself who was still with Sir Henry Taylor, roaming about the lawn as she often did, a shawl falling off her shoulders and a cup of tea in her hand, stirring vigorously and talking all the while. I slid through the gate and was trying to look nonchalant, which I thought was the only way I might get away with having been absent without leave for what I feared was about four hours, but as ill luck would have it Julia turned just at that moment from her excited conversation to gesture at the columns of roses that she had planted either side of the gate and there I was, framed in the middle. Of course she was a little startled and of course she asked me where I had been; and the odd thing was I never felt I could lie directly to Julia, not from any nobility of character I am sorry to say but because despite Julia's being impossible she believed that everyone in the world was basically good and it seemed too hard on her to contradict that idea. So I told her I had been to look at Mr Tennyson's house and I had climbed a tree and fallen out of it and then he had read his long long poem to me, all about suicide and gloom and the beautiful girl in the twilight, and that was why I was so late coming back. She did not seem too put out, just told me I must not run off again, but then she questioned me about the poem and even seemed a bit envious of my having had her Great Poet read just to me. Sir Henry looked much more outraged and told me I was naughty and ungrateful and should be ashamed of not doing my work. I did not see why he was cross because I was not his maid, but perhaps he felt that he should be stern and reproachful so that Julia did not have to be.

I got off lightly, I suppose. Honesty did seem in this instance to have been the best policy. I did not tell them about my pretence over the sewing, however. I thought it might be too much of a shock for them to hear all at once the true extent of my wickedness and in any case I did not want to give up my precious solitude, and I even thought I might go back sometime to see if I could hear more of the Great Poet reading although I hoped that perhaps next time he might choose to recite something a little shorter.

\* \* \*

One afternoon about a week after the tree incident I was reading Keats again, this time beneath the laurel bushes. The window of the parlour was just above my head, and on this hot afternoon it stood open. Julia had some visitors, as usual, and I heard the usual noises of tea being brought in and voices flowing out over my head, but I had become an expert in closing out everything but the words in front of me or I should never have got any reading done at all. One day, I thought, I shall have a room of my own, with books from floor to ceiling and a great cushioned chair and a door I can shut against the world. For now, though, I was happy enough reading about veiled Melancholy in the dappled gloom beneath the laurels, sitting among the dry rustling leaves, my back against the brick wall of the house, until I heard my own name spoken, and then I did listen.

'What will become of her? If she is to be a servant, I am afraid there is not such a thing as a good servant who is fond of reading.'

It was Sir Henry Taylor's voice. I held my breath. Thoughts chased through my head: *am* I a good servant? Do I *want* to be a good servant? Shall I pretend that I am not fond of reading, so that Julia will *think* I am a good servant?

*A servant is next door to a slave*, said Mammy's voice softly in my ear.

'Learning, though, Philip; that will help her in life—she may become, perhaps, a governess—that would be a great thing for her—'

I should say here that Julia always called Sir Henry *Philip*. I thought for a long time that it was simply another random manifestation of her strangeness, but I found later it was because years ago he had written a play in verse called Philip Von Something-or-other and being Julia she liked to cast her friends as romantic figures from history or legend. And her servants, as I was to discover.

72

Sir Henry snorted. 'If she is to be a governess will she be any happier than governesses who have not been beggars?'

Sir Henry was a kindly, clever man. So everyone said. Julia adored him, and she always listened reverently to his pronouncements. I began to feel sick. I would have to stop my lessons and be an under-parlourmaid all day long, every day, for the rest of my life. Or I would have to become a governess, which might be as bad, or worse, because of the loneliness. Poor Miss Berthold was caught somewhere between being a servant and being family, and not properly accepted in either camp.

Why did Julia not reply to him? She was never lost for words. Why did she not say what she thought? I could hear the clinking of the tea cups and Sir Henry drinking his tea with a loud slurp. I hoped his tea would choke him.

'Well,' said Julia at last, 'what will become of her, indeed? And yet—you know me, dear Philip, I always have more hope than reason.'

I swallowed and I hoped they did not hear me for my swallow sounded loud in my ears.

'Well, Julia, you must decide for yourself; but until you are sure of what you intend, you should guard yourself against petting the beggar.'

That word. It was the taste of bile in my throat; it was a clutch of fear in my stomach. I had a thousand times rather be a servant than be a beggar; but in the eyes of Sir Henry and everyone like him I would never be anything else. Beggar. *Beggar*. It was like a dirty stain I would never be able to wash away.

'*Is* she a good servant, Julia?'

That was a different voice. It was Mr Tennyson, who was also taking tea at Dimbola Lodge. I was surprised because he was not much of a talker really except as I knew when it came to his own poems.

'Oh, Alfred, Mary is—to tell you the truth she is rather naughty, now and then. You know that. Dear Philip is right, perhaps. Do you think so? Do you think I have done wrong in letting her have lessons with my boys?'

'Yes,' said Sir Henry.

'No,' said Mr Tennyson, at the same time.

Even with my heart thumping hard against my ribs I had a moment of feeling for Julia, for she worshipped both of these clever men, and now one said one thing and one said another. How was she to choose?

'But, my good man, if you will but listen to my reasoning—', said Sir Henry.

Here the Great Poet's practice in sweeping all before him when it came to reciting seemed to stand him in good stead. He simply talked on, paying no heed at all to Sir Henry's bleats about how servants should know their place and not be given ideas above their station.

'No. You have not done wrong, Julia. You act on impulse, in almost everything, I know, but your impulses spring from a kind heart and kind hearts are more than coronets. We should teach the orphan-boy to read. And the orphan-girl.'

'Mary is not exactly an orphan—', began Julia.

'The girl is clever. She has an ear for poetry and a heart to understand it. You would do wrong to stop her learning.'

There was more in the same vein, but Mr Tennyson won the argument. It was never mentioned to me, naturally, but I felt how close I had come to losing my new life and I was grateful to the Great Poet for ever afterwards, even though I could not always like every line he wrote; and even though I will always believe that John Keats was the Greatest of all Great Poets, still there is surely room for more than one great poet in the world.

# 10

I got away with the sewing ruse for almost a year. Now as I look back I think it extraordinary that I was not found out sooner. But of course one day Julia told Hilda to mend some more than usually distressed garment and Hilda said rather sniffily that she had understood sewing was no longer her job because the Irish beggar girl was to do it and then of course it all came out. Hilda was almost speechless with rage when she discovered what had been happening and her fury was doubled when she realised she was going to have to do the mending of Julia's clothes after all, and of course by now the clothes were in a truly dire state so her work was made that much harder. She never forgave me for that. But then I never forgave her either for referring to me in the way she did, so in that we were perfectly even.

I could disregard Hilda's wrath, but I did fear Julia's. However, when she confronted me about the sewing ruse I made a long impassioned speech to her about how I needed to have time to read and I laid it on so thick about how my soul craved beauty and how the works of Mr Tennyson and of Keats and Shakespeare were nourishing my heart and my senses and filling my mind with wonder that in the end she did not scold me at all but instead said that I had a pure and noble soul, and then she actually embraced me, she put her arms around me and patted my hair and murmured that I was as dear to her as though I were her own child.

When Julia said those words I felt tears brimming up into my eyes, and I laid my head gratefully against her stout shoulder while ideas of being actually adopted rushed into my head. Mr Cameron would be my father and Julia would be my mother and I would have my own bedroom and read books all day if I wished. I would never be a servant again and no one would ever refer to me as a beggar. I would wear beautiful clothes and eat sugar-plums and travel in first-class railway carriages. I bent my head and took her hand and kissed it, full of such hope that I hardly dared raise my eyes to hers, but believing when I did that I would see my golden future reflected in them.


Julia had not meant that, of course. Of course she had not. What was I thinking? True, I was not punished for my transgression; but I was to return to all my servant's duties, it was back to the sweeping and the dusting, back to serving meals and clearing them away, carrying cans of hot water upstairs for baths and then carrying it all away again, the sheer relentless repetitive labour, day after day after day. Moreover, Charlie was now old enough to go away to school, and Miss Berthold had been instructed to concentrate on Hal, who although his mama's darling was rather idle and lacking application, and she certainly had some work to do getting him ready for the day when he too would be packed off like his brothers. So my days of having proper lessons were over, and my mornings were no longer devoted to French conversation or Latin verbs or the rivers of the world. They were devoted to scrubbing floors and emptying chamber pots. *How are the mighty fallen*, said Hilda more than once to Mrs Lyle when she was sure I could hear her. *My disdain is my reply*, I thought to myself, but did not say. She would not have recognised the line, in any case, so there was more satisfaction in staying quiet and dignified.

Something had shifted, perhaps, after that moment when Julia took me in her arms, but it had shifted into an odd shape. I might be sweeping the crumbs from the breakfast table and Julia would press on me a new book to read; she would ask me what I thought of Miss Rossetti's new poem, and before I had answered tell me to set an extra place at tea because she expected Mr Dodgson to call. I was a servant still, and yet sometimes I was something else too. Not a daughter. She had a daughter already. A sort of distant relation, perhaps. A poor one, a dependent one, someone who should be constantly aware of her good fortune and on her knees thanking heaven for it.

*The need to be grateful all the time*, said Mammy in my ear. Her voice was full of disgust.


Of course I was relieved that I still had my place, that I had not been punished, and at least I still had books to read when I had the time and was not too exhausted to do so. So I did not sulk, I went on with my work, and I smiled and bobbed and did as I was told, but inside I sometimes allowed my thoughts to turn bitter. I was scrubbing the hall floor one afternoon and feeling just that bitterness, for it was hot summer and I would have liked to be down at the bay listening to the soughing of the waves, or under the green canopy of a tree reading *Goblin Market*, not on my knees on the hard tiles with my hands red and sore from the soapy water, hot and sweating and my arms aching with tiredness. The door bell rang and there was no one about to answer it. Billy—whose job it was, in theory—was probably away up on the downs, I thought, as I got to my feet with a groan as though

77

I were an old woman, for scrubbing floors is terribly hard on the back. He'll be up there with a cool breeze on his face, smoking, watching the gulls swoop and cry and not a care in the world. I pulled open the door and there was a girl about my own age, holding out a basket.

'I brought the fish up and I'm to wait for payment,' she said.

'You're to go round to the servants' door with deliveries,' I said.

'I'm to wait for payment,' she said. *Oi'm to wite fur poyment.* She was local, obviously.

'Yes, at the servants' door,' I said, not rudely, just wearily; but the girl looked almost as tired as I felt, and there was no one about. 'Oh, well, come through, then,' I said, and I let her come into the hall and was about to show her through to the kitchen when Julia came charging in from the garden and saw us. I was about to apologise but she held up her hand to me while she eyed up the girl with the fish.

'And who is this?'

'Mary Hillier,' said the girl. 'I brought the fish up and I'm to wait for payment.'

Julia put her hand under the girl's chin and tilted her face up.

'Beauty!' she said. 'The face of a Madonna!'

I couldn't see it myself. The girl was pretty enough, I supposed, but she looked a bit vacant. Julia, though, was smitten. As so often.

'I brought the fish...' began the girl again.

'Fish!' cried Julia, 'what do we care for fish, when there is such beauty in the world?'

The girl looked blank. This was not a question she felt able to answer, obviously. I sighed and took the basket from her, and carried it to the kitchen and got the fish-money from Mrs Lyle and by the time I got back into the hall the girl had been hired as a housemaid and Julia was explaining to her that she would start her work the next morning and was gaily brushing over any

78

possible objections from the girl's parents or current employer (her father was a shoemaker, I gathered, and she had work as a fish-gutter down by the bay). Of course no one stood a chance when Julia had made up her mind, and the household promptly gained another servant. It was faintly annoying to me that this girl was also called Mary; and a few months later a similar episode occurred and another pretty maid was hired who was, tiresomely, also a Mary. Most employers would have called us by our surnames only, so that we would have been Ryan, and Hillier, and Kellaway, which would at least have been practical. As it was, Julia called us all Mary, which was of course more polite, and in some ways more cheering, but it gave the impression, I always felt, that Mary was somehow a generic name for a servant in the way Mammy had told me that my father when he worked on the railways was often called Paddy even though his name was James. *Mary!* Julia would call, and one or other of us would always appear. It was as though we were interchangeable: shout *Mary* and a good-looking girl in a starched apron will materialise to do your bidding.

Mary, Mary, Mary. Pretty maids, all in a row. And quite contrary. Some of us, at least.

# 11

One of Julia's guests in the early part of the year I turned fifteen has stayed in my mind because he was the first person to take my photograph. He was a jolly bewhiskered man, who spoke with a strong accent of a type that I had never heard before, which turned out to be because he came from Sweden, and his accent was even more interesting because he now lived in Wolverhampton and had acquired some of the Midlands way of speaking too. He came to stay because he was a friend of the Tennysons and of Mr Dodgson, with whom he shared an interest in photography; but while I think for Mr Dodgson it was just a hobby, for Mr Rejlander it was his work. Portraits were what he liked—he was a painter too, but he said that he had once spent three weeks trying and failing to capture the folds of silk on a sleeve and then he had seen a photograph of the same thing and his eyes had been opened.

When he visited Dimbola he brought his camera with him, which was very interesting to me because I had never seen a camera before. It was a large wooden box which stood on three legs and there were bits of glass that came with it and bottles of strange-smelling fluid which he left in the kitchen and he warned us that they were dangerous, so Mrs Lyle put them on the top of the dresser well out of the way lest they should be mistaken for vinegar and we poisoned the family with a salad. While he was there he decided he would take some photographs.

'I would like to photograph the peasants,' he said to Julia. I was taking in the tea tray at the time and he looked up and saw me. 'Like this,' he said, pointing at me. 'The peasants of the Isle of Wight.'

'Mary's not from the Isle of Wight, Oskar,' said Julia, who was poking about among the ornaments on the side table, probably looking for something he wouldn't like that she could give him. 'She's from Ireland.'

'Ireland, Island, what can it matter?' said Mr Rejlander. He reached out and tweaked my dress. 'This one will be a good subject.' He bounced up from his chair, nearly upsetting the tea. 'Now, I will take the likeness! Now! Outside, outside, into the sunlight!'

Of course that was just the sort of thing Julia loved and outside they went, prowling round the garden looking for a suitable backdrop, while I followed reluctantly behind. As we came round the side of the house Louisa was there drawing water from the well, and it was decided that she and I together would make a suitable picture, so he lugged out his camera and set it up, and then he got us to drop the bucket down and haul it up again a dozen times until he found the perfect scene. He wanted Louisa to turn towards the well and me to stoop as though I was going to lift the bucket, and we were told we must stand very very still and look at the camera. It seemed to take for ever for him to be ready, and our arms were aching with all the work and our backs were hurting because of all the bending while keeping still, and moreover we were trembling on the verge of hysterics because Julia was flapping about behind him trying to see what he was doing and getting in his way, and when he put a big black cloth over the camera to keep the light out she tried to get under it too and he had to reverse out and they both got tangled in the cloth and you could see that he was getting quite cross with her but was too polite to show it. Then he said *now, as still as still can be, young ladies*, but because of his Sweden-and-Wolverhampton voice it sounded like *yong loidees* and it was too much. Louisa caught my eye and let a tiny choke of mirth escape and then I caught it from her and we were both shaking with the effort of not laughing. Then Julia started to get cross too, saying we were naughty girls and could we not see that Mr Rejlander was an artist and we would be immortalised for ever by his work?

At last we managed to be still long enough for the picture to be taken. Then we were allowed to go and as soon as we were round the corner of the house Louisa and I fell helpless with laughter, unable to stop, leaning on each other, gulping and wiping tears away and then starting all over again until at last we were weak and drained and hardly able to speak, and even then for hours afterwards as soon as one of us caught the other's eye we were liable to feel the giggles bubbling up inside and it took very little to set us off again.

I saw that photograph the next day, when Mr Rejlander had conjured up a picture from the wooden box and the glass. Louisa had done a much better job than I of looking serious. She had managed to control her face and only I knew that her chest was heaving with the effort of containing the laughter inside. Anyone who looks at me, though, can see that I was failing to suppress the merriment with which we were both still quivering. Mr Rejlander didn't mind, he said he liked natural poses and he was very pleased and he gave us both a shilling for our trouble and said he would like to photograph us again, which he did, and I forgave him the remark about peasants, not so much because of the shilling but because he was a kind and merry man and he said thank you to us both with much politeness afterwards. That was worth at least as much as the shilling to me.

While he was staying in Freshwater, Mr Rejlander photographed the Tennyson family. There was much talk about the plan, because while Mr Tennyson was generally against the idea of photography altogether he was very proud of his little boys and so he was brought round to the idea of a family portrait. I was much intrigued by this photography business and I asked Mr Rejlander if I could help carry his camera up to Farringford, the Tennysons' home, and he seemed pleased that I was interested and said yes before Julia or anyone else could point out that I was supposed to be beating the rugs and cleaning the drawing room windows that afternoon. So I walked with him (and of course Julia, who would never be left out of any project involving her beloved Great Poet) up through the green gate, lugging a bag full of mysterious bits of equipment and cloths while Mr Rejlander pushed his camera in a wheelbarrow through the woods, and Julia, wearing a red dress and a purple cloak, forged on ahead, pointing out the beauties of the woodland in case we should miss anything, and anticipating the joy the photograph would bring to the world, and begging Mr Rejlander to explain the intricacies of the camera to her without necessarily giving him a chance to answer beyond saying that he must have the apparatus set firmly on the ground and no light must get under the cloth.

Setting up the equipment was the easy part. Mr Tennyson was clearly regretting his decision to allow his photograph to be taken, and was muttering under his breath that the whole thing would be pandering to the Cockneys, who would rip him open like a pig if they got the chance. (Cockneys is what he called people he did not know who came to the Island to try to get a glimpse of him—thank goodness, thought I, that I had never chosen to speak like a Londoner.) So he was extremely grumpy;

and the boys, delicate creatures with their hair in long ringlets and dressed in velvet suits with lace collars, were looking hardly more enthusiastic. Poor Mrs Tennyson was trying to cajole them all into a better frame of mind, and she succeeded to some extent with the elder boy, Hallam, who at twelve years old was a rather serious, gentle lad who did as his mother and father bid him on most occasions. Mr Tennyson, however, went on grumbling like a great sulky child, while Lionel, who was ten and looked like an angel, just pouted and rolled his eyes and stuck his lip out until I could have slapped him, for poor Mr Rejlander was being his usual jolly self, polite and patient, and Julia was in a fever of anxiety lest the whole thing was thwarted, and I could not see why they did not all just do as they were asked and get it over with.

At last they were propitiated enough to be assembled and posed, and they managed to keep still until the deed was done. Mrs T gazed soulfully and adoringly at her husband, who stood rigidly with a slightly alarmed expression. Hallam held his father's hand and looked up at him solemnly. Lionel, his pretty head on one side, was still pouting. *Don't want to,* I could hear him thinking. *Why should I. Not fair.* It didn't take long, though, for Lionel to realise that his soulful gaze and big eyes and pouty lips worked very well for the camera, and he quite quickly came round to the whole idea of being photographed. He could break hearts, I think, one day.


Not long after Mr Rejlander's visit, Mr Cameron went back to Ceylon again, and left Julia in her usual state when he was away, drowned (as she constantly told everyone) in troubles and cares, fidgety and unsettled, being even more needy than usual with her friends, looking constantly for distractions. As a result she decided to visit her married daughter who lived in Kent, and for the week or so that she was gone the household relaxed into what was almost a holiday, that lightness of heart which servants have when the master and mistress of the house are away; as long as the place did not burn down we could all breathe freely, and raise our eyes from the ground and look about us. Of course we went on keeping the floors swept and the fires lit and everything ticking over, but by tacit consent no one had to rush or fret, and if a layer of dust formed over the furniture or there were muddy footprints in the hall, well, they would still be there tomorrow and everything could be set in order in half a day before Julia's return. We could dawdle over our duties or even neglect them altogether and no one seemed to mind too much.

Billy's role was of course quite superfluous when Julia was away, so he managed to spend hours at a time quite free. (He was by now far too tall to be convincing as a page, and he had somehow got himself promoted to Butler, although he did precious little buttling since he much preferred the horses and being out-of-doors.) He liked to roam the downs or stroll about the village or go down to the sea, and I liked to walk on the downs too, but the place I loved most was always the bay, that curve of shingle where the sea made its constant deep-throated roar. There was a vast white rock there shaped like an arch which stood in the sea, and I had a childish fantasy that if I could somehow get through that arch I would find myself in another world, an untraveled world that gleamed and beckoned to me. One sultry afternoon during Julia's absence, when the house and the rest of the servants seemed to have sunk into a comatose state, I persuaded Billy to come to the beach with me. I wanted to search among the pebbles for shells and for bits of glass that had been polished smooth by the sea. My favourites were blue; they looked dull and washed and cloudy, but if I dipped them back in the water they glowed again with a lovely deep transparent colour.

'Look, Billy,' I said, holding two pieces of sea glass up, one against each ear, 'sapphire earrings. Do they suit me?'

He looked up from the bit of fishing net he'd been trying to disentangle from a rock and when he saw me he straightened up and grinned.

'They do, Mary,' he said. 'Give them to me. I'll make them into proper jewels for you.'

I laughed and handed them over to him and forgot about them, but a day or two later he said to walk over to the stables with him and when we got inside he put his hand in his pocket and pulled out a little twist of paper and gave it to me. When I opened it there were the bits of blue sea glass wrapped delicately in bits of silver wire to make a pair of earrings, not like any I had ever seen, but I thought they were the prettiest jewels I was ever likely to have. I didn't ask where he had got the silver wire from although I did remember that a man had come to mend a chandelier a month before and I knew that Billy liked to snap up the odd trifle in case it came in useful later.

'These are beautiful, Billy,' I said.

'Put them on, Mary,' he said.

'But I've not got holes in my ears.'

He hadn't thought of that, but then he found a bit of twine and fixed the little hooks onto that and tied them onto my ears.

'There,' he said, 'you're a fine lady now, Mary Ryan.'

The sound of his voice as he said that suddenly made me feel strange, a bit shivery and hot at the same time. Billy was seventeen now and a handsome lad and I looked at his smiling mouth and all in a moment I wondered what it would be like to kiss him. I felt warmth rise through my face at the thought, and I turned my head so that he would not see my blushes. He reached out and flicked my nose and grinned at me the way he always did, and I said that I must get back into the house and I picked up my skirts and walked quickly away, but something had shifted inside me. I knew that Billy had an eye for the girls, and there were more than a few young ladies who would make eyes at him across the pews on Sundays, and now I felt a stab of jealousy when I thought of how Billy gave them his blue-eyed look in return. Some of them would walk out with him too, in the evenings, along the seashore or among the woods, and I had not even liked to think about that. I had always thought of Billy as mine; my friend, my companion, the person I trusted above all else. I did not want to share him with anyone else. My footsteps slowed. Perhaps I would go back to the stables now, hold out my hand to him, draw him close, raise my face to his—

I paused, ready to turn back. But then—Mammy had warned me often enough, when I was barely old enough to understand, not to be alone with men, not to let them touch me. She had explained very clearly what it was that men did to women given half a chance; and besides Mammy's tipsy lectures I had witnessed enough when we were in Putney to know a good deal on the subject; some nights in the boarding house there was enough of what Mammy called *goings-on* going on in the same grimy fetid room where we slept on our heap of rags. I knew where babies came from and I knew how they got there in the first place. I did not want to think of Billy acting like that, but he was a man after all, practically, and Mammy said all men were the same. If I went back, I was pretty sure I could get Billy to kiss me, but it would have to stop at kissing.

I closed my eyes and pressed my hands to my face. The thought of Billy's smiling mouth was pulling me back like a magnet, but Mammy's voice was saying in my ear *now, then, Mary, mind you don't let the boys be taking any liberties with you—*

'Mary!'

My eyes flew open and I thought I had gone mad, that I had conjured her up by thinking of her words.

'Mary,' she said again, impatient, beckoning to me from over the stone wall that bordered the lane, 'come on now, let me in the gate, will you, I've been walking a hundred miles to get to you and I'm ready to drop.'

In a daze I walked to open the wicket gate and I let her put her arms around me and I felt her kiss on my cheek.

'Well, my girl, you have grown into a fine lady, now,' she said. 'Will you not take me into the house and let me have a bite to eat?'

It really was Mammy. She looked older. She still had the boots and the plaid dress—could it be the same one? No hat, though, now, just hair almost entirely grey, deep lines scored into her forehead, a stale unwashed miasma about her. I stepped back from her embrace and led her round to the scullery door. Mercifully it was Mrs Lyle's afternoon off and it was only Louisa in the kitchen, getting the tea things ready for upstairs. She stared as I walked in, and I tried as hard as I could to look and sound as I usually did, though my voice was sticking in my throat and the back of my eyes were prickling.

'Louisa,' I said, 'can we spare a cup of tea and one of those muffins? You'll remember my—my mother. She's come a long way to see me.'

Louisa behaved beautifully. She hid her surprise pretty well, and poured a cup of tea, and I buttered a muffin and Mammy sat down at the kitchen table and began to eat and drink, not greedily or slurping her tea as I had feared but with exaggerated daintiness which was somehow worse. When Louisa went out with the tea tray I asked Mammy what she was going to do.

'I don't know yet, Mary,' she said. 'A bit of a holiday, perhaps. Here by the sea. I have a fancy to live by the sea for a while. It reminds me of the Old Country.'

'Where will you stay, Mother?' I asked uneasily.

'Can I not stay with my only child, now, Mary?' She had that wheedling note in her voice.

'I don't think so, Mother. I can't invite you to stay. This isn't my house.'

'Too grand for your old Mammy now, are you, Mary?'

'Of course not,' I said.

'I don't mind sharing your room, Mary.'

'I share the room with Louisa,' I said. 'There's scarcely enough room for us both as it is. Perhaps the hotel will have a room.'

I was thinking of Plumley's Hotel down the road, where Mr Dodgson always stayed when he visited. At that Mammy, half way through a second muffin, gave a laugh which turned into a cough, so I had to thump her on the back.

'A hotel? You have got fancy ideas, my girl. How am I to afford a hotel, do you think?'

I stood up.

'I'll pay, Mother. I have some savings. I'll pay for your room at Plumley's for a few days, so you can have a rest and a holiday.'

She eyed me craftily.

'Board as well as lodging?'

'No,' I said. 'I can't afford that. I'll bring you food from here if I can, but otherwise you can get a cheap dinner at the village inn.'

She poured herself another cup of tea and leaned back in the chair.

'This is a nice place you've got here, Mary. Easy work, I should say, good clean air, a mistress who isn't too fussy.'

'It isn't easy. Being a servant isn't easy. You know that; and you always said it was next door to being a slave.'

'So it is. It's not for me, Mary. But I'm glad you're settled in a cushy billet yourself, so I am. You keep it, my girl, just do as you're bid and know your place, and you'll be all right, I dare say.'

Just then Louisa came back and I went up to my room and got my wooden box out from under my bed and took out some money and went back down and gave it to my mother. She'd got Louisa to make a fresh pot and now she was eating one of the macaroons that I knew Louisa had been saving for herself.

'My mother is just going,' I said to Louisa, not meeting Mammy's eyes. 'She's taking a room at Plumley's for a few days.'

Mammy took her time finishing her tea and eating every crumb on the plate, but at last she gathered herself up and made for the kitchen door.

'I'll drop in to see you tomorrow, Mary,' she said graciously. 'Perhaps I'll come about teatime, since your friend has made me so welcome.'

I watched her go and then I sank into the chair she had just vacated and buried my head in my hands. Louisa came over and patted my shoulder.

'Are you all right, there, Mary?' she asked awkwardly.

I reached up and held her hand for a moment while I collected myself. I was heartily glad that only Louisa was there, and at the same time I was deeply ashamed of myself for wishing my mother a thousand miles away.

My mother stayed at Plumley's until my money ran out, and then she disappeared again, taking with her a shawl I had loaned to her, half a dozen macaroons, a game pie from the pantry, and, I strongly suspected, a silver tea strainer that we could never find afterwards. At least she was gone before Julia's return from Kent. I did not want them to meet again.

# 12

When we knew Julia was expected back there was a deal of getting the house all clean and ready for her, and our days of peace were over. As soon as she stepped back inside all was bustle and confusion just as it always was when Julia was present—baggage to be brought in, much exclaiming about the dear beloved house and the dramas of the journey—and in particular this time a deal of shrieking about one of the trunks which apparently held something very precious. Billy was deputed to unpack it with many injunctions and instructions to take the greatest possible care with the contents, and we thought it must be a Dresden china service or a set of Bohemian crystal glasses, so he was rather unimpressed when it turned out to a couple of wooden boxes and some plain glass cut into rectangles and a tripod stand. A camera, in fact. It was a gift, it seemed, from Julia's daughter and son-in-law, who had thought it might amuse her while Mr Cameron was away.

Julia was enthralled from the first moment she started trying to figure the thing out. It was all laid on the dining room table while she prodded it and puzzled over it, and tried to remember what Oskar Rejlander had said, and then Hillier and I had to take all the glass plates into the kitchen together with some bottles of various kinds and Julia came marching after us giving orders. There was a printed leaflet that gave instructions, but Julia was not the sort to bother with such prosaic matters as that. (In any case, she claimed, she already knew a good deal about photography, both from Mr Rejlander, and from an old friend she had met abroad, a Sir John Somebody who was an astronomer.) She rolled up her sleeves and off she went, pouring some vile-smelling liquid over the glass while trying to tilt it this way and that, to get it evenly coated and keep it all steady, and the stuff got all over her hands and clothes, making black streaks and stinking to high heaven, while Mrs Lyle tutted about her sink. Then it was back to the camera, getting it steady on the tripod, fitting the lens and peering in and screwing and unscrewing it, and within a couple of hours she was sure she had got the measure of it and she was burning to take her first photograph.

'It must be a portrait!' she said. 'Someone with a noble face—'

Billy and Hillier and I all glanced at each other, trying hard not to look noble in case she picked on one of us. We were saved, though; Julia, standing near the window, happened to see a herd of cows being driven up the lane with the farmer following behind.

'There!' she shouted. 'There, that man—oh, Providence has sent him—does he not have a look of Bolingbroke?' and with that she galloped out of the door and down the path, leaving the gate wide open, and was straight in amongst the cows, sending them into a panic while the poor farmer roared and cursed as they all turned tail and headed into Julia's garden.

'A look of who?' said Hillier.

'Bolingbroke,' I said. 'He's in Richard II.'

Billy raised his eyebrows at me. I stuck my tongue out. Outside voices rose while the cows bellowed and jostled and trampled the flowers underfoot, their hooves sinking deep into the beautiful smooth green lawn. After a while they calmed down and wandered over to graze on the vegetable patch, tearing up mouthfuls of carrot tops and beetroot leaves with evident relish, treading on the strawberries and breaking a dozen glass cloches that had been set over the lettuces. One cow effectively demolished a row of bean poles with a sweep of her horns, and a large brindled animal started eating the roses outside the drawing room window. The noise had brought the other servants clustering into the room to enjoy the show, but it was over fairly soon, after Billy and I went out and helped the farmer to get the cattle out of the garden and back along the lane into the field.

Julia was quite unperturbed by the damage; within a very short time she was back indoors, the bewildered farmer firmly in tow, and with promises of half-a-crown an hour the poor man was seated in a carved wooden chair and swathed in an old bedsheet fastened with a brooch, looking terrified while Julia ordered him to look this way and that way and keep still and move left and move right and keep still again. She moved her camera back and forth and side to side, she got under the black cloth and out again, fiddled with the lens, broke two glass plates by dropping them and a third by sitting on one, and at last took a photograph which she promptly erased by rubbing her hand over the glass.

She had started, though. Weeks, then months, went past while she tried and failed and tried again to produce an actual photograph, and we all began to think it was a passing fancy and nothing would come of it. Julia, after all, was given to enthusiasms into which she threw herself with the utmost abandon—painting, writing bad verse, making horrible wax flowers—and they were instantly dropped when something new came along. But this time she persevered.

'Curtains!' she said suddenly, one day, as I was bringing her coffee into the morning room. She was polishing some glass plates as though her life depended on it, using the ends of her shawl and adding new smears rather than taking any away. 'Have we any dark curtains, Mary?'

'The curtains in Mr Cameron's study are a very dark green, Ma'am,' I said cautiously.

'Then get them down, Mary. Get them down. I shall buy new ones before he is home—red, perhaps, less gloomy.'

'Very well,' I said. 'Shall I dispose of the green ones?'

'Dispose of them? No, no, I need them. That is the point, Mary.'

'Shall I have them cleaned?'

'No time for that,' said Julia. She had the gleam in her eye that always meant something was afoot. 'You will hang them in the fowl-house, Mary.'

'You want the curtains hung in the fowl-house?'

This seemed not entirely rational, even by Julia's standards.

'Just one, perhaps, for now. Rig up a line or something like that.'

I waited.

'The hens will have to go, I'm afraid.'

'All of them? Shall I have their necks wrung, Ma'am?'

She gave a little shriek.

'No, no! Set the poor creatures free—let them taste liberty! Let them roam at will, roost in the trees, live the lives that nature intended for them! The fowl-house is to be my studio, Mary, do you not see? That humble little place will exchange the society of hens and chickens for that of poets and prophets and lovely maidens. The curtain is to be my backcloth—and I will need a chair—and somewhere in the attic I have a trunk of shawls and cloaks that may be required—'

So the fowl-house was requisitioned and turned into a studio, and the coalhouse into a darkroom. Hal was cross because he had a small business going, collecting the eggs and selling the surplus, which was a useful income for a twelve-year-old. (His mother assured him that he would find the eggs laid about the garden, and that they would be worth even more because their providers would be enjoying health-giving freedom and thus laying eggs of peculiar deliciousness. In fact all the hens were consumed in very short order by foxes.)

By now Julia was sweeping all before her, dismissing any and every objection or problem out of hand, and once she had things organised to her satisfaction she started looking for models. Bolingbroke had got away from her, but she decided that children would be delightful subjects and she rounded up two or three local infants and imprisoned them in the fowl-house for hours, lecturing them on their good fortune in sacrificing themselves in the name of art in order to make them sit still, and she very nearly got a picture out of them when one child gave a splutter of laughter and set the others off so it was ruined. Undeterred, she sent a couple of the children packing and concentrated on one of them, a little girl, as being the most biddable.

'Just think, Annie,' she said sternly, 'of the waste of these very expensive chemicals if you were to laugh, or move—and of all the effort poor Mrs Cameron is putting into this work—you would not want to spoil it, now, would you? *Would you?*'

The child seemed suitably cowed by this, and at last Julia got her first success. She was in raptures, running all over the house to find suitable gifts to reward the little girl (or unsuitable, it was all the same to Julia). Then she disappeared into the darkroom and eventually she reappeared with a print. She announced that she would be presenting it to Annie's father, but first the entire household had to be summoned to admire and wonder at it.

'Beauty!' exclaimed Julia, never one to hesitate when it came to blowing her own trumpet. 'The sweet, sweet child—here she is—see what I have done, see how I have captured her expression—it is a triumph—oh, what joy, what delight—'

And so on. I looked at the picture, long and hard. There she was, Annie Philpot, her hair unbrushed, her coat collar slightly askew, looking solemn, her dark eyes shadowed, the faint hint of a frown on her brow. The others nodded and said the things they knew they must and drifted back to the kitchen or the garden or wherever they were supposed to be. Only I lingered on, looking.

'You like it, Mary?' she asked. It was a rhetorical question, I knew, but I answered it anyway.

'I think it is remarkable,' I said. 'I have not seen many photographs at all; I have little to compare it with; but this seems to me something extraordinary.'

She looked gratified, and patted my arm.

'This is my work. I have begun,' she said. 'I have found my métier.'

I was inclined to agree.


After that there was no stopping her. The fowl-house became the centre of her world, and she lured, commanded, bullied and cajoled everyone of her acquaintance and many complete strangers into sitting for her, generally in some sort of fancy dress. Mr Cameron, as soon as he returned from Ceylon, had to pose, of course ('look at him! a philosopher, with his beard dipped in moonlight!' shrieked Julia)—her sons—Dear Philip—Il Signor— local children—sisters and nieces, visitors, labourers, sailors, porters, unfortunate passers-by whom she would spot from her bedroom and hurtle down and out into the road to capture, dress in berets and cloaks and crowns, and oblige to sit completely motionless for interminable stretches of time. Once she saw the local policeman passing and rushed out to accost him, convinced that he would make a perfectly splendid Sir Galahad (although in the end he was rejected; he didn't have the calves, apparently). She brooked no opposition. Poor Mr Tennyson resisted as long as he could, saying he was not going to waste the precious hours of summer sitting in a fowl-house swathed in shawls, but inevitably she wore even him down in the end.

It didn't take long before Julia started on the servants. First she pounced on Hillier, draping her in sheets and taking a likeness of her full face. Apparently she was supposed to be St Agnes, virgin martyr, patron saint of chastity. Personally I thought Hillier looked a bit simple in that photograph, but Julia was in raptures. It was no surprise, really, the day she announced that she was going to photograph me. It was to be a biblical scene, apparently, something to do with Queen Esther, who appeared in one of the books of the Old Testament that had somehow escaped me. I believe it was Hillier's afternoon off, so it was Mary Kellaway and I who were ordered to the fowl-house one hot afternoon, to find Dear Philip already there, wearing a cardboard crown and a cloak and looking resigned. He was to be King Ahasuerus. It was not spacious inside the fowl-house—which had a glazed roof—and it was a hot day. With the three of us, and Julia, and the camera, it was stifling, especially when we were swathed in towels and shawls and robes.

'Now, Mary!'

'Yes,' we both said, together. Of course.

'You, Mary,'—this to Kellaway—'put this veil about your head—yes—so—and Mary,'—(my turn)—'you are to be Esther—'

She undid my hair, fanning it out about my shoulders, and seized a jewelled band to tie about my forehead.

'Now—loosen your dress, Mary, your throat must be bare—and now, Mary, swoon! Swoon!'

Mary Kellaway obligingly fell backwards into my arms. However, it turned out it was I who was to do the swooning while Kellaway supported me. We were posed at last, but apparently it would not do.

'Philip!' she shouted. 'Look kingly!'

Sir Henry gave his fishy smile, but it was not enough.

'A sceptre! Yes, that is it—you must have a sceptre!' Off she went to the house and flew back with the drawing room poker. 'Here—hold this—yes! yes! Now, Mary—' She poked me to make sure I knew it was I she was addressing this time—'swoon!'.

I did my best. I really did. I rested my head on Mary Kellaway's shoulder and closed my eyes. The minutes dragged by in the heat, and a fly buzzed irritatingly about the glass panes, and my neck, which was at an awkward angle, started to hurt, and I could feel poor Kellaway trembling with the effort to stay perfectly still, and I could hear Sir Henry breathing rather heavily in our direction, and all the while Julia exhorted us not to move even a fraction, until at long, long last she gave a triumphant cry and released us from the torment.

'I have it!' she said. 'Yes, I believe I do have a picture—now, no time to lose, I must get this plate to the dark room—Mary, come and help me, will you?'

This time I knew it was me she meant; Mary Kellaway had neither taste nor aptitude for helping with the technical side of Julia's pastime. The making of a photograph is a long process, laborious yet delicate, and I had been intrigued by it from the start. I had already been called upon frequently to help with the preparation of the glass plates, the stink of the collodion catching me in the back of the throat as I poured the viscous stuff over the glass while Julia tilted it this way and that to ensure an even coating, and then immersed it in the sensitising bath. After the exposure there was the developing—balancing the plate in one hand while the developing solution was poured—and washing, which necessitated endless cans of freezing well-water—warming the negatives before a fire—varnishing—until at last, assuming the glass had not cracked or the varnish had not destroyed the collodion—there was a picture. It was the printing, however, that

I really liked; and I was, I admit, intrigued to see this image Julia had made of me.

She pressed the negative onto the silver nitrate paper and we carried it out into the sunlight, and sat together while we watched the picture emerge. Sir Henry's face, Kellaway's face, my face, emerging from nothing, ghostly blurs gradually taking shape, sharpening, refining. The fringe of the white woollen shawl, the veins on the back of Sir Henry's hand, the loose strands of my hair. A photograph.

'Perfection,' gasped Julia. 'Oh, the nobility of dear Philip's face—and you, my beautiful girl—Queen Esther to the life—'

On she went. Apparently I was an exact representation of the audacious and irresistible heroine who averted the massacre of her people. I have no idea why Esther had to swoon to do this but then I am not convinced Julia did either. As it turned out this photograph was rather popular with the public when it was released into the outside world. At the time, though, I just gazed at it and thought: it is dreadful. Truly, truly dreadful.

It looked exactly what it was: an old man with a poker and two maids dressed up, inside a fowl-house. You could see the glass panes, and the old curtain from Mr Cameron's study I had rigged up myself, behind us. The varnish had cracked the collodion film as the image was being fixed on the negative and the cracks showed in the print. Worse than anything, though, was me. I didn't look like Queen Esther, whatever Julia might have said. I didn't look like Queen Anyone. I looked like what I was: an Irish servant girl wearing a woollen shawl and a stupid band round her head, a servant who can't wait to be released and get back to the pots and pans. I hated it. If Julia hadn't been there I would have destroyed it and pretended it was ruined as so many of her pictures were, by heat or dust or chemicals or carelessness. As it was I had to pretend I was happy with it. But

I didn't want to be in any more photographs. Not, of course, that I had a choice.

# 13

The Great Painter whom Julia always called Signor had a less romantic real name which was Mr Watts. One of Julia's beautiful sisters, Mrs Prinsep, who lived in London, had virtually captured Mr Watts some years ago and kept him as a house pet but he was allowed out now and then, and often he came down to Freshwater to see Julia. All the Pattle sisters idolised him and I once saw Julia actually kneeling at his feet to offer him a cucumber sandwich. He seemed a gentle sort of man, quite modest, and despite all this worship (or perhaps because of it) content to be dictated to by the imperious women who had surrounded him. His visits to Dimbola were always occasions of awestruck excitement for Julia and when he agreed to paint Mr Tennyson's portrait it was as though all her birthdays had come at once for naturally she took full credit for the arrangement and the thought of Il Signor and the Great Poet spending hours together actually in Freshwater, where she could get at them both within yards of her own house, made her dizzy with happiness. So Mr Watts turned up at Dimbola regularly over that summer; but it was not only the portrait painting for which the Seven Sisters could take credit. They seem to have arranged Mr Watts's private life as well for it was at the London home of Mrs Prinsep that he had apparently met a lady and very quickly became engaged to be married. He was at this time nearly fifty years old and when I heard the servants' gossip of his engagement I naturally assumed that some kindly grey-haired widow had agreed to take him on and nurse him tenderly into his declining years. I learned that the lady was also to visit us at Dimbola that summer, and I pictured her—a little plump, perhaps, faded, motherly, twinkling—and I was very happy for him. When the betrothed couple arrived, however, I was in for a surprise.

Tea was to be served in the drawing room as usual, and I followed Louisa who had the tea tray while I carried the sandwiches (foie gras and cress) and the cake (Madeira) and when I saw the scene before me it was only with great presence of mind that I did not drop the whole lot onto the Persian carpet. There was Mr Watts on the sofa and sitting next to him was a girl who looked scarcely older than I was. The Great Painter was looking at this girl as though she were a rare creature, a white gazelle, perhaps, or a bird of paradise, which he had managed to capture but which was now causing him some anxiety. Mr Watts had a greying moustache and a beard (of course) and a high forehead and he generally wore a sort of skull cap which I think was supposed to proclaim that he was an artist just in case there was anyone whom Julia had failed to inform of the fact. He was not a bad-looking man but next to the girl beside him he simply looked old.

She was not classically beautiful. She was pale, and her hair was an unremarkable brown, and her jaw was rather square. She was wearing a plain dark green dress, with hardly anything in the way of lace or ribbons. But when she turned to see who had entered, and then smiled (either at Louisa and me, or at the cake and sandwiches, it was hard to say) she gave off a warmth and loveliness that just made one want to smile back, and in fact I did smile at her, I could not help it, even though I had had it drummed into me a thousand times that servants did not smile but looked grave and respectful at all times. The way she turned her head, the softness and curve of her cheek, the expression in her eyes; all were irresistible. Louisa and I put our trays down and set the dishes on the tea-table and glided out of the room, but as soon as we were the other side of the door we looked at each other with our eyes wide and our mouths open.

'Well, my eye!' said Louisa as we went back to the kitchen. 'She'm a purty thing, ain't she? It don't se'm fitten, so it don't.'

(Louisa really did talk like this, and so did the other Island servants. Sometimes I had to ask what they had said, but usually I got the drift.)

The consensus among the servants was: firstly, that there was no fool like an old fool; secondly, that the girl was an actress and therefore no better than she should be; and thirdly, that it was all bound to end in tears. In view of what later transpired I should say that all those assertions were bang on the nail. Opinion above stairs, though, at the time, was quite different. Julia was clearly thrilled, for she loved matchmaking especially where there was an element of the fairy tale, and Cinderella's finding security and riches through marriage was one of her favourites. Of course Mr Watts was no Prince Charming but in Julia's eyes genius and fame were a fair match for beauty. There was another factor, too, perhaps—Julia herself had married, aged twenty-two, a man twenty years older than herself. Unkind people might have hinted that as the plain sister among so many beauties she had been glad to take any offer she could get; but it always seemed to me that despite the age difference the Camerons were very well suited and on the whole were very happy together. Both were eccentric, both were artistic and liberal in their outlook, and they tolerated each other's strange behaviour. Julia pined when Mr Cameron was away; he bore patiently with her enthusiasms and extravagances and crushes as he surely would not have done if he did not love her. So it was not perhaps entirely fanciful in Julia's eyes to imagine that the marriage of a young ardent girl to a much older man might be a happy one.

I don't know quite what Mr Cameron thought of the match. He generally avoided visitors when he could, and in fact he often did not emerge from his room at all, except sometimes in the very early mornings to potter about the lawns in his dressing gown. If he came across Miss Terry he looked at her with vague surprise, but one could hardly be sure that he had actually registered who she was. It was perfectly clear, however, what his sons felt about her.

Charlie, aged fifteen, arrived back from school for the summer holidays to find that a glamorous young actress, at something of a loose end while her betrothed was painting madly (he was prolific, Il Signor, he painted dozens of pictures every year, enormous biblical scenes and society ladies and naked nymphs), was quite often to be found wandering about the garden at Dimbola reciting lines from plays to herself, drinking tea in the shade, or just looking sultry while the youth of the village, like moths in the vicinity of a particularly vivid flame, spent an inordinate amount of time walking up and down the road and peering over the garden walls in the hope of catching a glimpse of her.

Charlie wasn't altogether at ease with girls. (I don't count myself; he was perfectly at ease with servants, in the sense of not really being aware of them as actual human beings.) I suppose being sent away to a school where there were only other boys was the reason. When he first saw Miss Terry he was quite bereft of speech; I was there, serving the luncheon, and Charlie was doing a fair impression of a goldfish, opening and closing his mouth silently while goggling hopelessly at Miss Terry, which was doubly unfortunate because Charlie had a slightly fish-like face to start with; while his brother, who was thirteen, couldn't even look at her without turning a deep shade of beetroot. She appeared to be serenely unaware of this, but when I leaned over to offer her some cold salmon she glanced up at me and gave me a wink which plainly said *Honestly! Boys! Aren't they just the living limit?* I bit my lip hard so as not to laugh but I winked back. I told you she was irresistible.

Later that day Miss Terry was sitting in the shade of a mulberry tree in the garden when I went out to hang some laundry. She jumped up and came over to watch, and she told me her name was Ellen, and asked me mine, and we got to talking quite easily; and after that first time we quite often chatted when there was no one else about, for I think she was lonely, surrounded as she was by so many people who were much older than she and a couple of mooncalves.

'You're the parlourmaid, Mary, aren't you?' she said to me one day. Before I could answer, she'd rushed on. 'Well, I can see you are, of course; but you sound educated—you sound like a lady. How did you come to be a servant?'

'Oh,' I said, not wanting to tell the whole story, or even much of it, 'Julia adopted me. I am a sort of daughter to her. But I did not want to live on her charity, so naturally I work a little in the household.' I was rather pleased with this version of events. It was not altogether untrue.

'That's commendable,' she said. 'And I suppose when you marry, you will know just how to run a household, having had the experience. I have no idea at all.'

'You will learn,' I said, wondering if she would.

'I don't think I really want to, though. I have my career to think of.'

105

'Will you be an actress even after you are married, then? Will Mr Watts mind?'

She laughed, although it was rather an uncertain laugh. 'Mind? What's it got to do with him?'

I didn't answer that one. I began to wonder, though, whether Ellen was not making a very great mistake, and moreover I wondered if she was wondering that too. The next time we talked in the shade of the mulberry tree I asked her straight out why she was marrying him.

'I have to,' she said. She looked a bit agitated when she said this. She may even have blushed.

'No, you don't. People break engagements. Some people don't get married at all. Some people get married and then are very sorry that they did.' I was thinking of my own mother and father.

'But,' she said, pressing one elegant white hand to her bosom, 'you see—he has already—kissed me. *Passionately*!'

'Even so—'

'So now I must be going to have a baby,' she explained, patiently. 'Because I have been kissed.'

I did not know what to say. Should I enlighten her? But she was older than I, and despite what I had said, I really was a servant, and it was not my place, surely, to explain to this seemingly sophisticated young woman—an actress, for heaven's sake—that you could not get a baby just by kissing, even passionately. So I hesitated, and then I was called from the house, and the moment passed.


I was busy all the rest of that afternoon. Mrs Lyle had decided that the silver must be cleaned and that was my job so I was imprisoned in the hot steamy kitchen, sitting at the long table with newspaper spread out to protect it, wearing a grimy apron, rubbing at spoons and knives and coffee pots and trays, surrounded by old cloths and acrid-smelling polish. I thought of Ellen's white hands with their clean pink nails like a row of shells, and I looked at my own hands as I worked, red and chapped, the black of the tarnish engrained into my skin and the nails filthy. When Mrs Lyle sat down for her cup of tea and her eyes started closing, I put down the sauceboat I was working on and tiptoed to the kitchen window. From there I could see Ellen, in her loose floating dress of lace and muslin, still reclining in the low rattan chair, a book lying unread on the grass beside her. She looked cool and clean and fresh and alluring. As I watched, I saw Billy saunter out into the garden, carrying a bundle of hazel twigs, and begin to put them in the earth to stake up the pea plants in the vegetable bed. I hadn't realised that Billy was helping out the gardener, but he did take whatever jobs he fancied and perhaps that day he fancied staking the peas just where he could get a good look at Ellen. She seemed entirely unaware of his presence for a while; then she glanced over towards him, picked up her neglected book, yawning prettily, and dropped the book again with a little flutter of her beautiful hands. Billy was there in an instant, picking up the book, dusting it off, presenting it back to her with a flourish, and I could see her smiling up at him, tilting her head a little, one hand playing with a stray tendril of hair that had fallen across her breast.

I had to go back to the silver then because Mrs Lyle had woken up and was demanding to know what I thought I was doing, staring out of the window while there was work to be done. I rubbed and polished all the rest of the afternoon, making every piece of silver as brilliant as I could, not missing even the tiniest trace of tarnish, so that even Mrs Lyle was pleased and said I was a grand lass when I put my mind to it. It was that or sweep the whole lot onto the floor with one vast satisfying crash.

As well as painting Mr Tennyson's portrait, Il Signor was, at that time, also painting his bride-to-be. I know both pictures. In the first, the Great Poet, against a background of dark leaves with just a glimpse of sky above, is facing the viewer, although he is not exactly meeting their eyes. Perhaps he is seeing something invisible to the rest of us; something that only exists in his mind's eye. He looks sombre, and he looks clever, and he looks mysterious. Is he about to recite one of his poems, perhaps? Or is he composing another? Either way, you can tell something important is happening inside that great distinguished head.

The second picture, the portrait of Mr Watts's teenage bride, shows Ellen leaning almost out of the picture as she presses forward to inhale some exotic blooms (although as far as I can tell they are camellias, which of course have hardly any perfume at all). The flowers fall against her creamy throat and bring out the warm red of her parted lips. Tucked away in one corner of the picture, almost invisible in her left hand, are some tiny violets. The picture is called *Choosing*. Glamorous waxy crimson flowers, or little modest sweetly-scented violets? What do you think, Ellen?

What would I choose for myself?

Oh, I don't know. Can I have both, please?

# 14

Mr Watts married Ellen Terry in February and they came to Freshwater frequently during the summer that followed. Of course Julia was mad to photograph Ellen, and Ellen was more than happy to pose. She was an actress, used to being the centre of attention, in fact she loved it, like the cat lapping the cream. When people looked at her she came alive, she glowed, she bloomed. Julia got her arranged, not, this time, in the fowl-house, but in one of the bedrooms at Dimbola. It was something about the wallpaper, apparently, Julia wanted a little pattern to set off the plainness of Ellen's dress, so the camera had to be lugged upstairs and Hillier and I were told to do that. Ellen was wearing a skimpy white shift, the lace-trimmed edges barely clinging to her shoulders, and her hair loose, and a string of beads round her neck. This idea, I gathered, was that the portrait should be a gift to Il Signor, the proud husband, who was nowhere to be seen that day; busy painting some magnificent allegorical scene, I supposed. Julia as usual was shouting instructions at Ellen while adjusting the lens—'Look up! Look down! Now, think of your joy as you contemplate your marriage, your life together with your lord, the great artist, the sublime Signor—oh, the bliss of the new bride, the blushing rapture ...'

Hillier listened to all this without much expression except vague puzzlement, while Ellen leaned moodily against the bedroom wall and fiddled with her beads. Julia kept up the tirade of instructions while darting in and out of the black camera-cloth, Ellen sighed and closed her eyes, as though trying very hard to think of something else altogether, and eventually the picture was done and Julia sailed off with the plate to do the developing. Hillier and I carted everything back downstairs again, and Ellen went off to put some proper clothes on. I caught up with her later that day; I had gone out to pick blackcurrants, and she was mooching about the garden.

'Have you seen the picture, Mary?' she asked me.

'No,' I said. 'How did it turn out?'

'Oh, it's beautiful,' she said, dispassionately. 'Perfect. I think I might use it as a publicity photograph, once I'm back on stage.'

'Then you will be going back to acting?'

I was surprised, but pleased. I had formed the unpleasant idea that Mr Watts would somehow be keeping Ellen to himself, to look beautiful, to model for his paintings, to adorn his life. A bird in a gilded cage, that sort of thing.

'Oh, yes,' she said. 'Soon, I should think. Very soon.' She laughed, but it wasn't the merry laugh I had been used to hear from Ellen.

'That's good, isn't it? You always intended to go on with your stage career?'

'Yes, I did. I shall. What have you got there?'

I offered her a handful of currants, and she ate one, puckering up her lovely face at the sharp taste. I ate a couple too, to keep her company.

'I'm glad you liked the photograph,' I said. 'Mrs Cameron has an extraordinary talent, I think.'

'I suppose so,' said Ellen. I saw that the beauty of the photograph had only struck her in relation to the sitter, not the artist. 'She's mad, though, isn't she, Mrs Cameron?'

'Not mad, exactly. Unusual, perhaps.'

'No, she's definitely mad,' said Ellen firmly. 'Quite mad. All the shrieking and the weird clothes, and she will keep *giving* me things. And she has no taste. A hideous shawl, a revolting carpet bag, a turquoise bracelet. What am I to do with them? I have tried saying that she really mustn't, too generous, I couldn't possibly, that kind of thing, but she takes not a bit of notice.'

Perversely, I felt quite protective of Julia at this criticism.

'She means well,' I said. 'She likes to be generous. You'll offend her if you don't accept the things she gives you.'

'Well, she offends me by forcing them on me,' said Ellen. 'I'll tell you what, Mary, you can have them. I'll leave them with you when I go.' She sighed, rather theatrically.

'And how is—married life?' I asked. I was ashamed of myself for wanting to know, really, but I couldn't help myself. What happened at night, when the distinguished painter was just a man growing old, a man with thin legs and not much hair and silver in his beard, and his wife was a girl so full of life and youth, a girl with soft rounded limbs and white sloping shoulders and a mouth that looked as though it would taste of peaches and honey? It was not a polite question, nor a dignified one. It was, frankly, prurient. In my defence, I was fifteen, and I really wanted to know. I wanted to know about how it felt to be with a man, and I hadn't found anyone of my own age who might tell me. Mammy's dire warnings had been graphic enough; it wasn't the details of the act I needed explained to me, but the feelings, the mystery, the wonder, the romance.

'Married life?' said Ellen, and she laughed again, that cold sound. 'I haven't the least idea, Mary.'

A few days after that, the newly-weds left. Ellen did leave the shawl and the horrid carpet bag with me as parting gifts, but I noticed she had taken the turquoise bracelet, after all.

Since the time in the stables when Billy had given me the sea glass earrings, I had not been alone with him. We had walked to church side by side on Sundays with everyone else; we had eaten together in the kitchen with the other servants, as we always did; he had winked at me when he caught me making a face at Hilda behind her back; but when he suggested walking up to the downs together, or down the road to the beach, as we had always used to, I had found I was too busy or wished to be alone or I asked Louisa to come with us. I could not quite explain to myself why I was being so evasive. Billy was still my friend, I supposed; but I was not so dependent upon his friendship as I once had been. Louisa, Mary Kellaway, even Hillier, were my friends now; Julia and Mr Cameron were, in my private thoughts, a sort of family. I was not a lonely twelve-year-old, abandoned by her mother, as I had been when we first came to the Island; I was nearly sixteen, independent, unafraid. I had met and conversed with clever, interesting people, I spoke as they did, I had read the books they had read. I no longer needed Billy Hemmings to be my defender against the world. I missed his company, though. Now and then.

I was in the hay loft one rainy afternoon, reading *Romola*, when I heard Billy singing in the stable below me. I had thought he was out, driving Julia over to visit a family called Liddell who always came to Freshwater for their holidays, but the rain must have cut the visit short. Billy had a sweet voice, and he often sang to the horses, old songs he'd known from his London days.

'*I seek no more the fine and gay*

*For each doth but remind me*
*How swiftly passed the hours away*
*With the girl I left behind me ...'*

I wriggled so that I could see him through a gap in the dusty floorboards. He was standing just below me, grooming the bay mare as he sang, and the horse stood calm and still beneath his touch, giving little whickers of pleasure. The rain had made Billy's dark hair wet and it was showing the shape of his head, and I could see the muscles of his shoulders moving under his shirt as he worked, and his strong hands working over the mare's glossy sides. I watched him for a while, and then I put my mouth to the hole in the floor and I started to sing myself.

*'Where have you been all the day, Billy boy, Billy boy,*
*Where have you been all the day, charming Billy?'*

He didn't stop the rhythmic motion of his hands over the animal, and he didn't look up, but I saw his shoulders shift, and then he sang back.

*'I have been to seek a wife*
*She's the idol of my life ...'*

I joined in, and we both sang:

*'She's a young thing and cannot leave her mother!'*

I saw him put hay in the manger and pour water in the trough for the horse, and then he swung himself up the ladder and appeared beside me.

'Now then, Mary Ryan,' he said, looking down at me where I was lying on the hay, 'and why are you not at work like a good girl?'

'But I am,' I said, widening my eyes at him, 'I'm dusting the parlour, can you not see?'

'Are you now? And does your mistress know you're dusting the parlour while at the same time you're up in the loft with a book I imagine you took from her own library?'

113

'No,' I said, 'but she's in the fowl-house with Hillier, making her pose as the Virgin Mary. She'll be busy for hours.'

'She should use you instead. You look more like the blessed Virgin than Mary Hillier does.'

'Oddly enough,' I said thoughtfully, 'I don't. Hillier looks like anything Julia wants her to be, in photographs. I always look like me. I don't know why that should be.'

Billy dropped to his knees and looked at me, turning his head this way and that. I kept still.

'You do,' he said. He put out his hand and traced the line of my mouth with his thumb. 'You look just like you.' Then he lay down on the hay beside me, propped up on one elbow so that he could still look at my face, and began to trace circles on the top of my shoulder where my dress had slipped. His fingertips felt slightly rough against my bare skin, and they set up little ripples and shivers that passed right through me. He went on doing this while the rain pattered down on the slates above us, on and on, the two of us lying close, so close I could feel the warmth that came from him, but the only place we touched was where his fingers were making their rhythmic circles. His eyes were half-shut now, the long dark lashes against his cheek, his black hair curling damply over his open shirt collar. Both of us were breathing differently from the way we usually breathed.

Then we heard steps below us from the stable, and the gardener calling.

'Hemmings! Are you there? I need that horse muck shifted onto the kitchen garden before I'm any older!'

I froze; Billy sighed, and flicked my nose, and rolled away from me, and was off down the ladder with a careless greeting as though he had just been getting hay for the horses and nothing more. I stayed there until I heard their footsteps receding and then I carefully brushed all the hayseeds off me and went back to the house. I might even have gone to dust the parlour. I wasn't concentrating, though. I wasn't thinking of anything but Billy Hemmings and his fingertips on my skin.

By the end of September, Mr Watts and Ellen were separated and the marriage was over. I don't suppose Julia ever gave Il Signor the photograph she had intended as a gift for him. It shows Ellen in all her lovely soft youthful beauty; and it shows her strength, her resolute jaw and straight brows and the fine column of her neck. Julia called the picture *Sadness*.

# 15

Julia's photography had taken over her life, and thus it had taken over the life of her entire household and frequently that of her friends too, of her visitors and her acquaintances and a good many of the innocent folk of Freshwater. No one was safe. Julia lurked in her bedroom, which had a fine bay window overlooking the road, and if she saw a handsome man, a pretty girl, a winsome child, or an aged person with an interesting face, she was out there in moments practically kidnapping them. Before they knew it, they were in the fowl-house, dressed up to the nines and being ordered to look sorrowful or noble or wistful or any combination of the above and then congratulated fulsomely on having had immortality bestowed upon them. She never stopped; poor Hillier was constantly being ordered into veils and robes and obliged to hang adoringly over small children or clutch stems of white lilies or just look moony; and to be fair, Hillier was very, very good at all of those. She had the gift of being able to stay still without complaining, and of making her face a blank onto which the viewer, or at least Julia, could project anything at all.

The photographs were turned out day after day, the prints hung or lay everywhere, Julia's clothes and hands were permanently streaked with black from the chemicals, and the carrier's cart called constantly bearing glass plates and bottles and reams of paper which she got through with immense speed, since for every successful print there were a hundred which she discarded. This not to say she was a perfectionist—most of her photographs were blurred, or speckled, or showed scratches and smudges—but it was the effect, she claimed, that she wanted, not mere precision, not slavish accuracy, but beauty.

'When I am focusing the lens, Mary, I find the point where I see beauty, and then I stop.'

I sighed. It was me she had inveigled into the fowl-house this time, to pose as the Madonna.

'*La Madonna Vigilante*, Mary, which means watching always.'

I knew that, actually, although I didn't say so. I had studied quite a bit of Italian with Miss Berthold. The child I was currently watching always was the small son of Mr Gould, a sailor from the village, and the wretched boy was fidgeting and struggling on my lap. He was probably too young to appreciate the finer points of producing a photograph using an orthoscope lens and the wet collodion method, and he had only submitted to the ordeal after being bribed shamelessly with quantities of strawberry drops, chocolate creams and molasses candy. Despite this sugar-laden feast, or possibly because of it, the child was not content to keep perfectly still while Julia spent forever adjusting the focus and shouting instructions (*move to the left, to the right, don't move, look down, look up, look at me!*) and I was finding it difficult to imagine myself as the Blessed Virgin because I was so irritated with the Holy Infant and his incessant wriggling. I tried to do what Hillier did and compose my face into a blank, but when I saw the finished picture I realised I had not been in the slightest bit successful. Freddie Gould had, of course, moved during the exposure, so his fat little face and mop of hair looked as though they had been caught in a high wind, and I looked—well, somewhere between mildly alarmed and frankly exasperated. In any case I certainly didn't look like anyone's idea of the Mother of God.

Julia was happy, though. She didn't seem to see the absurdity in the scenes she was so fond of, the Madonnas and the children dressed as angels or the carpenter wearing a coal scuttle on his head and told to imagine he was King Arthur. She was firmly convinced of her own brilliance, and when she discovered there was a national competition for photography that she could submit something to, she was fired up with the complete confidence that she would sweep the board. She chose two prints to send in, one of Hillier and little Freddie as the Virgin and Child (again) and one of Dear Philip, all noble brow and flowing beard (and no smile, which I felt was wise). Of course she was completely convinced she would win, and when the letter came she tore it open with a cry of triumph. This changed into a shriek of outrage when she learned that the prize had been awarded, not to her, but to some man, for a photograph entitled *Brenda*.

She railed for days against the injustice of it all. The Photographic Society of London as a whole; the miserable specimen who had created *Brenda*; the judges—in particular the judges—all were the subject of her derision, scorn, and bitterness.

'They clearly value details of table-covers and crinolines over art!' she wailed. 'They know nothing—nothing! of true beauty—they have no souls, no poetry, no vision—can they even see what is before them? Are they such pedestrian, limited, pathetic creatures, these judges, that they fix on pure manipulation, and ignore true loveliness? They do not value my work, they do not value *me*!'

It did not take long, however, for her spirits to reassert themselves. She dismissed their criticism ('too manifestly unjust for me to attend to it at all; and although they may not value my work yet, I know it is valuable; I *know* it, Mary! I *value myself*, you

118

see!') and she redoubled her efforts, taking picture after picture. She went on being Julia, passionate, imperious, vital, despotic; and I went on assisting with the preparation and the printing, and submitting now and then to being dressed as the Queen of the May or as some dying heroine, garlanded with flowers or swathed in white, never really liking the results but resigned to this being part of my work as much as raking out the coals or setting the table for dinner. In any case, my mind wasn't on it, really. My mind was on Billy Hemmings.

Billy and I were meeting now, not every day, but when we could. We went walking on Sundays, up onto the high down, and sometimes down to the beach if I could slip out late at night; but mostly we met in the hayloft over the stable. We'd got beyond the circling of fingertips on the shoulder, but not as far as Billy would have liked. We went a little further every time we were together, finding out as the weeks went past about each other's bodies, about the things we could do to each other. Billy had certainly had some practice; I had none, but I learned fast enough.

'I'll take care of you, Mary,' he said, every time we got close. 'I won't let anything happen; I'll be careful—'

Nevertheless I always made him stop before we got quite to that place he, I, both of us wanted to be. It wasn't exactly that I didn't trust him, but I did not want to take even the slightest risk of getting a child. I liked to believe that I was thinking of Billy as well as myself every time I said *no, no further*—for I was reasonably (if not entirely) certain that he would offer to marry me if I became pregnant, and then how would his grand dreams fare, his plans to travel to America and make his fortune? But mostly I said no for myself. Like Julia, I valued myself too much.

Julia meanwhile was seeking another audience for her work, one which she was sure would be more appreciative and discerning than the philistine creatures of the Photographic Society of London. She sent some pictures to Berlin. ('Germany is the very home of photographic art,' she announced. 'There they will have a true appreciation of my work.') And in reply she received a letter which took a deal of puzzling out, written as it was by a German gentleman who was translating his own words with, we surmised, the help of a dictionary rather than a native speaker.

'*He will take the utmost sorrow to place the pictures ...*' read Julia, her face puckering like a cross child. 'Whatever can he mean? And this—Mary, can you figure it out? *The rooms are filled till the least winkle!* Winkle? The man is insane!'

I took the letter from her. (I had been sweeping the hall when the letter was brought, and she had run and pounced upon it instantly, and as she always needed an audience for her dramas I was handy.)

'Look,' I said, 'his grasp of English may be shaky, but this part is clear enough: *he sends his extra*—er—*ordinarest respects to the celebrated and famous female photographs ...* and the other bits—when he says *sorrow*, perhaps he means *care*? he is taking care to place the pictures ...'

She snatched the letter back.

'Yes! Oh, Mary, of course that is it—well, I knew, of course, that they would value my work—oh, the dear, dear man—I still don't know what he means by winkle, though—'

'I think it may be *der Winkel*? meaning corner?'

'Really, Mary? Does it? Well, that would make sense. However did you know that?'

'Miss Berthold was Prussian,' I reminded her. 'I picked up some German words from her.'

She had lost interest already, however.

'A medal, look, he says I have a medal—bronze, to be sure, but nevertheless—a medal! This will be a poke in the eye for the London Society, oh yes, indeed—', and off she hurtled to find Mr Cameron to share the blissful news. Her husband was a never-failing source of praise and enthusiasm, always her most constant admirer, and if he also smiled quietly to himself sometimes at her wilder excesses it was always a smile of affection, not of disdain.

Julia's career was launched. She started winning real recognition—after the bronze, she won a gold medal from Berlin, and then prizes began to come from English institutions. I was pleased for her, naturally, and I was not surprised, for although I found some of her dressing-up scenes (as I thought of them privately) ridiculous, I felt quite differently about her portraits, the pictures that weren't sentimental set pieces. She made a likeness of her long-suffering husband in which she somehow managed to capture all the kind, wry, patient gentleness that I always saw in him. The lines that scored the skin around his eyes showed exactly how his face creased when he smiled; the mouth twisting a little beneath the unkempt white whiskers, the mane of hair flowing back—it was him, my dear Mr Cameron, it was so perfectly him. Then the picture of her friend Mr Trollope, wearing (thank goodness) not a robe or a cardboard crown, but his everyday hat and spectacles, in which you could see the drollery and cleverness, see the man who created a whole world of people whom one recognises and loves or despises or aches for; and portraits of Charlie and Hal, of Lionel Tennyson (still pouting gorgeously), of her beautiful niece Miss Jackson, all mesmerising, direct and truthful pictures. The eyes, the mouths, the light. I thought them vastly superior to all the pictures of us, the pretty maids, posing droopily or sulkily or wistfully in dressing-up clothes. I thought those portraits wonderful.

# 16

All the photographs of me, however, were the dressing-up kind. She liked to take scenes that illustrated poems, plays, songs, legends, stories, and the more romantic or sentimental the better.

'The Queen of the May!' she would shout at me, or at Hillier 'Friar Lawrence and Juliet!' It wasn't just me and Hillier and the local infants, either. Dear Philip, for example, was often in the dressing-up pictures, and he was a good sport, I will say that, always game, and never loth to don an embroidered blouse in the interests of art. Mr Cameron, too, was constantly ready to oblige with the biblical or Shakespearean or Arthurian stuff. The difference was that whereas Sir Henry, like Hillier, was rather good at keeping a straight face, dear Mr Cameron was perfectly hopeless.

He would always do just as Julia commanded, meekly allowing himself to be draped in shawls or gowns or whatever was required, and he would sit or stand or stoop, as Julia frisked about tugging clothes into place, tilting hats, pushing and pulling us this way and that, issuing instructions and admonitions, for what seemed like hours, and he never complained or grumbled, but just when at last everything was arranged to Julia's satisfaction it would all go wrong. We would all be exhorted to hold our breath, to stay immobile, not to let even the flicker of a change come over our faces; and then, just as the lens cap was removed and the breathless hush of exposure was begun, Mr Cameron would catch my eye and then would begin to shake helplessly, biting his lip, his eyes creasing into merriment, a great guffaw finally breaking out, so that the whole thing was spoilt and Julia would start to scold him and he would apologise humbly, wiping away the tears of mirth, and we would settle back into our places and try with all our might to do as we were bid and not to let the sheer absurdity of what we were doing or what we looked like take us over again. Sometimes we were successful; sometimes it took half a day to get the photograph done. Mr Cameron would collapse into laughter and then I am afraid I would follow suit and Julia would be outraged, but she never gave up; she kept on and on, undaunted, relentless, unswerving. Focused on her Art. Always.

'What are you reading, Mary?'

I should have been dusting the library books, but I had picked up Mr Cameron's Shakespeare and sunk into the window seat and had not noticed Julia coming into the room in search of her husband. I jumped up, guiltily.

'The Tempest.'

(By now, I didn't really like calling Julia Ma'am. I didn't think it suited her. Or me. Mostly I didn't call her anything.)

'Ah, the Bard, the Swan of Avon—now then, let me see—The Tempest—yes, I have it: this Island is full of noise—how does it go?'

'*Be not afeard: the isle is full of noises,*

*Sounds and sweet airs, that give delight, and hurt not,*' I quoted.

'Yes! That could be our own Island, Mary, could it not? Yellow sands,' she said vaguely. 'Wild waves—oh! oh, oh! Prospero and Miranda!'

'Yes, that's right—and Ariel, and Caliban, and Ferdinand—it starts with a shipwreck—'

'Yes, yes, I know that, but only think, Mary, what a photograph that would make, you as Miranda, dear Philip, perhaps, as Prospero—he visits tomorrow, he must be our Duke of—where was it—'

'Milan,' I said, as if it mattered, for she was off, full of plans, and not only for this particular picture. She had found a gallery in London who were to sell her photographs, and she was preparing for an exhibition there. This forthcoming event was naturally a spur for a new flurry of activity in the fowl-house; poor Hillier was hardly ever out of a white nightgown and a wreath of flowers for days at a time, no visitor or casual passer-by was safe, and now she had seized on the idea of some more literary scenes involving, of course, a good deal of dressing-up and looking soulful, noble, tragic, romantic, or whatever high-flown emotion was required at the time.

So Dear Philip was seized upon virtually as soon as he arrived the next day and off we all went to the glass fowl-house once more. I, as Miranda, was dressed in a horrible shapeless dress of white wool which Julia unearthed from one of her innumerable trunks, while Prospero wore a dark cloak and a rather rakish velvet beret. He was seated; I was to kneel at his feet, my hair loose, while he clasped my hands and looked wisely into my eyes.

'Now, Philip, you are both noble and powerful, and yet thoughtful and tender—oh, wonderful, my dear man, you are Prospero to the life! And Mary, you are perfectly innocent and soulful, full of wonder at what you hear—yes—that is it—just push your hair back a little, look up—now, do not move, do not breathe—'

We were both pretty practised at this by now, Sir Henry and I, and we managed to get ourselves arranged to Julia's liking and actually to keep still while she took the photograph. I was not tempted to laugh as I would have done had it been darling Mr Cameron I was gazing up at so soppily, so it was all soon done and when the photograph was developed Julia declared herself thrilled.

'Dearest girl, just look at you—a perfect flower, so virginal and sweet—this will certainly go up to Colnaghi's—it will have a prominent place, no hiding this *in der winkel*, isn't that right, Mary?'

I laughed at this, as I knew I must, but I wasn't feeling particularly mirthful. It was another ridiculous scene. There I was, kneeling humbly on the floor at Sir Henry's feet; and I knew the pose was because of the play, of course it was, for Prospero says to his daughter *sit down for thou must now know further* and Julia was always keen on getting the scene arranged according to whichever legend or poem or myth she was currently enthralled by; but I always seemed to be, in her photographs, sitting or kneeling or lying, a humble, penitent, vulnerable figure, probably with a man looking down at me. Women, as well as servants, must know their place. They can hardly help it, really. There's never a shortage of reminders.


Julia was to exhibit around fifty photographs at the London gallery. She was thrown into a fever by the need to choose, and as she was firmly convinced that every one was a masterpiece it was a hard task. There were to be a range of her portraits, which I still considered her best work—Mr Cameron, Mr Tennyson, and Sir

Henry, of course; Julia's handsome friend Mr Palgrave, wearing an exotic turban from his travels in Arabia; Il Signor, and the old ones of Ellen and Mr Trollope. The dressing-up pictures were not neglected, however; she chose several of Hillier (including one of the silliest pictures the poor girl ever sat for, wearing a crown and flanked by a couple of the usual local infants), the Prospero and Miranda which I so disliked, and the Esther and Ahasuerus which I disliked even more.

Of course it shouldn't have mattered to me what I looked like in the photographs. I would never know the people in London who would look at them. The interminable posing and the stupid clothes and the hot cramped fowl-house were just part of my job, I reasoned to myself, and if great poets and artists and travellers and writers were not too grand for that, who was I to object? They had little more choice than I in the arrangement, faced as they were with the irresistible force that was Julia. And Hillier never minded all, just sat patiently, made her face a blank, and then complacently received Julia's praise.

'It's better than scrubbing the floors,' said Hillier, with a shrug, when I had asked her if she wasn't being driven stark staring mad by all this Madonna and Angel and Divine Love stuff. She had a point, I suppose. Nevertheless, I felt a shudder of distaste whenever I looked at myself in those pictures; Mary Ryan, the helpless victim, swooning, dying, pleading, adoring, and always in relation to some man or other. Always less, somehow, always *lower*.

However, Julia had her photographs chosen now, so I assumed there would be a welcome lull in the dressing-up. Arrangements were being made for the journey to London, packing cases arrived to transport the pictures, letters and telegrams flew back and forth. She was to stay with her sister, Mrs Prinsep, in Little Holland House, of course, the exhibition was to last weeks, and everyone the Pattle sisters knew would be invited to see it and to dine while Julia was there. (Mr Cameron refused to accompany her; he pleaded his usual indisposition and said London disagreed with him, which made Julia cross, because she didn't like to travel alone, but he was immovable.) Eventually everything was got ready, the photographs were all carefully packed, until Julia changed her mind about her selection and unpacked everything and started again. Then, the day before she was to leave, she announced that she wanted to take one more photograph.

It was to be yet another silly romantic scene. Two little girls, the daughters of the Master Gunner up at the fort on the cliff, had been roped in, poor dears, for what Julia vaguely said was to be a tableau depicting wandering minstrels, this being because Julia had found a lute in a rag-and-bottle shop and wanted to use it. The children were given free range of the dressing-up box, and I was to supervise them, and we were all to be in the fowl-house as soon as we were ready. Julia, usually so certain of what she wanted from her models, was for once a little vague, the arrangements for the London trip being at such frantic last-minute stage, and I was looking forward to Julia's having gone and left us all in peace for a while, so I was feeling a little less mutinous than usual as I turned out the vast trunk with its ridiculous clothes, the lace and feathers, the velvets and brocades. Katie and Lizzie, who were rather sweet, were in ecstasies. The idea was for Katie to hold the lute, while Lizzie and I would look as though we were just tuning up to sing. Lizzie found a bombazine dress and an old hat of Julia's, all bobbing feathers, which she was determined to wear; Katie chose a striped skirt and a cotton blouse; and they twirled and giggled and marched up and down singing, while I put on a dark blue velvet dress as being the least bizarre garment I could find and sat at the dressing table to brush my

127

hair, wondering if I might get through the session in time to meet Billy in the the hayloft later.

'Look at this cloak, Mary!' said little Lizzie, holding up a length of gold satin. She draped it around my shoulders. 'Now you look like a queen!'

'And there's a crown here!' said Katie, bringing out the tawdry squashed cardboard thing poor old Hillier had once been obliged to wear. 'What about this?'

'I'm not supposed to be a queen,' I explained. 'We're supposed to be minstrels. Musicians, singers.'

'But you *could* be a queen,' insisted Lizzie.

Katie drew out some white ribbons and held them against my dark hair. 'Like this,' she said. 'Then we can be very queenly minstrels.'

I laughed. 'Yes, you're right,' I said. 'We can be queenly minstrels, can't we? Why not?'

I helped the girls to get ready, brushing out their hair until it stood in clouds around their faces, securing the too-big clothes with pins, adding brooches and bracelets. They stood solemnly until I told them to turn and admire themselves in the looking glass. Their eyes widened; they smiled and preened and practised walking around the room in a dignified manner so that their hats and clothes should stay in place, while I swept my hair up and fastened it with long pins, and then tied one of the ribbons around it, and tucked in a few sprays of white silk flowers. I turned my head this way and that, to check the effect. The little girls stood behind me, watching, rapt.

'Ready?' I asked, and we made our way downstairs very carefully so that we should not trip over our skirts, and processed across the garden towards the studio. Billy was pushing a wheelbarrow full of seed potatoes along the path, and when he saw us coming he stopped and assumed an expression of exaggerated awe.

'Who are these grand ladies, now?' he asked, as Katie and Lizzie beamed and blushed and gazed adoringly at him. He looked around, and saw a clump of jonquils in the border, and he picked three, handing one to each of us in turn; and then he made a flourishing bow, and gave me a wink, and went on his way. He was whistling. Charming Billy.

Julia got us posed against the dark curtains, Katie in the centre with the lute, little Lizzie at her elbow, I on her other side.

'Stand there! Look at me, now, girls,' said Julia. 'That's it, now, Mary—'

Something wasn't right. You could always tell.

'The flowers, yes, the flowers!' She picked up the jonquils Billy had given us, lying now on the table where we had dropped them when we had come in to the studio, gave them to me, and dived beneath the black camera cloth to assess the effect. 'Hold the flowers, Mary, yes, pale against the dark dress, just so, and—I think—' She emerged, flushed and eager. 'Turn your head a little Mary—further—' Back she went under the cloth, so that her voice was muffled. Although still strident. 'Ah—now, still, still as statues! Lizzie, keep your hands just so—now, think beautiful thoughts, my dears, hear the song you are about to sing, and do not even breathe—'

I thought of a poem by Miss Rossetti that I had read the day before, and the lovely words floated through my head as we stood there, and for once I did not mind as the long minutes drifted past me.

*We weep, because the night is long*
*We laugh, for day shall rise;*
*We sing a slow contented song,*
*And knock at Paradise ...*

It was done, and the little girls and I trooped back across the garden and upstairs to change back into our everyday clothes, so

129

that once again they were just village children in cotton pinafores and I was just a parlour maid in a white apron. I repacked the trunk and took down my hair and plaited it, as I usually did, and Katie and Lizzie scampered off to their home and I went downstairs to set the table for luncheon. Julia bustled into the dining room, waving a print, as I was folding the napkins.

'What do you think, Mary? The little one has moved her hands, of course, but it has its merits, I think.'

I looked. I saw the little girls, solemn and sweet, tricked out in their dressing-up box finds. My cloak and the children's skirts were soft and blurred. And I saw myself, half-turned away from the camera, looking down, holding Billy's flowers.

'Will you take it to the exhibition?' I asked.

She pursed her lips.

'No, I think not. I have decided on Mary Hillier as the Angel at the Sepulchre, after all. It has more feeling.'

I nodded.

'Then may I keep this one?'

She looked surprised.

'If you wish, Mary. I shall make another print, in any case. Now—oh, heavens, the carrier will be here directly to take the heavy luggage and I must have my hatboxes brought down from the attic and I think I will pack my striped purple gown after all, for of course we are to have some grand parties while I am there—'

Off she flew, leaving the photograph behind. I slipped it into my apron pocket, and later I put it between two layers of tissue paper and then pressed it between the pages of Christina Rossetti to keep it safe.


I took it with me to the hayloft.

'What do you think?'

I showed Billy the photograph. He was lying by my side, stroking the skin just above my stocking top; but he glanced up, looked at the picture, and then sat up straight.

'Mary Ryan.' He whistled. 'You are a bit of jam, aren't you?'

'A bit of jam?' I pushed his hand away. 'Is that what I look like?'

'You do. The jammiest bit of jam I ever saw.' He stretched out his hand for me again, but I rolled out of reach. 'What? What have I said?'

I stood up, and brushed the hay from my skirts. Then I picked up the picture, and put it back inside the book, tucked it under my arm, and started to climb down the ladder.

'Come on now, Mary—'

I reached the bottom of the ladder, and walked out into the sunshine.

'You look like a lady!' he shouted after me. 'Is that what you wanted me to say?'

I went back into the house. Hilda was in the corridor from the kitchen. She gave me a look as I passed, and I guessed that my hair was coming adrift and perhaps there was still a dried grass stalk there or hayseeds clinging to my clothes.

'You hussy, Mary Ryan,' she breathed, as I passed. I ignored her and went on, head held high, hoping I could head up the servants' staircase without being seen and get to my bedroom for a few minutes' peace before it was time to serve the tea, but when I got to the top of the stairs Julia was there with a tottering pile of clothes in her arms, trying to reverse into her own bedroom and dropping various unmentionable garments as she bumped against the door. I put the book into my apron pocket and went to her rescue, picking the things up and holding the door open so that she could get through.

131

'Oh, Mary,' she panted, 'thank you, dear girl. If you could get these things packed then I am almost done. There is just my travelling case for the train, and my jewel box—you can do that next.'

I began to fold the clothes and lay them flat in the trunk, smoothing them as I did so, fastening buttons and ribbons as I knew a lady's maid would do.

'Is Hilda travelling with you to London?' I asked, hoping the answer would be yes. A few weeks without Julia or Hilda would be very welcome. No photographs, no shrieks, no dramas; no cold looks, no sniffs, no muttered insults …

'Oh, Hilda,' said Julia, ruining my neat pile of nightgowns by dropping a heap of crumpled petticoats on top of them, 'I shan't need her in London. Sara has maids aplenty.'

I sighed. This was bad news. Still, I had become adept at keeping out of Hilda's way by now. Julia's own absence would be quite restful, in any case. I started on the petticoats. She had begun rummaging in a drawer for hairpins and combs. Then she gave a shriek, the shriek she always gave when a brilliant new idea had come to her.

'You, Mary!' she said, spinning round and scattering pins as she did so, 'you must come with me! I shall take you to London. Oh, what a splendid notion!'

# 17

Julia told me to pack and to prepare to leave at an early hour the next morning. I was ready long before I needed to be, and waiting in the hallway; Julia, naturally, was late, running up and down stairs in search of unsuitable gifts for her sisters and brothers-in-law and nieces and nephews, thrusting oddments into embroidered bags, wanting tea now and cake for the journey, while the minutes ticked by and her husband and sons and servants tried to get her organised and I worried about missing our ferry and hence our train. At last by some miracle she was persuaded to leave behind an umbrella stand she had been determined to take as a present for Mr Prinsep, had her cup of tea forcibly removed from her hands, and was bundled into the waiting trap by Mr Cameron (still in his dressing gown, of course, bless him) while he gave her many soothing assurances that he would take care of his health, remember to take his medicine, and drink his soup.

'I shall write every day!' she cried as we jingled away from Dimbola and along the road towards Yarmouth, 'every day, my love! Now, do not forget the soup!'

Billy was driving the trap. I watched the back of his head as we jolted along. He said nothing, and when we reached the ferry he did not meet my eyes, although he handed me down from the

trap just as he handed Julia down. I watched him drive away.
He didn't look back at me.


During the whole of that journey—the ferry crossing, the railway
to Brockenhurst and then to London—I was almost feverish with
excitement and apprehension. I was going back to London! a
place I hardly recalled now, just dimly remembered. I had faint
blurred memories: long rows of houses, the rumble of carriages,
the wide sweep of Putney heath, the room in the lodging house,
the kitchen at Ashburton where Mammy and I had slept among
the black beetles. I wondered if I might pass my mother in the
street. I imagined seeing her, falling into her arms, both of us
weeping with joy. I put the absurd thought away. Of course we
weren't going anywhere near Putney.

When the train arrived at Waterloo Bridge Station, the swirl
and noise seemed overwhelming. A hansom cab took us across
the great river and along the crowded streets. We sat amid the
piles of Julia's travelling cases and bags (her trunks and the tea
chests holding the photographs having gone separately by carrier)
while Julia talked all the way, pointing out everything we saw as
we passed. I looked out at the avenues and houses and churches,
the great buildings, the glittering shops, but I could hardly take
it in. The cab headed out westwards through Kensington, and
the streets grew gentler and leafier as we left the seething city
behind. I began to feel slightly sick. We were approaching Little
Holland House, and I had no idea what would be expected of
me. Was I here as a guest? As a servant? Or perhaps as something
in between, some unspecified creature like a governess, part of
no tribe at all?

The cab turned into the drive and drew up at the front door,
and Julia bounced out of the hansom, already calling and talking

before the door was even opened, while I cautiously followed, keeping well back, wondering if perhaps I should be going round to the servants' door, of which there was sure to be one at the back of the house. I stood, irresolute, on the threshold, clutching my bag, while Julia and her sister embraced and what seemed like a crowd of other people emerged, all talking and laughing and exclaiming at once. Among them I saw Mr Watts, who of course lived here on what seemed to be a permanent basis; I wished for a moment that he had still been married to Ellen, for then I would have had a friend, although I was glad for her sake that she had escaped. One of the beautiful nieces was there too—Miss Jackson, the daughter of another of the starry sisters—and there was Mr Prinsep, a big man with a woolly white beard, whom I remembered meeting in Freshwater; and the Prinseps' grown-up son, Valentine, who was (of course) an artist. They were not complete strangers. I had seen them before; the point was, they had not seen me. Not as myself. They had seen me as a parlourmaid, and why should they remember that? No one recalls a parlourmaid. And of course if they did remember me, that would be even worse than not being remembered ... I began to back out of the door. If the hansom had not already departed, for two pins I should have got in and gone straight back to Freshwater.

'And whom have we here?' said Mrs Prinsep, noticing me at last.

'Oh, yes, did I not wire you, Sara? Ah, no, for there was no time,' said Julia gaily. 'I decided right at the last minute to bring Mary to help at the exhibition. You remember Mary, of course?'

I could see that Sara had no idea at all who I was, but she was gracious enough to take this news calmly.

'Delighted, of course,' she said. 'Well, we will put you in—let me see—the Yellow Room, I think. Where is your luggage, my dear?'

Julia's own bags and boxes had been lugged into the hallway by this time by a couple of brawny footmen. Julia, Mrs Prinsep, Il Signor, and the rest of them all looked at me enquiringly. I clutched my horrible carpet bag a little tighter. Inside it were my parlourmaid's dress, my white apron, my nightgown, and all the underwear and stockings I possessed. I was wearing my Sunday dress, a brown check, the blue cotton having been grown out of long ago. That was my entire wardrobe. The women facing me were all dressed in velvets and silks, flowing graceful exotic clothes that spoke of people who would never doubt themselves, would never feel inferior or insecure. I stood there in my cheap ugly dress, and a tiny silence fell. Julia was staring at the carpet bag, as if for the first time; it was the one she had given to Ellen, who had so disdainfully passed it on to me.

I raised my chin.

'I have not brought anything else,' I said. 'I prefer to travel light.'

'That's the spirit!' said Valentine Prinsep heartily. 'Now, here is a girl after my own heart. I made my Italian tour with hardly more than a valise or two. Travelling light! Why, it frees one so.'

I gave him a grateful look.

'Exactly,' I said, hoping that my face was not burning too visibly.

'Oh, quite,' said Mrs Prinsep quickly, 'very sensible indeed, Miss, er—'

'Ryan,' I said. 'Mary Ryan.'

'Miss Ryan. May we call you Mary?'

I gave a stiff nod. I did not quite trust my voice, by now; but I was determined not to cry.

'You would like to see your room, I'm sure—and then please join us for tea, shall we say in half an hour? In the conservatory?'

\*\*\*

The Yellow Room was yellow with a vengeance. The walls were painted a deep glossy shade of sulphur; the curtains were gold brocade; the bedspread was amber velvet; there was a dressing table draped in primrose-coloured net. The furniture was black lacquer with gold inlays, a huge vase of sunflowers stood in the corner, and there were Indian brass plates and bowls on every available surface. The basin and ewer on the washstand were decorated with stylised daffodils. The very light was yellow. My reflection in the gilt-framed mirror showed me a face that looked as though I had developed jaundice.

I took out my pathetic handful of shabby clothes, and put them away. Even the drawers in the chest were lined with printed paper in delicate shades of saffron and honey. Then I sat on the bed and tried to compose myself. I looked around me and for a moment I longed for the cramped attic room at Dimbola, with its naked walls and dusty floorboards and my own hard narrow bed and Louisa's alongside. Absurd, I told myself. Here I was, in a beautiful house, with interesting artistic people; I should be grateful.

*Always the need to be grateful,* said Mammy's voice. I didn't necessarily want to hear her, but she still spoke to me now and then.

There was a tap on the door. It was Miss Jackson, clutching an armful of clothes.

'I just wondered, Miss Ryan,' she said, coming into the room without being invited, 'if any of these would be useful. I think they would suit you, rather—and I have far too many clothes, really, we all have—' She spread the garments out next to me on the velvet bedspread, and I looked at the beautiful things, coloured like jewels, smelling faintly of sandalwood. I had to stop myself touching them. 'And you are about the same height as me, I think, perhaps just a little taller, and certainly as slender, so I feel sure they would fit you—'

'You are very kind,' I said, perhaps more coldly than I intended. 'But I could not possibly accept your charity.'

'Charity? Oh, no, I did not mean—I only thought that perhaps you might like—' She stopped, and started again. 'Mary—may I call you Mary?—my sisters and cousins and I swop clothes all the time, you see, we're always doing it. I just thought it might be fun to do the same with you, as you're going to be staying with the family.'

'I'm afraid I don't have anything to offer in return,' I said, still resisting the temptation to put out my hand and stroke the treasures lying beside me. 'So it would hardly be fair.'

'But it would give me such pleasure,' she said coaxingly. 'Please say you'll try them, at least. You could put on this blue, now, and come down to tea in it.' She picked up a dress: it was quite plain, with a round neckline, a row of tiny buttons down to the waist, and a full sweeping skirt. It was the colour of the sea glass I used to search for at Freshwater Bay. I looked at her as she held the dress up against herself. She was like a painting, with her high cheekbones and deep-set eyes. Suddenly I wanted, more than anything, to be Miss Jackson. I wanted her ethereal looks and her confidence and her big warm loving eccentric family and her beautiful clothes. Slowly, I stood up, and she helped me unhook the back of my brown check and I stepped out of it and into the blue dress, and allowed her to fasten it for me.

'Goodness,' she said, stepping back to look at me, 'that could have been made for you, Mary. Here, let me tighten the belt—there! Perfect.'

I moved towards the looking glass, and the dress rustled a little, the silk touching my skin like fingertips.

'Say you'll wear it!' she said. 'You do look very lovely.' She did not make me feel as though she was bestowing a cast-off on a beggar child. Secure in her own beauty and charm, she sounded genuinely admiring. If I had refused, it would have been I who would have felt ungracious and condescending. That's how I put it to myself, anyway. I thanked her, trying to sound as though it were not unusual for someone to casually give me a new dress, and then I brushed my hair and swept it up into a chignon as I had done for the Minstrels photograph, and we went down to tea together.

If I had not had the benefit of Miss Jackson's dresses during my stay at Little Holland House, I should have felt very differently about my time there, I think. Perhaps Julia would have realised my predicament at some point and set about acquiring some new clothes for me, but it clearly had not occurred to her that someone who is dressed as a servant is likely to be treated as a servant and will almost certainly feel like one. How odd, that she, with her eye for beauty (as she was so fond of reminding everyone) did not see that. But then, Julia's focus was on faces, always—the immortal faces she was so determined to capture with her camera. The view from behind the lens, I suppose, is distorted. Inevitably. The photographer sees so much; but always through a glass, darkly.

The conversation in the conservatory was at its usual level wherever the Pattle sisters were—voluble, excitable, overpowering, with much gesturing and exclaiming, accompanied by the tinkling of gold bangles and silvery laughter—but when Miss Jackson and I walked in the hubbub suddenly died and everyone turned to look at us. There was a moment of silence. Then the gentlemen—Mr Prinsep, Valentine, Il Signor—all sprang to their feet, and Mrs Prinsep said, 'Well, my dears, how very delicious you both look!' and then she went on pouring tea and the conversation resumed. Valentine handed me a cup and started telling me about his time in Italy. He was a nice man, in his late twenties, I judged, with a craggy face and dark curling hair and beard. I was grateful for his attention, especially as his traveller's tales meant I hardly needed to talk myself, apart from the occasional expression of surprise or admiration. I sipped my tea, and nodded, and smiled, and listened. The day was fading now, the skies outside were darkening, and over his shoulder I caught a glimpse of someone reflected in the glass of the conservatory: a young woman, elegant, graceful, wearing an expensive blue gown, turning her slender neck to listen to her companion. She looked poised, composed, at ease. I looked at my reflection, and smiled.

# 18

Little Holland House was hardly little by most people's standards. It had once been the Dower House to an even grander place, and it had been altered and added to over the years. It was pretty, gabled and rambling and russet-roofed, its gardens romantically overgrown and shaded by ancient elms. Inside it was a maze of rooms and passages, with sloping floors and low ceilings, twisting stairs and unexpected corners. The Prinseps had knocked down some interior walls, built a conservatory, and transformed it from a pleasant, old-fashioned, rather quaint English house into a world of its own, a sort of enchanted kingdom.

My own violently yellow bedroom was an indication of the Prinsep taste in interior design, for everywhere was rich with colour: walls were painted in heliotrope or Venetian red or emerald green, the drapes and curtains were of velvets and brocades in shades of violet or copper or magenta, the sofas were draped with Kashmir shawls in every exquisite pattern imaginable. In the dining room, Mr Watts had been commissioned to paint vast allegorical murals (in fact, it was that commission that had led to his coming to visit for a few weeks and then to his staying for years). There were tessellated floors and Turkish carpets and woven rugs; embroidered cushions, curios of silver and bronze, tables inlaid with mother-of-pearl, stained glass that threw gorgeous patterns of coloured light across the rooms. And through this palace of delights, trailing scarves and perfume, dazzling everyone, moved the starry Pattle sisters; not only Mrs Prinsep—Sara—but, as often as not, Julia and Mia and Louisa and Virginia and Sophia. (Adeline, the eldest sister, was dead, I learned.) They had all been given nicknames, Miss Jackson told me, by their adoring circle; Sara was Dash, for her energy and élan; Virginia was Beauty, and so on.

'And Mrs Cameron?' I asked, curious to know where Julia fitted in this constellation of loveliness.

'Aunt Julia? Oh, she's Talent,' said Miss Jackson.


The exhibition was to be at a gallery called Colnaghi's in Cockspur Street. It was not due to open until a few days' time, but of course Julia was determined to get in early and tell the gallery owner exactly how she thought the photographs should be displayed, and no doubt explain his own job to him in no uncertain terms.

'My idea, Mary,' said Julia, over breakfast that first morning, 'is that you will greet people as they enter the exhibition, make them welcome, answer their questions, and then when they buy a print,'—of course she said *when*, not *if*—'you will write the receipt, and arrange the delivery for after the show closes.'

I nodded. I was relieved to find that I was to have a proper role, a role which was not being a parlourmaid or a lady's maid or something of that nature. I had not slept very much, that first night, partly because of the strangeness of the room, but mostly because I was trying to work out where I fitted in this peculiar household. The awkwardness of my arrival, the absence of luggage, my shabby dress, the fact that Julia had not forewarned my hosts of my visit, made my face burn whenever I thought of it, and when Miss Jackson had pressed her cast-off clothes on me I had prickled with resentment at being an object of charity; but then she had seemed genuinely kind, and during the evening, dressed in my new gown, I had been treated with perfect civility and even warmth. I had felt like a guest, almost like an equal, and that feeling, like the glass of champagne I had been served before dinner, had gone to my head with a delicious dizzying sensation.

I put the parlourmaid's dress and apron back in the carpet bag and hid it under my bed. I did not want any of the Prinseps' maids discovering it.


Julia took me with her to the gallery on that first day. It was a dignified place, calm and spacious, with white-painted walls and a hush inside like a church. Mr Colnaghi, whom Julia called by his first name after what I think was really a very short acquaintance, was charming, bowing and agreeing with everything Julia said as she announced her instructions.

'The pictures of the children here, Dominic—grouped, you see—then the allegorical studies in a line there, where they receive the natural light—or, no, now, let me see, the grand portraits of my dear friends, perhaps there instead, with the others over towards the door—'

Mr Colnaghi followed her as she roamed about, making notes and looking thoughtful. Julia explained my intended role, and he politely agreed that a gallery assistant would be most helpful. He showed me a splendid mahogany desk with a high-backed chair, placed near the door, where I might sit, and explained the system of sales and what would be expected of me. All in all the morning was very satisfactory for us both; I was pleased that I had not only a useful role but also a title—Gallery Assistant sounded rather grand, I felt—and on our way back Julia expressed herself delighted with the way the exhibition was to be run, and extolled at length the professionalism, thoughtfulness and good sense of Mr Colnaghi. My own respect for him was only enhanced when I discovered later that he had completely ignored Julia's demands, a fact she never really noticed since he had somehow managed to convince her that the quite different way he had hung the photographs had been her idea all along.

Mrs Prinsep had a programme of social events planned for Julia's visit—dinners, luncheons, soirées, picnics—to which her friends, who all seemed to be poets or painters or novelists or musicians, would be summoned to renew their acquaintance with her sister, and it seemed to be vaguely expected that I would be part of this gaiety.

'Does everyone in London visit at Little Holland House?' I asked Miss Jackson that evening, as she scribbled a list of guests for a forthcoming party: Mr Burne-Jones, Mr Dodgson, Mr Rossetti. I had thought Dimbola dazzling enough, but the Prinsep household was Dimbola concentrated. I was beginning to see that Mrs Prinsep collected famous people with the same unremitting passion as Julia—indeed, I was to learn, all the Pattle sisters did so. It was their life's work.

'Pretty much,' she said. 'At least, everyone of genius. It's known as Pattledom, you see; my mother and her sisters are acknowledged leaders of artistic society—the only society that matters.'

She sounded very serious; I had a terrible desire to laugh, but I controlled it, and offered to write the invitations out in my best copperplate hand.

'I shall be able to look forward to seeing some old friends,' I said, carefully addressing an envelope to Mr Trollope.

Miss Jackson looked at me, a little surprised.

'Oh—I had forgotten—quite a few of our friends visited Aunt Julia in Freshwater, didn't they?'

'Constantly,' I said. I met her eye. Did she even remember that she herself had seen me there, that I had opened the door to her, curtsied to her, served her with tea, flattened myself against the wall as she passed? And yet, oddly, in Julia's studio I had felt that I was not just a parlourmaid; there I had been a model, just as Miss Jackson herself had been. I had talked with Mr Tennyson about his poems; I had conversed with writers and painters and musicians. I felt a little flame of defiance rise inside me. I was not afraid of clever artistic people, nor of rich beautiful women with soulful expressions, and not even of famous men with beards. No one who had spent seven years with Julia Margaret Cameron was likely to be afraid of anything much.


Mrs Prinsep and Julia had decided between them to give an evening party the day before the exhibition opened, and it was to be a pastoral affair. They ordered several sofas to be carried out onto the lawns, and footmen arranged chairs and cushions beneath the trees, rigged up awnings improvised from silk shawls and bedspreads, and hung lanterns like golden globes in the branches of the apple trees. The food was to be a cold collation, served from a long table in the conservatory, and one of their circle, a singer, was to be concealed among the shrubbery while she sang operatic arias. The day had been hot and the warmth lingered into a still, balmy evening. Perhaps, I thought, even the weather was in thrall to Pattledom.

I asked Miss Jackson's advice as to what I should wear. We discussed the relative merits of the blue silk and a green velvet affair with a gold sash; but in the end, the evening being so balmy, I wore a loose-cut dress in rose-coloured lawn, with floating sleeves that fluttered around my bare arms. It would have felt extraordinarily daring, worn anywhere else, I thought; but here in the garden of Little Holland House everyone was dressed unconventionally: most of the women wore trailing robes and gowns with no stays or corsets beneath, Miss Jackson had bare feet, the men were in artists' smocks or embroidered coats, Il Signor wore something that looked like a monk's robe. They all seemed to know one another, and they were all brilliant, or beautiful, or both.

I walked carefully among these glittering people who were scattered like stars across the grass. Miss Jackson had made sure she was with me when I first stepped into the gardens, and Valentine had brought me some iced wine; but now Miss Jackson was surrounded by an animated group of young people, and Valentine was stretched full length upon the grass with another man beside him, both talking and waving their hands at the sky, and I felt the usual chill clutch at my stomach. I recognised Valentine's friend, Mr Burne-Jones, and Miss Jackson's cousins Adeline and Isabella. They had all visited at Dimbola; would they, if I were to speak to them, turn and say *oh, but surely, you are the parlourmaid?* Would they instinctively hand me their empty glass and wave me away, or stare coldly because I had addressed them as an equal?

I drifted back in the direction of the conservatory, thinking that in some ways it would be easier to be serving the patés and tartlets and junkets, to be taking wraps and clearing plates, than it was to be fearing that no one would talk to me, and fearing even more what would happen if they did. Perhaps I could simply melt away into the trees, stay there drinking cold wine and listening to the disembodied voice singing *Soave il vento* until all the guests had gone. I turned and began to move towards the darkness at the edge of the lawn.

'Miss Ryan—over here, come.'

It was Valentine, beckoning me.

'Mr Prinsep?' *Look like a lady, Mary Ryan, don't curtsey, just incline your head graciously ...*

'See, Ned,' said Valentine to his friend, 'isn't Miss Ryan just the perfect type of dark-haired loveliness?'

Mr Burne-Jones scrutinised me from his recumbent position.

'Exquisite,' he said lazily, 'really, Val, where do you find such beauties?'

'Oh, Mary's visiting with Aunt Julia, aren't you, Mary?'

I decided that it was too awkward to stay standing above them while they discussed me, and so I sank onto the grass beside them.

'I am,' I said, 'and I shall be working at Colnaghi's gallery during Mrs Cameron's exhibition.'

'Are you a photographer, too, then, Miss Ryan?'

'No—I assist Mrs Cameron with the technical side of her work, and I model for her photographs.'

Ned Burne-Jones sat up.

'I imagine you make an ideal model. Have you ever sat for an artist?'

'Mrs Cameron is an artist,' I said quickly, 'so, yes, but only for her.'

He gave a snort of laughter.

'I see. I stand corrected. Well, should you decide to model for a painter, don't forget me, will you? I'd love to paint that face.' He placed his hand against my cheek. 'You have the eyes of a temptress, Miss Ryan.'

I removed his hand and stood up.

'I'll bear that in mind.' I stopped myself adding *sir*. 'Forgive me, I believe I see someone I know.' I smiled down at them in what I hoped was a warm yet sophisticated manner, and moved away.

'Aha!' said a voice. 'The woodbine spices are wafted abroad, and the musk of the rose is blown, eh, Mary?'

It was the Great Poet. He had materialised out of the dusk in his black cloak, and my heart lifted to see him. Despite his sulks and growls, his oddness, his irritation at small things, he at least always saw me as a person. Not as a beggar, not as a servant, but as me, Mary Ryan, a girl who had fallen out of a tree in front of him, a girl to whom he had read his poems and then asked what she thought and listened to her answers. I could have flung myself into his arms. Instead I laughed and stretched out my hand to him.

'I am weary of dance and play, Mr Tennyson. The brief night goes in babble and revel and wine.'

He tucked my hand into his arm and we began to walk along a gravel path over which night-scented stocks were spilling and releasing their incense into the still air.

'I had not realised there was a party,' he said. 'I would never have come if I had; it is not to my taste. But I am in London to see my publisher and it seemed courteous to call upon my old friends.'

'I am very glad to see you, sir,' I said truthfully. 'May I get you some wine? Some food?'

'No, no,' he said, 'but I shall smoke, if you do not object,' and he drew out his pipe and we sat together on a stone seat beneath a canopy of pale roses, the scent of which was soon completely smothered in the comforting familiar smell of his tobacco.

Of course he did not stay unnoticed for long. There was a shriek, and a cry, and a stout figure in crimson stripes came speeding towards us.

'Hello, Julia,' he said, resignedly.

'Alfred! You naughty, naughty man!' she scolded. 'You are in London and you did not let me know!'

'But I am here, nevertheless,' he pointed out.

Another robed figure loomed up: Mrs Prinsep, all wisps of silk chiffon and gracious welcoming noises. Mr Tennyson got to his feet and executed a bow over her hand.

'*Principessa*,' he said.

'Have you brought dear Emily?' inquired Julia.

'No, she is indisposed—and she prefers to be at home, you know.'

'Alas!' said Mrs Prinsep, not altogether convincingly. 'Poor Emily. How sad that she cannot be here! Well, Alfred, you must let us take care of you in her absence. Now, you will dine with us soon, I insist; just a small party, for I think that is what you prefer. A few friends, a good dinner, and I know Thoby has some really excellent claret he has been saving until your visit ...' and she took his arm and led him away, with Julia on his other side, both sisters talking at him at once. I stayed on the stone bench, watching the guests begin to pull shawls and coats about them, and then slowly drift back indoors, until the chill and the dropping dew drove me too to stand and walk towards the lighted windows. Shadowy figures came out to carry the sofas and chairs indoors; lanterns were extinguished, cushions and wraps and half-drunk champagne bottles retrieved. In the conservatory, the food had been cleared, the tablecloth removed, the crumbs swept away. Ah, the silent army of servants. The Pattles and the Prinseps and the Camerons, modern and free-thinking and bohemian as they were, still needed those invisible others to maintain their beautiful artistic lives. I skirted the outside of the house, took the servants' stair and went to bed.

# 19

For my first morning at the gallery, I chose, from my delightful new wardrobe, a muslin blouse with long tight sleeves and a flowing skirt in a dark mulberry twill, and I put my hair up in a chignon. Demure, yet ladylike, I hoped. Julia had decided she would only come to the gallery in the afternoons, so off I went alone in a hansom, back towards the city and to Cockspur Street. I was a little apprehensive at first, but as soon as people began to arrive I found that being a parlourmaid had been excellent training for this type of work; in fact this was a good deal easier, since I did not have to take anyone's coat or hat, or curtsey, or submit to being teased or patted or ignored; I merely said a polite good morning, smiled, noted purchases, took money, and wrote receipts. I found I was perfectly able to answer any questions about the photographs, for I knew a good deal about Julia's methods. The morning was pleasantly busy, and Mr Colnaghi congratulated me on my knowledge and expertise, which pleased me immensely.

There was something of a lull towards the end of the morning, and a maid brought me a cup of coffee and some sweet biscuits. The novelty of being waited on thrilled me, and I was beginning positively to enjoy myself. I drank my coffee, and put the receipts neatly in order, and checked the list of sales. A few more visitors arrived in a group, and asked me about the pictures, where they had been taken and who the subjects were. When they had thanked me and wandered off to look at the show, I noticed that a young man had entered the gallery unseen, and was now standing in front of one of the photographs. He stood very still, his back turned to me, so that all I could see was that he was tall and broad-shouldered; but the striking thing about him was his hair, a mass of tangled light brown curls, worn rather long. I watched him as he stood there, wondering why he was so absorbed. Then a woman swathed in furs came up to me, asking about the photograph of the dear little angel, as she put it (actually the wretched Freddie with a pair of turkey wings strapped to his shoulders) and I was engaged for a quarter of an hour while she explained that the picture spoke to her of heaven and told me a long sentimental story of a dead infant sibling, and I took her money and wrote her receipt and noted her address for the delivery. When at last she had gone I saw that the young man was still standing in exactly the same place, as though transfixed. I wondered if he were quite well, or if perhaps he had fallen into a cataleptic trance.

Just as I began to feel that I should go over to him and enquire if he needed assistance, however, he turned and came towards me. He had the sort of good looks that men who have grown up in prosperous families often have: fair skin, clear hazel eyes, an aura of health and strength, the long stride of an athlete.

As he drew near he gave a sort of start, almost as though he recognised me, although I was very sure that I had never seen him before.

'Good m-morning,' he said, and cleared his throat several times. 'I should like to buy the picture—the photograph over there. N-number twenty-three.'

I looked at my list and my heart sank.

'*Prospero and M-miranda*,' he added. Oh, goodness. Dear Philip all wise and kind and me kneeling winsomely at his feet in that unflattering dress. There is no accounting for taste.

'Certainly, sir,' I said. 'May I take your name?'

'Henry,' he said. I looked up enquiringly. 'Oh, C-cotton. Henry Cotton.' He spoke with not quite a stammer, but a slight hesitancy in his speech, which was rather charming. He started fishing in his pocketbook for money, while I made out the receipt. 'It is you, isn't it?' he said suddenly. 'You are the M-miranda in the picture?'

Rather reluctantly, I admitted that I was. He took his receipt, I wrote down his address, and he thanked me, but he didn't move, just stood irresolutely in front of me, until a couple approached to ask about buying *The Angel at the Sepulchre* (again, no accounting for taste) and Mr Cotton wandered disconsolately away.

I should have thought no more about this strange young man, but the following day, almost as soon as the exhibition opened, he was back, prowling moodily about the walls, and then just as yesterday he settled in front of another picture and stood and stared. This time it was *If you're waking, call me early, call me early, Mother Dear,* in which I am depicted lying on my deathbed in a frilled nightgown with a rather pretty white lacy pillowcase beneath my head, philosophically contemplating my own early demise. By the time Mr Cotton came over to me, I had guessed that he would be buying this one too. I decided that he must be a photographer himself, and keen to copy Julia's methods; her pictures were, it's true, very different from the stiff formal pictures so many professionals turned out. The blurs and the smudges, the immediacy, the arresting nature of her portraits—they were worth studying, certainly. Julia may not have been the Beauty of her family, but she was, indisputably, Talent.

'It's Mr Cotton, isn't it?' I enquired.

'Yes. Oh, yes.' He was staring at me again. I smiled up at him; he really was rather handsome.

'To be delivered to the same address as the first purchase?'

He nodded. 'And—might I ask your name, M-miss—?'

'Miss Ryan,' I said. 'Here is the receipt, Mr Cotton. I hope you enjoy the picture.'

'Oh, I shall,' he said, in a slightly strangled voice, and once again, when other customers approached, he wandered off, clutching the receipt as though it were a holy relic.


Mr Cotton came back the next day, and the next, and bought another photograph each time. He had clearly become obsessed with the whole subject of photography and Julia's pictures in particular, so on the fifth day, I thought I should offer to introduce him to Julia, for if he wanted to study her methods I felt sure she would be generous with her knowledge. As I wrote out yet another receipt I told him that Mrs Cameron would be coming in to the gallery that afternoon, if he wished to meet her.

'I believe—I believe I may have a c-connection with M-mrs Cameron already,' he said. 'My father, you know, was in India, and I think he knew the Pattle family there.'

'Indeed?' I said, interested, recalling the story of Mr Pattle's corpse and the brandy-filled coffin. 'I am staying with the Prinseps, at Little Holland House.'

'Are you, Miss Ryan?' He looked immensely pleased at this news. 'Then—yes, I will return this afternoon, and hope to have the honour of m-meeting Mrs Cameron.'


When Julia bustled in, Mr Cotton was waiting, indeed pacing about, obviously keen, I supposed, to learn more about the wet collodion method and the rectilinear lens. I effected the introduction, explaining that Mr Cotton was interested in photography and had already purchased five of her pictures. Naturally Julia was thrilled, and launched immediately into a discourse on focal lengths; but rather to my surprise, Mr Cotton did not seem as enthralled by this as I had imagined, and when she stopped for breath (as even Julia had to, sometimes) he said quickly that he believed his father may have once, many years ago, met her father, and explained the Pattle connection.

'Oh, yes—Cotton, Cotton,' said Julia vaguely, not really sounding as though she recalled any such name, but of course she was always delighted to add an attractive young person of good family to her collection—especially this one, with his glowing looks and his romantic curls—and within a short time he was being invited to dine at Little Holland House that very evening.

It was, as Mrs Prinsep had promised, a small party, at least by the standards of Little Holland House: herself and Mr Prinsep, Julia, Valentine and his friend Mr Burne-Jones, Il Signor, Miss Jackson, myself, Mr Tennyson, and now Mr Cotton. Mrs Prinsep had not seemed at all put out by her sister's announcement that she had met a handsome and interesting young man with a refreshing interest in photography and had issued an invitation to him to dine *en famille*. Her household existed for just such moments. There was even a sense of glee, perhaps, when a new prize came into view, for Sara Prinsep was not the only hostess in London who prided herself on running a salon; Mrs Carlyle held 'at homes' where people would come to meet her famous husband at their Chelsea house, and the Countess of Airlie was putting up strong competition in Kensington. Tonight's guest list was not unusual—Il Signor and the Great Poet were established

154

lions, Mr Burne-Jones had the whiff of danger as part of the Pre-Raphaelite Brotherhood, and an unknown young man would add a further pinch of spice to the gathering. Julia's instincts for collecting interesting people were generally faultless. She had certainly had a good deal of practice.

The weather had turned, and rain had been falling all day, so there would be no sofas on the lawns or lanterns in the trees tonight. When I arrived back from my day at the gallery the long table in the dining room was being set, and there was barely an hour until the guests were expected. I resisted the compulsion to offer to help the servants who were scurrying to and fro with linen and silver and plate and flowers, and went up to my yellow room to change. My drawers and petticoats and stockings had been taken away and washed and returned, and were neatly folded in the lacquer chest, smelling of lavender. My borrowed finery was brushed and pressed and hanging in the cupboard. A torn hem on the blue dress had been neatly mended, I noticed. There was a fire burning briskly in the grate, a welcoming sight on the chilly summer evening; hot water and scented soap and clean towels were already on the washstand. I shivered with delight at this luxury; perhaps also with a little shame. Someone else now was doing these things for me, and I was becoming used to it.

Downstairs, the guests were arriving. I would not be hesitant or awkward tonight; these were all people I knew, now. Mr Watts and Mr Tennyson I thought of as friends, Valentine Prinsep was kind, Miss Jackson, I felt, almost sisterly. I was wearing the blue silk dress which I loved and which made me feel graceful and grown-up, and I approached the salon, where a champagne cup was always served before dinner, with a feeling something like happiness. Voices and laughter were chiming from within, and I paused just on the threshold to take in the scene. I suppose no

155

one had seen or heard me arrive, for in that moment Julia's voice rang out.

'Oh, indeed, it is remarkable; she was a beggar-child, you know, and the mother, I'm afraid, a drunkard, quite irredeemable ...'

I stopped. I took a silent step backwards, away from the glimmering candles and the cultured voices, back into the shadows.

'You have done wonders, Julia.' Mrs Prinsep, this time. 'I did not know about the mother. Dreadful. Well, it is *entirely* to your credit that the girl is so presentable ...'

Then Miss Jackson, with her little musical laugh.

'Oh, and my old clothes, of course—she would hardly be acceptable in society without those—fine feathers, you know, make—'

I did not wait to hear any more. I grasped the door handle and turned it so hard that they would hear it rattle, and stepped into the room, my head held high. I saw that Mr Cotton was there, and that he stood in the group with Julia and Mrs Prinsep and Miss Jackson. It was he to whom they had been explaining my origins, it seemed. I did not look at him, or at them; I took a glass of iced champagne from the footman who stood next to the door—not meeting his eyes, either—and walked steadily over towards Mr Tennyson, who was standing by the window staring gloomily out into the rainy evening.

'I dislike the city, Mary,' he said, with no preamble. 'I will go back to Farringford, tomorrow.'

As soon as he said this I too was filled with a desire to be back in the place I knew, in the house I thought of as my home, with the attic room and the old stables and the sea sounding at the end of the road. I missed Louisa, and Billy, and Kellaway, and Hillier. I even missed Mrs Lyle, her lilting Geordie voice, her rough kindness.

'*I loathe the squares and streets,*

156

*And the faces that one meets,*

*Hearts with no love for me,'* I quoted.

He nodded. 'You know my poems well, eh, Mary?' He patted my arm. 'Come back with me, if you like. I suppose Julia can spare you.'

I drank my champagne, a little too quickly. Oh, how tempted I was. To travel in friendly silence with my Great Poet, to smell the salt and seaweed as we boarded the ferry which would clank and chug its way towards the long misty line of the Island, to see the trap waiting at the quayside, to get back to Dimbola Lodge and put on my parlourmaid's dress and to be certain of my place.

And yet. There was still a hard bright flame in me, somewhere, that was not quite extinguished even by the ice and glitter of Little Holland House.

'I shall stay to finish my work at the exhibition, sir,' I said. 'I have a part to play there. But I shall look forward to being back in Freshwater as soon as it is over.'

I was still resolutely not looking in Julia's direction, and I managed to avoid her until the gong was struck for dinner and we all trooped into the long low room, with its dark blue ceiling studded with gold stars and Signor's frescoes covering the walls. Never afraid of a vast subject, he had chosen as his theme the History of Civilisation, with the Pattle sisters, swathed in exotic drapery, depicted as, variously, Mother Earth (Virginia), Sophia (Art), and Mia (Assyria). I was seated between Valentine and Mr Watts, and mercifully at the other end of the dining table from both Julia and Sara, although rather alarmingly I had the larger-than-life representation of Julia (Hindustan) dead opposite me on the painted wall.

Il Signor was in a talkative mood, explaining to me at length that his artistic goal was always to emulate music by suggesting thoughts or emotions, and I was grateful to be able to listen to

157

him and to Valentine (talking of his own artistic goals, involving painting entirely devoted to nature) in turn. Neither gentleman required me to say very much in response, which was just as well since I was distracted by seeing that across the table from me Miss Jackson was engaging Mr Cotton in a conversation which seemed to be absorbing them both. She was looking even more ethereally beautiful than usual, in a gown of white satin with jasmine woven into her hair like Queen Guinevere, and Mr Cotton himself could certainly have modelled for Sir Lancelot. I would not be at all surprised, I found myself thinking, if Julia were to hit on the same idea and pounce on them both for one of her medieval romance photographs.

The dinner dragged on. I found I could not eat much, because my stomach was in a knot of fury still from the words I had overheard. Afterwards, inevitably, we were all shepherded into the drawing room (no conventional ladies-withdraw-while-men-drink-port stuff here in Arcadia) to hear Mr Tennyson read and then listen to Miss Jackson declaim some theatrical stuff that Julia had beseeched her to recite. I found myself a seat at the back of the room, composed my expression into what I hoped was one of interest, and began to calculate how long it would be before I could return to Freshwater without its seeming that I was running away. I would not afford them that satisfaction, I thought grimly. Beggar child I might be, daughter of a drunken mother, but I would not be crushed by them. More champagne had been brought in, and I drank another glass. The entertainment ended, and the guests all began to mingle again. Mr Cotton began what looked like a good-humoured discussion with Valentine and Mr Burne-Jones, until Mrs Prinsep fixed him in the beam of her ineffable charm and swept him away to talk again to Miss Jackson. It seemed that Julia's latest captive was regarded as a trophy worthy even of the Pattle sisters. He looked a little dazzled, or perhaps daunted. It struck me that he was at ease with men but somewhat uneasy with women who were, perhaps, an unfamiliar species. Something about him reminded me of the Cameron boys when they had first seen Ellen Terry: thrilled, amazed, and terrified.

At length the party began to break up. Mr Tennyson was the first to leave, which he did in his usual manner, abruptly, with a few gruff thank-yous and nods before he donned his rusty black cloak and disappeared. Valentine and Mr Burne-Jones went off together in pursuit of further entertainment in town. Mr Cotton began to make his farewells, thanking his host and hostess, bowing over Miss Jackson's hand. He came to me last. I held out my hand, but he didn't take it, instead swallowing hard once or twice, and then saying in a low voice, 'Would you—would you show me to the door, M-miss Ryan?'

'Of course,' I said. I walked ahead of him out of the drawing room and along the passage towards the entrance hall. A footman stood ready with his coat, helped him on with it, and then opened the door. Mr Cotton bowed to me, moved to go, and then suddenly turned back.

'M-mrs Prinsep has been kind enough to invite me again, to dine one day next week,' he said in a rush. 'Perhaps—that is, I hope I shall have an opportunity to talk to you then, M-miss Ryan—there seemed to be no chance, tonight—'

I looked at him directly, trying to read his face. His voice, his eyes, his gaze, all spoke of openness, honesty, truthfulness. But he was a gentleman, a toff, he was one of them. They all dissembled, every day, they seemed warm and generous and yet they were not.

'But of course,' I said. Even to my own ears, I sounded wooden. The footman stood, impassive, motionless, holding the door open to the damp summer night. Mr Cotton seemed to hesitate, and then he put on his hat and reversed awkwardly out into the night and the door closed behind him. The footman and I looked at each other. I knew his name: Joseph. He was about seventeen, I thought. My age.

'What do you think?' I asked him. 'Is he sweet on me? Or has he fallen for Miss Jackson and wants to ask my advice on how to court her? Or neither; perhaps he is just out of his depth among all these mad people and needs someone ordinary to talk to?'

Joseph grinned.

'Sweet on you, I reckon, Miss Ryan,' he said. 'They all are. Mr Valentine can't take his eyes off you, nor his friend.'

'Really?'

'I should say. Watch out, though, Miss. Those artists'll have you take your clothes off soon as look at you, wanting to paint you. That's what they'll say, anyhow.'

I laughed. 'Thank you for the warning. I'll be careful. And, Joseph—'

'Miss?'

'Would you call me Mary, from now on?'

'Couldn't do that, Miss Ryan,' he said. 'More than my place is worth.'

Of course it was. I had longed, suddenly, for the companionship of someone who knew what I knew, came from where I came from, worked as I had worked. I wanted to feel that I belonged somewhere. But he was right. He would lose his place if he was heard being too familiar with a guest. I was a little too high for Joseph now and far, far too low for my hosts. I felt close to tears, but I didn't want even Joseph to feel sorry for me. I blew him a kiss and then I went back into the beautiful drawing room to make my goodnights as politely as I could.

# 20

Mr Cotton was back at the gallery the next day. I was surprised; I had, in the small hours of the night, surmised that perhaps he had taken a few too many glasses of champagne last evening, and his apparent keenness to speak to me again would have dissipated in the cold light of day. His interest, if interest it was, would presumably have been quenched now that he was, thanks to Julia and her family, aware of my terrible origins.

He circled the walls, but he had already bought all the photographs that had me in them. He studied the pictures in turn, but whenever there was a gap in the flow of visitors coming to speak to me at my desk, he would drift over and begin a conversation. He told me a little of his upbringing—he had been born in India, like Mrs Cameron, but schooled in England, staying with relations in the holidays. He liked to swim and to fish; he had been walking in Switzerland and had climbed in the Alps; he had studied at King's College in London. Now he was considering his future career, and was about to take his examinations for the Indian Civil Service, although not perfectly convinced that this was where his future lay. He did not ask me about my own childhood—from delicacy, perhaps, or disdain—but he did ask me about the Island, and Mrs Cameron's household, about how I had come to model for the photographs and how I knew Mr

Tennyson and his friends so well. He was a good listener—perhaps his own slightly awkward speech helped him to be so—and I found that, somehow, I liked to talk to him and to listen in my turn. It struck me again that he was, although outwardly a confident man, extremely shy when it came to talking to women; he had hardly known any, had spent his schooldays and all his childhood and youth in the company of other boys. Perhaps a woman who was not of his own class seemed less daunting. Over the days that followed I began to look forward to seeing him at Colnaghi's. I almost thought of him as a friend; and yet I did not want to allow that thought in. I had thought Miss Jackson my friend, too, but I had learned my lesson. I would be more guarded in future.

The evening that Mr Cotton was to dine for a second time at Little Holland House would be the last day of the exhibition. I had established with Julia that I would be returning to Freshwater alone the following morning, while she stayed on a little longer with her sister. The prospect of going back to the Island filled me with such relief that I was almost carefree, that final day. Julia was delighted with the way the exhibition had gone—she had sold many of the photographs, but even more pleasingly for her there had been much interest and acclaim for her work. *The Illustrated London News* had praised her artistry, and she read the critic's words out again and again to anyone who would listen.

'And listen to this, Mary,' she said. 'Here—let me see—*the pictures ... the photographer has captured ... ah, here we are! the young ladies of various types of rare and refined female loveliness, or, at all events, possessed of a charm of expression which we suspect ordinary male photographers would fail to educe.* Well may they say that! Ha! At last someone realises that I might have skills not *in spite of* being a woman but *because* of being one!'

162

The dinner that evening was to be a sort of celebration of the end of Julia's exhibition. The usual household would be there, of course, together with another of the Pattle sisters, Mia (Miss Jackson's mother), and the guests were to include—as well as their new find, Mr Cotton—two of the particular prizes of Pattledom: Mr Carlyle and Mr Browning.

Thomas Carlyle, the Sage of Chelsea, was famously irascible, and on that account I hoped that I would not be seated next to him. Julia had told me that she wished very much to photograph him, but he had always resisted.

'I blame that shrewish wife of his,' she had said. 'She makes his life very difficult, and artists need a proper environment in which to create; not the noisy, cramped, dusty place she runs. Alas! But I will succeed in taking his likeness one day, you may be sure. That face is one of the utmost nobility. I shall capture it if I have to wait a decade.'

I had, I found, escaped being placed next to Mr Carlyle, but instead was seated next to the shrewish wife. Mrs Carlyle was, like her husband, from Scotland. She had smooth brown hair framing an oval face, and an expression of militant intelligence in her dark eyes which was both attractive and daunting. On my other side was Mr Browning, whose face I knew from one of Julia's photographs. Mr Cotton was seated on the far side of Mr Browning, so that I could not speak to him without leaning inelegantly forwards or backwards, and in any case the two men were quickly engaged in conversation with each other.

'And who are you?' inquired Mrs Carlyle of me by way of an introduction.

'I am Mary Ryan; I have been acting as a gallery assistant at Mrs Cameron's exhibition,' I said, liking the sound of the words.

'Ah! You have an occupation,' she said, 'then let me advise you, young lady, to pursue your work and not to let yourself become a drudge to some man who will turn your life into an incessant treadmill of servitude.'

'I hope very much to avoid that, Mrs Carlyle,' I said fervently; and then, I hardly know why, I told her that for most of my life I had been, and still was, Mrs Cameron's servant, a parlourmaid, and well used to the never-ending tyranny of housework. Somehow I no longer cared to pretend.

'Then you will know exactly what I have to contend with, Miss Ryan!' she cried, sounding more friendly than her brusque manner had initially suggested, 'Oh, the endless battles with coal dust and bed bugs! and the black beetles in Cheyne Row are like an army; they fight on every front.'

'It will always be a losing battle, I fear. At Dimbola Lodge we pour boiling water on them every day but their numbers never lessen.'

'Aye, so it seems.' She heaved a sigh, and threw a malevolent glance towards her husband who was eating silently on the other side of the table while Julia explained to him in detail exactly how important it was for the nation that she should be allowed to take his photograph, he responding only with an occasional shake of the noble head. 'If the beetles were all I had to contend with, I would be a happy woman, however! The noise of the streets drives my husband to distraction every day and I pay the price. He cannot sleep at night and he cannot write by day, and the end of it is that he shouts and rants at me, constantly, as though I am likely to be able to do anything about it!'

There were a few more laments of this nature. Mr Carlyle gave no evidence of having heard; he was either not listening or had made his mind up to ignore his wife. Instead—having eaten his dinner—he embarked on an extensive discourse on the French Revolution which brooked no interruptions at all, not even from

Julia, who was obliged for once to have her own attempts to speak disregarded.

'And so, Miss Ryan,' Mrs Carlyle said at last, 'you live on the Isle of Wight? You will know our friend Alfred Tennyson, I dare say?'

'I do indeed. Mr Tennyson's house is very close, and he is frequently at Dimbola.'

'Writers and artists abound there, I believe, as they do here. There—' She waved her fork at Mr Browning—'there's another one for you. Robert!' she called. 'Here's a young lady well used to conversing with poets.'

Mr Browning turned politely to me, and asked if I was a guest at Little Holland House, and I explained the Gallery Assistant role once more. Luckily I recalled a good deal of his work—I liked his collection entitled *Men and Women* very much, and Miss Berthold had been an enthusiast for *Sordello*, so I was able to tell him this and we talked very comfortably for a while.

'*Sordello!*' said Mrs Carlyle suddenly. 'What *is* that, Robert? A man, or a city, or a book? I could not tell, at all.'

'Well, Jane,' he said, 'then perhaps you should read it again.'

'No, no, no,' she said, in some alarm. 'That is exactly what Alfred said to me when I told him I did not care for that long, rambling thing that he insists on reciting every five minutes—what is it?'

'*Maud?*' I offered.

'*Maud*. Exactly.' Mrs Carlyle shuddered. 'On and on it went … you would think I might be quite used to interminable monologues by now,'—here she looked across to where Mr Carlyle was still holding forth—'but even I have my limits.' I found myself warming to Mrs Carlyle. She was a refreshing antidote to the uncritical worship that the Pattle sisters lavished on the men of genius whom they enticed into their orbit.

Mr Browning asked me if I had enjoyed being a model for Mrs Cameron.

'Sometimes,' I said, 'although it can involve dressing-up in odd clothes and then just trying to be very, very still for a long time. It isn't always easy.'

He gave a rueful laugh.

'I can sympathise heartily, Miss Ryan,' he said. 'The last time Julia stayed here, she announced that she would and she must photograph me, wrapped me in a cloak and told me to sit quite still while she fetched something of vital importance. There I was, trying not to move, waiting patiently. I heard the clock ticking the minutes away, and she did not return. Still I sat, and sat, and sat, until at last Mr Prinsep came in and asked me whatever I was doing, and I told him, and he sent to find Julia. It turned out she had got distracted and forgotten all about me.'

Mrs Carlyle gave a sympathetic snort at this, and Julia must have heard her name mentioned, for she shouted down the table over Mr Carlyle.

'Now, Robert, I have quite decided I shall make a photograph to illustrate one of your poems! No, do not say anything; I absolutely insist. What shall it be? *My Last Duchess*, do you say?'

'Oh, I don't really think—' began Mr Browning, but fortunately, perhaps, for him, Mrs Prinsep was rising and announcing that we must all make our way to the drawing room for a little theatrical performance. The Carlyles, clearly united in their wish to avoid this if in nothing else, made their excuses and departed, and the rest of us were subjected to a one-act play depicting the murder of Amy Robsart (played by Miss Jackson in a gown of gold brocade with her hair loose) by Lord Dudley (played by Mr Watts in a red coat and a high collar). I managed to tuck myself away on a window seat from where I had a slightly obscured view of the actors (I did not mind that) but an excellent view

166

of the rest of the audience, who provided, I felt, an altogether more interesting entertainment.

Mr Cotton was watching the play; Mrs Jackson—Mia—was watching Mr Cotton; and Mrs Prinsep was watching Mrs Jackson. At length Sara leaned over to whisper something to Mia, she too directed her gaze at Mr Cotton, and then both looked over at Miss Jackson. They looked complicit. They smiled, small discreet smiles. Oho, I thought. Mia has her eye on Mr Cotton as a match for her daughter. Sara has the same idea.

Somehow I did not care for that thought. Miss Jackson was extraordinarily beautiful, it was true, hauntingly lovely, and accomplished, and exquisitely dressed, and above all part of this dazzlingly glamorous family. She had the face of a Madonna—oh, so much more than I, or even Hillier, ever would—but I somehow felt that she had a tiny vicious streak. Mr Cotton, I thought, was too good for her.

When the silly play was over, the guests began to depart. I said goodbye to Mr Browning, who bowed over my hand and said kindly that he hoped to see me in Freshwater; and once he had left I glided over to where Mr Cotton, the last guest to leave, was thanking his hostess, his stammer as always more pronounced when he was speaking formally.

'You are most welcome, Mr Cotton,' said Mrs Prinsep, at her most gracious. 'We hope to see you again very soon. Now—I will ask my niece to show you to the door—I am sure she would be happy to do so—'

'Let me save Miss Jackson the trouble,' I said quickly. 'I will show Mr Cotton out. It is my job, after all.' I hoped Julia had heard that. I hoped they all had.

Neither Mrs Prinsep nor Miss Jackson could really object without looking and sounding foolish, although Miss Jackson shot me a look full of venom. As last time, therefore, it was just Mr

Cotton and I who walked together along the passage and into the hallway where the footman, as always, was standing by the door.

'Don't wait, thank you, Joseph,' I said. 'I think Mrs Prinsep needs you in the drawing room.'

Joseph bowed to us both. As he passed me he gave the merest suggestion of a wink.

'I have so enjoyed the evening, Miss Ryan,' said Mr Cotton. 'M-may I ask how long you will be here in London?'

'I leave tomorrow,' I said. 'The exhibition is over; I shall travel back to the Island in the morning.'

'Tomorrow? Oh, I had not realised—that is, I had thought you were—can you not s-stay a little longer?'

'No,' I said firmly. 'I must go.'

'But—perhaps—that is—Miss Ryan, m-might I—no, of course, no, I have no right—'

Whether it was my sympathy for his hesitant speech and his look of real dismay, or some other less worthy motive, I cannot say, but I stepped towards him so that I was standing very close, put one hand on his arm, and raised my other hand to place one finger on his lips.

'Shhh,' I said. Then I placed one hand on each of his shoulders, and looked into his eyes.

It was enough. He lunged towards me, aiming clumsily for my mouth, and our teeth clashed.

*Oh, no. This won't do,* I thought. *This won't do at all.*

I drew away from him, just a little, and then I put my hands up either side of his face and slid my fingers into the tangle of soft brown curls. I leaned up and brought my lips close to his ear. His skin smelled of expensive soap.

'Wait,' I murmured, very softly, and I felt him quiver as my breath landed. I let my cheek touch his, and I whispered 'wait', again, and we stood still for a long minute, close against each other, silent apart from his ragged breathing; and then I began to drop tiny kisses along the line of his jaw, drawing nearer to his mouth, and then I let my lips touch his, soft, lightly at first, then clinging, then pressing, and at last I parted my lips and he gave a sort of tiny groan from the back of his throat as we kissed, properly, deeply, warmly.

It was a start. He had a way to go, but I felt he had the makings of being a good learner.

I should have been ashamed of myself, really, because I was teaching him how to kiss just as Billy had taught me (along with a lot of other things) and I won't say I didn't think of Billy at that moment. In the arms of one man and thinking of another. You hussy, Mary Ryan. But, I reasoned to myself, it's for his own good—he hasn't had much teaching in this field yet, it's clear, if any, and everyone has to learn from someone. It was for my own good, too—if he desired me, if he wanted to please me, he had better learn how to do it properly, and he would certainly thank me; and perhaps some other woman would thank me in the future, for no woman wants to be practised on, after all —but then Henry started to kiss me again, and I stopped thinking about anything else. As I had surmised, he was a quick study.

# 21

I left Little Holland House early the next morning, once more in my brown checked dress and carrying my carpet bag. The hansom took me back through the city and over the river to the railway station and I bought my ticket and felt, as I waited, my usual delight in watching the locomotives as they stood breathing steam under the high glass roof, admiring their gloss and strength. And then I started thinking about Henry Cotton.

We had stayed in the hall last night for—well, it was hard to say how long, but perhaps for ten minutes, until a sudden noise of footsteps made us spring apart as Mrs Prinsep appeared from the gloom of the corridor. I did not know if she had seen us locked in each other's arms. I thought not, but Henry's flushed face and my disheveled hair may have given her some hints what had just passed. She gave me a look not unlike the look Hilda had once given me when I had passed her with wisps of hay still clinging to me, but naturally Mrs Prinsep was far too well bred to make any remarks about hussies, even if her thoughts were running along the same lines. She merely asked Mr Cotton if he had found his coat, gave him a gracious smile, and bade him goodnight. He gave me a slightly anguished look, muttered something about not having realised the time, and melted into the night.

'Well, Mary,' she said, with a slight edge to her voice, 'you have an early start tomorrow, have you not? You had best be off to bed, now.'

When I reached my yellow room, Miss Jackson was in the corridor. She was standing artistically by a window, as though looking out at the moon, but I had the distinct impression that she had been waiting for me.

'I don't suppose I shall see you in the morning,' she said. 'So I shall say goodbye now.' I held out my hand, but she did not take it, just inclined her head towards me and then turned to walk away. 'You can keep the clothes, by the way,' she said over her shoulder, 'they are all rather dowdy and quite out of fashion, but I don't imagine that will matter in Freshwater.'

I instantly decided that nothing would induce me to keep her cast-off dresses. I folded them all with meticulous care, and laid them on one of the chairs for her—no, of course it would not be her—for one of the servants to find. When I rose the next morning, those clothes were the first thing I saw, and as I packed my own few shabby scraps of cotton into the carpet-bag the lovely things lay just in my line of vision. I resisted until the very last minute, and then on an impulse I stuffed one dress, the blue silk, into my bag and walked out of the bedroom before I could change my mind. I might never have such a dress again, and beggars can't be choosers. Although, I reflected, I had by now made at least some choices in my life: I had, after all, chosen to change the way I spoke, and chosen to study and learn and read. And I had chosen to walk with Henry Cotton to the door last night and stand close to him and look into his handsome face and make it inevitable that he would kiss me.

All the way back to the Isle of Wight, as I gazed unseeing out of the carriage window, I thought about him. What can one tell about a man from his kisses, I wondered? A young man (he was three years older than me, I now knew, but in some ways he seemed younger) with, it seemed, hardly any experience of female company, finds himself alone with a girl who makes it clear that she wants to be kissed. What else is he to do? He might even now be regaling his friends with the story of a little conquest, hearing them laugh and congratulate him on an opportunity grasped. There was none of the danger that would have attended such a thing happening with a girl of his own class—say, for the sake of argument, someone like Miss Jackson—for then he might certainly have felt obliged to make her an offer of marriage. A servant, however, a girl from a lower class, was quite different; no danger there—and Julia and her sister and niece had made sure he understood that was exactly what I was.

Something, though, made me think that it was more for him than an opportunity grasped. It was not casual, that embrace, it was passionate. Even now I felt my breath catch as I recalled how he had held me, pressed against me, his mouth seeking mine, and the little sound he had made in his throat as he kissed me, and how he had murmured my name into my hair as though it were a sacred word. I hoped he would think of me sometimes, as perhaps the first woman for whom he had felt that passion.

Nevertheless, I reminded myself, it hardly mattered. I would not see him again.


There was no trap waiting for me when I disembarked at Yarmouth, so I found a carrier's cart that was about to set off for Freshwater and asked if I might ride among the boxes of fruit and sacks of flour. I had somehow imagined that Julia would have wired ahead for Billy to meet me, but it seemed that she had not.

Walking back into Dimbola Lodge, I felt as though I had been away for months or even years instead of the few weeks it had actually been. Louisa was pleased to see me, and Kellaway and Hillier too, I thought. They all asked me excited questions about London, about the city and the exhibition and the place I had stayed. I told them what I could, but I found that I was making my account, not exactly untruthful, but slanted a little away from reality. I said that I had worked at the gallery, had helped Mrs Cameron, seen just a little of the great city streets as I had driven through—but I did not say that I had dined with the family, dressed in borrowed finery, and drunk iced champagne under the stars. I did not say that I had, at various times, felt hot with shame, giddy with delight, cold with anger, shaken with pleasure. I did not show anyone the blue silk dress hidden in the box under my bed. I made sure they believed I had been there simply as a servant. That we all understood. The rest, I was not sure I could explain, even to myself.

The household was of course beginning to prepare itself for Julia's return the following week, but it was still in that pleasant, relatively peaceful state it always assumed when its mistress was away. Mr Cameron as usual kept largely to his own room, emerging now and then to hunt for a particular book or pour himself a glass of something sustaining. I bumped into him one afternoon, as I was lethargically dusting the library and taking the chance to snatch a few minutes' reading when I thought I would not be disturbed.

'Ah, Mary,' he said, 'seen my copy of Keats anywhere, have you?'

I went to the table where I had that minute laid down the book he sought.

'Here, sir.'

'Good, good. Just fancied I might read the Ode to Autumn, you know, since it will be that time of year before too long.'

'Mists and mellow fruitfulness. The fumes of poppies. The soft-dying day.'

'Exactly. Although,'—he peered at me closely, his kind eyes wrinkling behind his gold spectacles—'you look as though the Ode to Melancholy might be more the verse for you, today. In the very temple of delight, you know.'

'I am well enough, sir, thank you,' I said, but I could hear my voice shake a little.

'Life here a little stale perhaps, after London?' he suggested.

'Oh, no—I am glad to be back here, really. I was longing to be home—although staying at Little Holland House was, certainly, an experience.'

'Bit overwhelming, the Pattle girls. Can't stand them when they get together. And I never go to London at all if I can help it. Far too many people, and all those grey buildings and the smoke and the noise.' He sighed. 'Ceylon, India, Mary, those are the places for beauty.' He started to amble towards the door. 'Get out and have a walk, my dear, clear your head. Or take a glass of brandy. Or both.'

When he had gone I put my duster down. I thought I might follow his advice. There was a decanter on the desk, and I poured myself a little glass of brandy and drank it down, and then I walked out and went swiftly towards the servants' door. Unluckily, Hilda was in the passage. I was beginning to think she must lurk there in the sole hope of catching me doing something I shouldn't.

'And where are you off to, Ryan?' she asked.

'I'm going out,' I said. 'On Mr Cameron's advice.'

She looked incredulous, but she could hardly stop me.

'If you're looking for that ne'er-do-well Hemmings you're so fond of, he's probably somewhere with his new strumpet,' she said, and there was a little note of triumph in her voice. 'He hasn't wasted any time since you've been gone, you may be sure. You aren't the only pebble on the beach, my fine lady.'

The fact was that I had not seen Billy since my return from London. Oh, he had greeted me from across the stable yard, waved his hand, nodded at me across the kitchen table when he came in for the servants' supper; but he had not sought me out, we had not been alone, we had not exchanged more than a word, hardly even a look. I had supposed he was sulking because I had been away and had an adventure while he, despite all his talk of America, was still in Freshwater. I had thought he would come round in time. I had been looking forward to telling him all about Little Holland House, about my yellow room, my dresses, the parties and the champagne and my hosts and the famous people I had met. (There would be no need to tell him about Mr Cotton, of course, who was safely in the past.) I had imagined regaling him with these stories, sharing the absurdities and glamour and eccentricities of my hosts, describing Il Signor in his monk's robe and the beautiful Miss Jackson walking barefoot with jasmine in her hair. I had imagined him laughing, ruffling my hair, kissing me, telling me I was worth a thousand Miss Jacksons.

I went past Hilda without replying, ran through the garden gate, and took the path that led up towards the high down. I felt the need for wind in my hair and sun on my face, for the loneliness and wildness of the place. If Billy had found himself another girl to take to the hayloft, why should I be surprised? Had I thought of him as mine, waiting faithfully, like a devoted dog? That was hardly Billy's style.

I half-walked, half-ran, up the path through the field, past the fort that clung to the edge of the rocks. Up on the down, the wind was blowing from the west, and the turf was short and springy beneath my feet. The chalk cliff dropped away, sheer and terrifying, and the wrinkled sea lay far, far below. By the time I reached the highest point where the fire beacon stood I was out of breath, and I stopped to do what I always did when I was there: I revolved, slowly at first, looking at the world spread out around me, the ocean and the land and the sky, the misty horizon where they faded into one other. Quite alone, my arms spread wide, I turned and turned, faster and faster, until everything blurred and I was dizzy and at last I stopped to feel the world still spinning beneath my feet, and then I lay down on my back on the turf and stared up at the clouds scudding fast across the sky.

I had been so relieved to escape from Pattledom, so desirous of being back here in a place I had believed I belonged. Now, if Billy was not my friend and ally, I felt empty and alone, and I wondered if I would ever truly belong anywhere. I thought of Mr Cameron longing for the east, of Billy longing for the America of his dreams, of Mammy longing for the old country. I thought of Henry Cotton and the look of yearning and despair he had given me as Mrs Prinsep banished him into the darkness. Aching pleasure turning to poison. Were we all forever wanting to be elsewhere, sure that a happier place existed if we could but get there? Mr Cameron was right. In the very temple of delight veiled Melancholy has her sovereign shrine.

# 22

I lay there for a long while, watching the sky, and at last I closed my eyes against the huge emptiness above me and drifted into a sort of half-doze. It was as though the sadness in my heart had exhausted me, and I had a hard knot of sorrow inside me which tears might have dissolved, but tears would not come. I do not know for how long I lay there, but I woke with a start, because a large black-clad figure was bending over me.

'Mary. Do you want to walk with me a little way? Or do you prefer to stay here?'

One of Mr Tennyson's qualities was that he never seemed surprised by anyone else's behaviour, however strange. Finding his friend's parlourmaid asleep on the downs in the middle of the day did not seem to perturb him in the slightest. I scrambled to my feet.

'Yes, please, I should like to walk.'

'Good.' He set off at a stride, heading towards the Needle Rocks with his long cloak flapping behind him like a giant bat. I ran to catch up. On we went, heads down into the western wind which was blowing more strongly now. It always felt slightly alarming to me, that walk, with the sea closing in on either side of us as the land narrowed, like a terrifying dream in which one might find the earth disappear beneath one's feet. We didn't speak as we walked. The wind would have whipped our words away in any case. At the furthest point we stopped to catch our breath, looking down at the new fort and the sharp white rocks around which the grey-green water seethed, and then we turned and made our way back. With the wind behind us it was easier, and we could even talk a little.

'Clears the head, Mary, I always think, being up here,' he said, swishing his walking cane at the gorse bushes as we passed.

'Does the poetry come more easily out of doors?' I asked.

'Always. The sea, the sky. Just walking. There is something about walking that sets the mind free.'

We tramped on, mostly in silence, except that now and again he would mutter a few lines out loud, disconnected phrases that were taken by the wind before I could catch them. A gale was coming, and the clouds had overtaken us by now, building up in vast dark towers that blotted out the sky. When we reached the point where we began to descend once more towards the bay, he stopped. The sea was rolling, now, great waves crashing in against the grey rocks below.

'*Break, break, break,*
*At the foot of thy crags, O Sea!*
*But the tender grace of a day that is dead*
*Will never come back to me.*'

Those words I did hear, clearly enough, and it was as though Mr Tennyson was speaking them because he knew what I was feeling. Somehow the knowledge that at least one person understood me made the knot inside me begin to loosen a little. Full of gratitude, I looked up at him, and then I saw that there was a deep anguish written on his own face, a pain that I had never imagined that a person who was (as I thought then) practically old could ever feel. He had known a great loss, I thought, some terrible unimaginable sorrow that racked his heart. Because it seemed natural I put my hand in his, and we stood there together gazing at the relentless sea. Perhaps I began to grow up a little, in that moment, when I realised that other people might feel deeply, might ache and mourn; that love and passion did not belong only to the young; that the world did not revolve solely around Mary Ryan.

I had no idea what he was thinking, or of whom, so I just leaned my cheek against his shoulder and said nothing. After a while he put his arm around my shoulders, and kissed the top of my head, and then he disengaged himself and we began to walk onwards.

I was late back, of course. I should have been in an hour before to serve the tea, and Hillier had had to do it all herself and was sulking, but I promised to make it up to her by doing the tea by myself for the next two days and she relented quite quickly. She was sweet-natured, Mary Hillier, with a disposition I almost envied. She was not like me; she did not seem to resent her position, or dream of another life. She just went placidly about her work, submitted with a good grace to being dressed up and photographed, and philosophically accepted Julia's raptures and scoldings alike. When Julia returned a few days later, full of glee about the success of the exhibition and brimming with new ides for photographs, Hillier was ordered straight back into her modelling role.

'I'm to be someone called Sappho tomorrow,' she told me, resignedly.

'Sappho? Goodness,' I said. 'What will she dress you in, do you think?'

'A nice printed frock, I do hope.'

'I should have thought a flowing robe of some sort would be more suitable for Sappho,' I said. 'Something rich, in crimson or gold ...'

'I should like a printed frock,' said Hillier dreamily.

Julia did photograph Hillier as Sappho the next day. I was not present when she took the picture, but I was busy in the morning preparing the plates, and then later pouring the developing solution and the varnish. As the image began to emerge—that magical moment that I always loved—I saw Hillier's familiar face taking shape, her rounded cheek and the slightly drooping set of her mouth. Then the rest of the picture came into view—and there she was, in a printed dress which I recognised, because it had been altered from an old one which had once belonged to Julia's married daughter. It was the most un-Sappho-like garment I could have imagined, but Hillier was thrilled for she was allowed to keep it and she wore it every Sunday from then on.

We all went to church on Sundays, naturally. There were no exemptions, not for staff nor for the family (apart from Mr Cameron who was an out-and-out atheist, something that gave Julia pain, I think, although naturally he was always forgiven). Julia herself was certainly devout—all those Madonnas and angels— and she would occasionally fall to her knees and pray out loud in a quite public and dramatic way. I was more of Mr Cameron's way of thinking, myself, but I did enjoy going to church. It was a social occasion, really, particularly for us servants—a chance to wear our best outfits, such as they were (generally the only garments we owned apart from our work clothes), chat with each other as we went to and from the church, and see all the folk of the parish. I found some pleasure in the ritual of the service, too, the familiar words and the hymns; and I liked the building itself, the ancient pillars, the vaulted roof, the narrow arched windows and the gleam of coloured glass.

We walked there every week—not Julia or her family or her visitors, of course; they did not walk, Billy drove them in the trap—but we servants walked, marching along through the village and the lanes to where the church stood above the old causeway that crossed the river. That Sunday was warm and pleasant, but there was a chill inside the church, as there always was, the chill of cold damp stone that had stood through the centuries, and I drew my shawl tight around me as the Rector entered and the service began.

Two rows in front of me sat Billy, and across the aisle from him was a girl I knew slightly. Elsie—a fair-haired creature, pretty enough, I supposed, in an insipid way—worked in the shop along the road from Dimbola Lodge. From where I was sitting I had a perfect view of the pair of them: she kept glancing across at Billy, then whispering behind her hand to the girl next to her, and now and then Billy would return her look. Although I couldn't see his face I knew he was smiling. Once she dropped her hymnbook and Billy stooped to pick it up for her, causing more agitated whispering and a smothered giggle. Elsie, I supposed, was the strumpet Hilda had mentioned. In fact Hilda, across the aisle from me, was watching them too, and with a good deal more satisfaction written on her sharp face than I was feeling.

When we all trooped outside after the service Julia cornered the Tennysons by the lychgate and started on about a new idea for a picture illustrating one of his poems.

'The Gardener's Daughter, Alfred! I can see it now—Mary under a cloud of roses—'

She looked towards Hillier. Mr Tennyson looked towards me. Hillier and I both pretended not to hear and edged away. There was a young man standing awkwardly nearby, looking at Hillier, turning his hat round and round in his hands, and I recognised him as a lad from the village who worked as a jobbing gardener at Dimbola now and then.

'Oh, look, it's Tom,' I said, giving Hillier a little push in his direction. 'Go on, cheer him up, say hello. You know he's sweet on you.'

Hillier blushed faintly, but she didn't object. I left them and wandered off round to the back of the church to look at the river. The tide was up, and a solitary skiff was sailing downstream, towards Yarmouth. I began thinking of the journey I had made to London all those weeks ago. *This way for England!* the ferryman on the quay at Yarmouth had shouted as we went aboard. I had been so anxious then about what might await me, and so relieved at last to return—but now, perversely, I wished with all my heart that I were back at Little Holland House. Freshwater seemed so provincial, so far away from the glamour and danger of that enchanted place. I wondered if Henry Cotton had been kissing any other girls since that evening we had stood together in the darkness of the hallway. I had a sudden memory of the feel of his mouth on mine and the way he had said my name. If he had I hoped at least that he had not been kissing Miss Jackson.

A step on the gravel path behind me made me turn. It was Billy, and as far as I could see he was unaccompanied by the strumpet. He followed my gaze out towards where the little boat glided along leaving a silver trail in the water.

'Planning to sail away, Mary Ryan?'

'I might be.'

He kicked at some moss on a nearby gravestone.

'Had enough of this place, I dare say? A bit too grand for it, now, are you?'

I laughed. 'Hardly. How could Mary Ryan be too grand for anything?'

'You went off to London town readily enough. You were gone for weeks.'

'Mrs Cameron took me there, to work for her. I wasn't there for pleasure. Anyway, Billy Hemmings, I hear you amused yourself well enough while I was gone.'

I hadn't meant to say that; the words just came out. He looked me in the eye for the first time.

'Ah, well,' he shrugged. 'That means nothing.'

'I'm not sure the young lady in church would like to hear you say that.'

He moved a step closer to me.

'Mary—'

At that moment a voice called for Billy—Mrs Cameron was ready to leave—the trap must be brought round—and he gave me a rueful grin and sauntered away. As I walked back through the village, Hillier fell into step beside me, chattering about Tom and how he had looked and what he had said and how he planned to seek work on the new railway that was to be built out to Freshwater. I made encouraging noises but really I was only half-listening. Billy and I were almost friends again now, I felt, despite the strumpet (whom I thought was probably quite a nice girl, if rather ordinary). If I put my mind to it, I thought, I could certainly see her off. If I chose to. The fact was that I hardly knew if I chose to or not.

'But do you think I should?'

I had lost the thread of what Hillier was saying. 'Should what?'

'Walk out with Tom Gilbert. He do say he will call for me on my afternoon off.'

'Yes, of course. If you like him.'

'I like him, right enough. He's a steady young man, I do believe.'

'Then walk out with him. Perhaps he's the one for you, and you won't know until you try, will you?'

She looked much struck by this idea.

'That is true. I won't know until I try.'

Louisa and Kellaway joined us then, to discover what we were talking about, and Hillier told them about Tom Gilbert, and there was much excitement and giggling and exclaiming; and then we all linked arms and walked on, laughing and talking as we went, the four of us, matching our steps, raising our faces towards the sun.

# 23

Billy started walking out with Elsie from the shop on a regular basis, and he seemed quite taken with her. I told myself that she was welcome to him, but I had to admit to myself that I missed our old friendship, the teasing and laughter and closeness. When we talked now, if we talked at all, it was stilted. I had not thought that Billy and I would ever lose the bond of our shared memories, the things we never spoke of but would surely never forget—the time of the lodging house, the cold and the hunger and the fear, the fetid room where a dozen strangers slept, muttering in their sleep, the scrabble of the rats below the floorboards. We both knew how far we had come, and we knew how easy it would be to find ourselves back in that terrifying world. Neither of us had family to fall back on. We were both alone, apart from each other, and I had believed that we would always be close. And of course we weren't meeting in the hayloft any more, and I missed that too. One afternoon, though, when I was picking peas, Billy materialised close by, ostensibly to mend a hole in the garden fence.

'Saw you up on the downs yesterday, Mary Ryan. Walking with Mr T.'

'I expect you did. We walk up there quite often.'

'You want to be careful. Old men are the worst.'

'No, they're not. Young men are the worst.'

'He's old enough to be your father.'

I put the pea-basket down and straightened up.

'If you are suggesting that Mr Tennyson might get fresh with me, that just shows how your mind runs, Billy Hemmings.'

'What's he want with you, then? The pleasure of your company?'

'Yes, as a matter of fact, just that. Is that so hard to believe?'

'Mary. You're being daft, girl. What's he want walking and talking to a parlourmaid if it isn't what we all know he wants? He's a gentleman. People say he's met the Queen. He's the Poet Whatever.'

'Poet Laureate, I assume you mean. I realise that, obviously. And what do you mean, *what we all know he wants?* I suppose you and others have been gossiping. Well, you can gossip all you like. I've nothing to be ashamed of. I'm not surprised that Hilda and Mrs Lyle are saying that sort of thing, but I didn't have you down as such an old woman, Billy.'

He flushed.

'You've a sharp tongue, Mary Ryan.'

'I need one. I've to contend with idiots like you.'

I picked up my basket and turned to walk away, but he stepped up behind me and grabbed my arm.

'Come on, now, Mary.' He turned me to face him. 'I'm looking out for you, that's all.'

'I don't need you to look out for me. I'll look out for myself. Now let go of my arm.'

He dropped his hand, but he didn't move away, just stood, looking into my face, and then he grinned.

'Ah, Mary,' he said, 'don't let's quarrel.' He flicked my nose, the way he used to when I was ten and he was twelve. I stuck my tongue out, and he laughed. 'That's more like it,' he said. 'Meet me in the hayloft later? Just to talk. We won't do anything you don't want to do.'

'I'll see,' I said. 'I might, if I'm not too busy.'


I decided, of course, straightaway, that I would definitely not go to the hayloft. I didn't want Billy to think I would come back to him at the snap of his fingers. Then he winked at me across the servants' supper table and I saw Hilda intercept the wink and purse her lips. Hilda had me down as a minx already, and if she was spreading gossip about me, well, then I would give her something to gossip about. As soon as the supper was eaten, I stood up and said that I was going out for a walk, and would Billy care to walk with me? He jumped up, nearly knocking his chair over as he did so. I saw a few glances exchanged around the table. Hillier's eyes widened as she looked at me and Mrs Lyle made a clicking sound with her tongue. Well. Better that they all thought I was after Billy than that I was an old man's darling. Poor Mr Tennyson. He was not really old, of course, but he was, as Billy had pointed out, certainly old enough to be my father.

'This is like old times, Mary,' said Billy, sliding his arm around my waist as soon as we were out of the kitchen door.

I removed it.

'I just want to walk, Billy,' I said.

'Aren't you coming to the hayloft?'

'No,' I said firmly. 'Look, it's a beautiful night. Let's go up to the downs and look at the moonlight on the sea.'

I heard him sigh, but he fell into step beside me, and we took the path towards the high down. The moon was so bright that night that we had no trouble seeing our way, and we climbed fast, and when we were far above the sea we stopped to catch our breath. The moonlight made a dazzling path across the black waters, and ghostly streaks of cloud drifted across the sky.

'Look, Mary,' said Billy softly. 'Look over there.'

A tiny glimmer of light was racing in sudden streaks where a cluster of hawthorns grew. As I looked another and then another joined it, little magical dashes, gleams that came and went.

'Fireflies,' he said, and put his arm around my waist once more. It felt solid and strong. This time I didn't remove it. We stood quite still and watched the fireflies while the moon sailed serenely overhead and the sea made its far-off lonely soughing sound. After a while I began to shiver; it was late now, and the soft night air was growing chill. Billy wrapped both his arms around me and held me close so that I began to feel warm again, and when he started to kiss me I kissed him back.

# 24

'In the manner of Perugino!' shouted Julia.

It was a few weeks later, and I was in the fowl-house wearing the shapeless white woollen dress that Julia deemed suitable for almost any woman of a maidenly and submissive type. I was doing my best, but, alas, Perugino seemed to have been unaccountably omitted from my studies. I had no idea who he was, and I had to confess as much to Julia after the third photograph had been ruined because I was not looking sufficiently Peruginesque. She was becoming exasperated.

'Come now, Mary,' said Julia briskly, 'Perugino, Italian Renaissance painter, fifteenth century. Or sixteenth. I forget which. You have the look of his Madonnas, I fancy. Now we are trying for the Annunciation. The Angel of the Lord has just appeared to you—'

I tried to concentrate on the large vase that Julia had placed before me to represent the Angel Gabriel.

'That's good,' said Julia encouragingly, 'yes, your hair is falling just so, but do try for a more spiritual expression—'

I tried.

'No! No no no no *no*. The blessed Angel has just told you that you are to bear a child. I do not know why you cannot get this right. In fact you have been quite distracted for a while, now I come to think of it, and not yourself at all. You are not ill, are you?'

'No,' I assured her, 'I am not ill.'

'Good. You look perfectly well to me, I must say. Now just try harder, Mary!'

Julia was right. I had been distracted for some time, in fact ever since the walk up onto the downs with Billy. When he had kissed me beneath that brilliant moon, I had felt a rush of longing and relief and gladness that after all it was me he wanted, not the insipid Elsie, and when he spread out his coat on the grass beneath the hawthorn trees I lay down with him, pulling him to me. We held each other tight, kissing fiercely, and he tugged at our clothes, his skin hot against mine.

'I'll be careful, Mary,' he muttered, as he had done before. 'I won't let anything happen.'

But it did happen, of course. He wasn't careful and neither was I. All those hours we had lain in the hayloft, touching, kissing, gasping, sighing, so close, yet always holding back—it was as though they were always going to lead to this moment.

Afterwards it was too cold to linger up there; we dressed as quickly as we could and then ran back down to the house, hand in hand. I had to creep into bed quietly so as not to wake Louisa. I wanted very much to tell her what had happened, and I thought of waking her, but common sense asserted itself. The fewer people who knew what I had been up to, the better. Gossip was one thing, but you can always deny gossip. True confessions are harder to laugh off.

When I awoke the next day, I half-wondered if I had dreamed it all. Billy's cheerful wink at me over the breakfast table, however, seemed to indicate that it had all been real. And now the fear and the self-reproach began. How could I have been so stupid? Hilda was right. I was a strumpet. Worse, I was a fool, a fool in the way women have been since time immemorial. What would happen to me if I were with child? It wasn't as if Billy was in a position to provide for a wife. I would be turned off without a character, for everyone knew that is what happened to servant girls who were caught out. Even Julia, generous, unconventional, scornful of society's norms, would surely not keep me on if the worst really had happened. I would starve, or die in childbirth lying on filthy rags in some sordid room, and if I survived I would have no alternative but the workhouse, and there I swore I would never go. I would be begging for my bread, just as Mammy had done, begging with a baby in my arms, a poor despised creature, the lowest of the low. My looks and my voice and my book-learning and my silk dress would be no help to me then.

I kept out of Billy's way for the best part of two weeks, making myself busy, inventing tasks that kept me indoors. Eventually, though, he cornered me as I was hanging out the laundry.

'All right, then, Mary?'

'I don't know,' I said, facing him, as I supposed I had to. 'I don't know if I'm all right. I might be pregnant, Billy.'

Was it my imagination, or did he flinch slightly? At any rate he looked stricken.

'Are you?'

'I don't know. I said I might be. I mean, nothing's happened yet to prove I'm not.'

'If you are, Mary—'

I put my hand up and backed away from him.

'Don't say it. Don't say anything.'

I turned and walked away, head held high. I might be terrified inside, but I was certain of one thing: I did not want a husband who would marry me because he had to.


That night, as we undressed for bed, Louisa asked me what was wrong.

'You looks pale, Mary. You ain't yourself. You got a pain? Is it the monthlies?'

I smiled wanly at her.

'If only it were, Louisa. Oh, if only it were.'

Silence fell while she digested this.

'Mary,' she said at last, 'if you'm in the family way, I do think there is a way to get rid of it. 'Tis something my cousin telled me once. A very hot bath, and a deal of gin.'

That sounded reassuringly like the sort of thing my mother would have suggested.

'Then I'll try it,' I said. 'Though how I'm to get enough hot water upstairs for a decent bath without the Family seeing I can't imagine. Let alone the gin.'

'Leave it to me, Mary,' said Louisa. 'We might have to tell the other two. But we'll do it.'

By *the other two* she meant Hillier and Kellaway. The four of us had become close by now, a little group who relied on each other, laughed and sighed together, teased and comforted one another. They were my friends; and now, when I needed them, how extraordinary they were. A whispered conference was held late that night, the four of us in the tiny dark attic room. The next morning, a synchronised exercise took place: when the hot water was carried up for the family, we all managed to take an extra can and pour it into the servants' tub on the top floor, then Kellaway caused a distraction by pretending she had spilled some and needed more; and as Mrs Lyle was tutting over that and fresh water was boiling Louisa was in the pantry sliding a flask of gin into her apron. Hillier reported to the rest of the servants that I had been sent out by Mrs C on an errand to Farringford and would be gone all morning, and I, following Louisa's instructions, undressed and slid gingerly into the scalding water while she poured me a tumbler of gin. I lay there flushed and sweltering amid the curling wisps of steam, and sipped and sipped, and felt the fiery liquid slide down my throat and into my stomach, and as soon as I had finished it she poured me another, and I stayed there perspiring and drinking gin until the water began to cool.

As soon as I stepped—rather shakily—out of the bath and Louisa wrapped me in the thin towel, a flower of scarlet blood bloomed on the cotton rug beneath my feet. I gave a gasp, and so did she, and she hugged me, and then said she would go and tell the others. I don't know if it was Louisa's remedy that did the trick or not—from things I have read subsequently I don't think there's much likelihood that gin and hot baths do anything except make one feel temporarily very relaxed and subsequently rather delicate, but I have never forgotten how those young women gathered around me, took risks for me, and cared for me.


'Now, once more—try bowing your head a little, Mary,' said Julia, not giving up. 'Just think, imagine, how must the Blessed Virgin have felt at that moment?'

I had a fair idea of how the Blessed Virgin might have felt, frankly; pretty much as I had felt three days ago, before Providence and my friends came to the rescue. I bowed my head and crossed my hands reverently across my breast, and at last Julia got her picture, and when it was developed she did say that she was pleased with it.

'Ah, the great Perugino!' she sighed, holding the print up to the light so that it might be better admired. 'Mary, I was right; you have the look that the Italian masters worshipped, and see what I have done, see how I have made the light fall upon your expression of divine rapture.'

I looked. Julia might have seen rapture, but all I could see on my own face in that photograph was divine relief.

# 25

Julia did not like people to elude her. She was very used to getting her own way in most things, and when it came to photography she was by now convinced that it was not only her duty but her God-given right to capture the eminent men of genius she so adored. Of course she had got many of them already, but one who had thus far escaped was her old friend Sir John Herschel, whom she and Mr Cameron had known for many years. Now in his seventies, and living in Kent, Sir John rarely left home, and Julia's repeated attempts to lure him to Freshwater had failed. Winter passed, and with the coming of the spring she made one of her sudden decisions and dashed off a letter to Lady Herschel, explaining its contents to me as she sealed it and I waited to take it to the post for her.

'I shall be no trouble to them, you see, Mary, no trouble at all. I have written that all I require will be a dark room with one window that I shall cover with yellow calico. I shall take all the equipment; they will hardly have to put themselves out in the slightest.'

I rather doubted that. Julia's presence generally meant upheaval and disruption wherever she was. Still, her intentions were good, and it seemed the Herschels were resigned to their fate, for Julia received an invitation by return and within a day she was busy packing her camera and her chemicals and making arrangements for her journey.

'Do consult Bradshaw's, Mary, and find out the trains to wherever it is—let me see—Hawkhurst, I believe—shall we have to go to Tunbridge, do you think?'

I went to find the timetable.

'You will need to go to Staplehurst,' I told her. 'That is the nearest station. The journey is rather tortuous—up to London and then out again on the south-eastern line.'

'Well, it must be done, and after all a journey is always an excitement. You had better write down all the times and connections, and then run along and pack, Mary.'

I sighed. Hilda was Julia's lady's maid, after all, and I did not really see why I should have to do Julia's packing when that was clearly Hilda's job. In fact I suddenly decided that I would not.

'I'll tell Hilda to pack for you,' I said.

'She has packed for me,' said Julia, her face red from wrestling with the camera tripod. 'I meant, pack *your* things, Mary. I shall need you to come with me to Kent to help with the photographs.'

A journey! Oh, my spirits leapt at the prospect. An escape—the ferry, the trains, new places. Exactly what I wanted. And yet—the last time Julia had taken it into her head to take me on a journey, she had sprung me on her hosts with no warning, and it had been a cause of deep mortification.

'Are Sir John and Lady Herschel expecting me to accompany you?' I asked.

'What? Oh, I dare say I may not have mentioned it, but they will not mind, Mary, Sir John and I are very old friends, far too old to stand upon ceremony, which I detest in any case, all the ridiculous formalities of written invitations and so forth—no, no, true friendship rises above such matters ...'

Her shawl had come adrift. I bent to pick it up, and then I put it round her shoulders and fastened it with her brooch.

'Nevertheless,' I said steadily, 'I should very much prefer it if they were expecting me.'

'Oh, very well, Mary,' she said, a little pettishly. I knew that she considered herself above such trivial things as ordinary social rules, and resented having to consider them. 'You can send them a wire, if you like. But then get back here and help me with the glass plates. I shall take quantities. I do not intend to skimp.'

I composed the words for the telegraph wire carefully, and I was rather pleased with the result. I wrote as though the message came from Julia herself—an uncharacteristically polite and tactful Julia, perhaps—explaining that she planned to bring her photographic assistant, a young lady, with her, and she hoped that it would not impose too much upon their kind hospitality to include Miss Ryan as well as herself. Then I wrapped all the glass plates to guard against breakage, checked the chemicals were safely sealed in their bottles, found some calico to screen the darkroom window, and at last went to pack for myself.

I got out the revolting old carpet bag again. By now I had two Sunday dresses, the brown check and another, which I preferred, in pale grey with a white collar. It was somewhat puritanical but I liked its shape. I decided that I would take my dark working dress because of the chemicals, but that I would travel in the grey. The blue silk was still in the box under my bed, and as it hardly took up any room I packed that too. I had no idea what awaited me in Hawkhurst, but I felt that this way I was prepared for all eventualities.


The journey was, as always with Julia, somewhat fraught: porters had to be found at every change to carry the crates of equipment and her trunks, as well as the bulging bags she had brought to carry a variety of wraps and cloaks that she thought she might need in which to swathe poor Sir John, and an ancient hatbox which held a collection of glass animals that she was convinced would be the very thing as a gift for our hosts. It seemed a miracle that we arrived at Staplehurst with all our possessions still with us, and it took three traps to transport us from the station. We arrived in a procession, like a caravan of camels, trundling slowly along the country roads and lanes, and at last up a winding gravel drive to Collingwood House.

I thought it a very beautiful place. It was of soft weathered brick and classical proportions, and on the pillared porch stood our hosts: Sir John, who had a handsome, crumpled face, and brilliantly piercing eyes beneath a shock of white hair, and his wife, somewhat younger—in her fifties, perhaps—who had a sweet expression and a comfortable figure. They seemed genuinely pleased to see Julia, and I could see why, as she sprang at them all excitement and squeals, for there was no mistaking the real warmth and affection she always showered upon her friends.

'And this must be Miss Ryan.' Lady Herschel was holding out her hand to me. 'You are most welcome, my dear. Oh, how lovely you are! Come inside, do, and we will have tea at once, and then you shall settle in.'

She had a soft Scottish lilt to her voice, which reminded me of Mrs Carlyle, although Lady Herschel was altogether a gentler person.

'Yes, Mary is to help me; she is very accomplished at all the photographic processes now,' said Julia, and I thought, hoped, that I detected a tiny note of pride in her voice.

'Indeed!' said Sir John, also shaking my hand. 'Then we must have a long talk, Miss Ryan, over dinner; I should be glad to have your views on the possibility of colour reproduction, which has been occupying me much of late.'

Inside, the house was every bit as delightful as its exterior had promised. I had never been in such a place: Dimbola was pleasant, if often chaotic; Little Holland House was glamorous and exotic; but this, with its high ceilings and perfect proportions, its tall windows and graceful sweeping staircase, was all light and elegance. We took tea in a parlour where the spring sunshine streamed in through gauzy curtains, and then I was shown to my bedroom, which had a soft faded carpet and a shelf of interesting books and fresh flowers by the bed and looked out upon a view across the weald of Kent. This, I thought, was the sort of house I should wish for, if a genie or a leprechaun should ever appear to grant me a wish. I leaned on the windowsill and allowed myself to imagine, for a while, living in a house of my own, a house with gardens full of bright flowers, windows through which sunlight fell in stripes across the floor, rooms with pretty furniture and everything arranged to my taste, a house I would drift through wearing a silk gown, where I would welcome friends, where I would live with—oh, let me see, three or four beautiful children, and a cat. And—I mentally added as an afterthought—a handsome husband.

Really, Mary Ryan. I washed, and brushed my hair, and changed into the blue silk dress, and when the gong sounded I walked down the curving stairs to the dining room. It was not like Little Holland House, full of noisy eccentric guests; it was quiet, with just ourselves at dinner, and birdsong outside the windows. It was not, in fact, Julia's natural milieu, but something in the warmth and gentleness of Lady Herschel's manner, and the evident respect Julia had for Sir John, seemed to bring out the best in her, and she talked away with far fewer shrieks and exclamations than were usual.

Julia and I rose early the next morning, and set about creating a darkroom from the Herschels' dressing room. They seemed remarkably calm about the whole thing, even when Julia spilled some silver nitrate on their very pretty Turkish rug. Then we hung dark curtains in their drawing room to create a suitable background, got the camera assembled, and I spent an hour in the kitchen preparing the plates, much to the dismay of the Herschels' cook and kitchen maid. The chemicals do have a very strong smell, it is true, which does not altogether enhance the preparation of an elegant luncheon.

In the afternoon we made a start. Sir John sat patiently on a hard chair while Julia darted back and forth, fiddling with the lens, and I adjusted the curtains to see if we could get more dramatic lighting on his face. At last Julia took two photographs, and I went off to develop them. We spent another extremely pleasant evening with our hosts, but when Julia looked at the photographs again the next morning she was not happy.

'I have not captured the divine essence of the man!' she wailed. 'I must show his other-worldly brilliance—a halo should glow around that splendid head.'

'Perhaps if he could fluff up his hair,' I suggested. 'I mean, that would create a sort of halo effect.'

'Ah! Yes—Mary, that it is it! His hair!' and she galloped off to find our subject again. He was resting with a handkerchief over his face, but Julia seized him and announced that she was going to wash his hair. With only the mildest protests he was led off upstairs, jugs of hot water were brought, and Julia herself soaped and rinsed and poured and then tousled him dry until a brilliant white cloud stood around his face. I felt I should apologise to Sir John for this treatment, but he bore it nobly, and when the photograph was done Julia was satisfied at last. She promised to make the prints as soon as we were back on the Island, and to send them to the Herschels within a very few days. I thought our hosts both looked more than a little relieved that the ordeal was over.

As we were due to depart first thing the following morning, we dined early. While Lady Herschel asked Julia about her children and her garden, Sir John and I conversed on subjects ranging from the moons of Saturn to colour blindness and the Iliad via the use of hyposulphite of soda as a photographic fixative.

'You are a most interesting lady, Miss Ryan,' he said at one point. 'Is photography to be your profession? Will you follow in Julia's footsteps?

'I do not have Mrs Cameron's eye for beauty,' I said, regretfully. 'I admire her art, her genius—but her skill is not something I could aspire to.'

We bid each other goodnight, and retired, but Sir John's question stayed with me as I undressed and hung my blue dress carefully in the cedar-scented wardrobe. *Is photography to be your profession?* Well, no, being a parlourmaid is to be my profession. I had no money, no family, no status. Julia's passion for photography, in the view of most of her class, was an eccentric hobby, no more, and she was free to indulge it because as far as I could see she did not need to earn a living, for she had Mr Cameron and his coffee estate. I felt a sudden fear at the prospect of being a servant for the rest of my life. I had tasted something different now, not just slightly different, but another world. This sunlit universe was light years from Putney Heath, of course, from the grinding sordid life I had once lived, but it was also far, far above the invisible, meagre, exhausting life of a servant. This was a world of good food and wine, books and ideas, music, art, and poetry, warm clean spacious houses full of beautiful objects, soft carpets and glowing candles, silk gowns and Kashmir shawls. I knew that world now, and I wanted to live in it myself, and I feared that I would never be allowed into it for longer than a few brief moments. I had disguised myself in a pretty dress, conversed and laughed and looked like a lady, but of course I was nothing but an imposter.

When we arrived back at Dimbola late the following day, I had hardly time to take off my hat before Hillier was drawing me aside with a thrilled look on her face.

'There's a letter for you, Mary. It came yesterday.'

She sounded awestruck. Servants hardly ever received letters. Mrs Lyle had a daughter in Newcastle who wrote to her now and then, and that was a definite mark of status. No one below stairs else had ever received a letter, as far as I knew.

'A letter?' I repeated, stupidly. My heart gave a jump. It must, it had to, be Mammy. Who else would write to me? She was writing to say that she was coming to see me, that she would settle down, that she would be near me forever ...

'Where is it?'

'On the hall table,' said Hillier, in the same reverent tones as one might refer to a high altar. I thanked her, and went to the hall. There in the silver tray on the side table lay a long envelope addressed to me in a clear strong script. I picked it up, my hands shaking slightly. The writing was in black ink, the envelope was of thick cream-coloured paper, and when I turned over I saw that it was sealed neatly with an embossed circle of red wax.

Well, of course it could not be from Mammy. She couldn't write, for one thing, and if she had asked someone else to write on her behalf it would hardly be someone who used expensive note paper and a seal. I swallowed hard, and tore it open.

*Dear Miss Ryan,* it began. And then—

*Mary. My Miranda. Do you remember me? Are the moments we spent together burned as clearly in your heart and your brain as they are in mine?*

*Mary, I have decided on my future. I have passed the examination to enter the Indian Civil Service, and I have secured a post in Midnapore, to be taken up this autumn. I am shortly leaving London to visit my grandfather in Devonshire, and after that I shall be making preparations for India. There is much to be done, but I am resolved.*

*I remain yours—*

*Henry John Stedman Cotton*

I read and re-read the letter, standing there in the hallway at Dimbola. What did Henry Cotton mean by writing such a missive? Why would he tell me that he was going to India? I supposed it was a farewell. He still thought of me—that much was clear. I could not help being glad of that—he still troubled my dreams a little, even though I had tried resolutely to get him out of my mind. But I hardly knew what to make of his letter. I half-thought that I should burn it, put it right out of my thoughts, rather than allowing any fanciful notions to be provoked by these few and rather random words. I didn't burn it, though. I put it in the box beneath my bed in my attic bedroom, and every now and then, when I was alone, I took it out and re-read it.

*I remain yours.* Do you, Henry? Do you? It seemed unlikely.

# 26

There was a loud and excited shriek from Julia as I collected her morning coffee tray. This was not in the slightest bit unusual—she was opening her post and she always liked someone on hand to regale with any news or gossip, however uninteresting to her audience—but the shriek was even louder than normal.

'A letter from Mia, Mary! My niece is to be married.'

'Miss Jackson? That niece?'

'Yes, you will remember her, no doubt. She's visited here, and she was staying with Sara when you were at Little Holland House with me. Didn't she give you some clothes?'

'Yes. She did.'

'Well, she is to marry in—let me see—well, this summer. All rather unexpected but they seem pleased enough. The young man is not from a hugely wealthy family, although I think there is property, but he has prospects at least—'

'Happy news, then,' I said, since something seemed to be expected of me.

'Indeed! Such a beautiful girl, exquisite, all grace and spirituality, with the face of an angel—oh, he is a very fortunate man, this fiancé—'

And so on. I had to listen politely while Julia went on about Miss Jackson and her many perfections, and all the while I had a cold feeling inside. So she had ensnared Mr Cotton at last, I supposed. He was eligible, he was handsome, and he was there. Pattledom had woven its spell and he had been drawn in to that world of art and elegance and refinement, the salons and the suppers, the wit and charm and general consciousness of superiority. Well, and what was that to me? He would be bound to marry someone, that was clear, and why should I mind if it was Miss Jackson more than any other who would be going to India with Henry Cotton? When I finally escaped with the tray I was in a thoroughly bad mood without being exactly able to explain to myself why.

About this time I began to consider the idea of becoming a governess. Ever since I had overheard Julia discussing my future with Dear Philip I had kept the idea in my mind, but whenever I had thought closely about it I had ended by dismissing it with a shudder. It was not only that the position of a governess was a lonely one, awkwardly in a no-man's-land between the drawing room and the kitchen, treated as a servant yet lacking the camaraderie of the servants' hall which at least gave us ties and even friendships. It was also that I did not think that I had the right qualities to teach. Miss Berthold had been patient and gentle, rarely raising her voice, never allowing herself to be provoked by her pupils' obtuseness or insolence. Patience, I had to admit, was not, perhaps, my strongest virtue.

On the other hand, the wages of a governess were considerably more than those of a parlourmaid. She was likely to have her own room, enough money for more than one new dress a year, even the possibility of saving a little for the future. And then, there was the appeal of the work itself—there would be the chance to read and study rather than dust and clean and fetch and carry.

There would be a little status. One would be addressed as Miss Ryan, not just as Mary. I began to picture myself in a pleasant, airy schoolroom, with one attentive pupil, a little girl, perhaps, who would listen obediently to my every word. I would introduce her to poetry and novels, show her maps of the world, explain scientific theories. I would be treated with respect by the family—charming, cultivated people, who would invite me to dine with them and their guests, and there would be evenings of intellectual conversation. They would have a wide group of friends who would become my friends too. They might take me on their travels to accompany my pupil. *This is Miss Ryan,* they would say, *she is travelling with us to the south of France, for we simply cannot do without her, and little Annabelle is quite devoted* … That was the sticking point, really, for already I was regarding the fictional child as something of an annoyance. Still, perhaps she would have a maid as well as a governess, and surely I would be strolling down the Promenade des Anglais unencumbered by Little Annabelle for at least some of the time.

Once this attractive picture had lodged in my brain, I started to wonder how I might take a tentative step in that direction. I did not want to even suggest to Julia that I might relinquish my current position. Here at Dimbola I knew that I was in many ways fortunate. I was part of the household, I had friends, the work was not as arduous as it might have been in many establishments. I would do nothing to jeopardise my place here. It was my home, or at least the only home I had. Yet I kept thinking that I would like to just try out my idea, dip a toe in the water, as it were, without commitment, for it might open up the world to me. *You won't know until you try, will you?* I had said, laughing, to Hillier. Perhaps I might follow my own advice. Perhaps I could treat a job as though it were a man; walk out with it for a while, without committing myself to anything like a marriage. But how?

The answer came to me quite quickly when Mr Tennyson was visiting. He and Julia had almost fallen out, because she had recently come across a party of excited Americans wandering about the streets of Freshwater looking for him, and she had not only directed them to his house but had written a letter for them to take with them so that they might have an introduction. Why she would do such a thing I had no idea since she must know that he hated being hunted by admirers, and inevitably he had roared at them and sent them packing. Then they came back to Dimbola to complain and she had rushed over to Farringford, the hopeful Americans still in tow, to remonstrate with him.

'Alfred,' she had said severely, 'these good people have come three thousand miles to see a lion, and they have found a bear!'

There was a bit of to and fro with this argument, but at last he saw the funny side and relented and consented to receive the star-struck visitors, and to show there were no hard feelings on either side he came to Dimbola the next day to drink tea. While I was in the room handing round the seed cake he began a lament about his sons, who had now both been sent away to school. Mrs Tennyson had not, I knew, really wanted the boys to go away at all, and I think it must have been a shock to the boys themselves, for they had been cosseted and adored all their lives, and kept in their sailor suits and ringlets right until the day they left home. Mr Tennyson had eventually insisted that they must go; but he was often worried about Hallam's health, which was rather delicate, and now he had withdrawn Lionel from school because he was being bullied.

'Until we find a place more conducive to his temperament, he will be at home, and I will have to teach him myself. Left to his own devices he will just escape out of doors to ride his pony or climb trees. I exhorted him the other day to apply himself, and sent him off to my library, but then I found him reading *Don Quixote*.'

'Oh, then, surely that is most promising—' said Julia enthusiastically.

'The *unexpurgated* text,' said Mr Tennyson sternly. 'He requires guidance in his choice of books, I fear.'

I had to take the tea tray away at that point, but an idea was forming. Lionel was must now be twelve. He would be an ideal pupil for my first attempt at teaching, I thought—a well-brought-up boy, old enough to be sensible, young enough to be (I hoped) obedient, perhaps even a little in awe of me. I considered approaching the Tennysons with my plan, but then, I thought, they would be sure to discuss it with Julia, and that might look as though I had been deceiving her; whereas if I approached Julia first, she might be affronted that I was ungrateful enough to even consider leaving her employ. No, I decided, I would have to take an informal approach.

On my next afternoon off I slipped through the green gate from the Dimbola garden into the Farringford estate. There was a lane that ran along the edge of the woods, and I knew that Lionel liked to gallop his pony along that lane whenever he could. Sure enough, after I had walked along the track for a few minutes, I heard the thud of hoofs and a dappled pony came charging towards me, with Lionel, wearing a scarlet coat, in the saddle. I put up my hand to wave, and he pulled the horse to a halt.

'Yes?' he said loftily.

'Lionel,' I said, 'how are you? Your father told me you were home from school for a while.'

'Did he?' Lionel scowled down at me. 'Why is my father discussing my schooling with you? You're a parlourmaid at Dimbola. I've seen you there.'

'I am not solely a parlourmaid,' I said, with dignity. 'I am a photographic model and assistant to Mrs Cameron.'

'Well, whatever you are, I don't see it's any business of yours. And you shouldn't address me as Lionel. I am Master Lionel, to you.'

This was not going as I had hoped, but I persevered.

'Master Lionel, then. I thought I might be able to offer you some help with your studies, until another school is found. I expect your father is anxious that you should not neglect your reading, isn't he?'

Lionel's scowl grew even darker.

'Papa's always grumbling at me. I hated school, and I hate it at home almost as much. I don't see why I am never to have any fun.'

'It doesn't seem fair, I agree. That's why I thought I might help—might make things easier for you. If your father knows you are studying he won't grumble at you any more.'

'I suppose.' He kicked moodily at the pony's flanks, and it skittered sideways. I jumped nimbly out of the way.

'You see, Lionel—Master Lionel—I often talk to your father about books—poetry—and I am sure I could help, by reading with you, and giving you ideas for things you could say to him to show you are applying yourself.'

'Really? You talk to my father?'

'I do.'

'Well—I still don't want to spend all my time indoors reading stupid books.'

'Of course you don't. In fact I could only spare an hour or so each day myself—and it doesn't have to be dull, really, I can make it fun. It will be a secret, you know, just between us. Why don't we try? We can stop if you don't find it helpful.'

His scowl began to clear a little.

'All right,' he said. 'I don't mind trying. If it's to be fun, and if you think it might make Papa pleased with me.'

'Splendid,' I said. 'Well, why don't we meet tomorrow, at about this time? Can you think of somewhere private we could use?'

'There's a summerhouse in the garden,' said Lionel, evidently now warming to the idea. 'My father had it built, but he never goes in it since a Cockney came and smashed a window. You can get to it through the woods.'

The next day I pretended to Mrs Lyle that Julia had sent me on an errand to Farringford and slid out before I could be asked any more. Lionel, bless him, was there on time.

'What am I to call you?' he asked as I entered the summerhouse.

'Miss Ryan. Or Mary. As you choose.'

'I shall call you Mary. And you can call me Lionel,' he said graciously.

'Then, Lionel, suppose we start? Here, I have brought some books.'

I had given some conscientious thought to what I would teach my first pupil. Impressing his father seemed to be his chief wish, and as I knew something of Mr Tennyson's preferred reading (apart from his own works) I had made a preliminary list: the Iliad, Malory, Milton, Shakespeare. I was familiar with all of those—although I did not read Greek to any great extent, so had only read the Iliad in translation. I had decided at last on Milton, and had managed to smuggle a copy of *Paradise Lost* out of Mr Cameron's library.

I asked Lionel to read the first part of the poem out loud. It was rather hard going—he stumbled over the words, and after two pages began to yawn and fidget. I stopped him and asked for his thoughts on what he had just read, and he looked quite blank.

'I don't know what it means,' he said. 'I suppose it's about God, and some bad angels.'

'Yes, well done—'

'And an infernal serpent. I like the sound of him.' He picked up a wooden toy sword that had been lying abandoned on the floor of the summerhouse. 'If I met him I should fight him—like this!' He jumped up and started running around the little cabin, making wild thrusts with the sword at the imaginary serpent.

'Shall we read a little more?' I said, severely. He subsided back into his seat, but the scowl was beginning to appear. We went on in this way for half an hour or so, but keeping Lionel's attention was a good deal harder than I had imagined. He sighed, and he wriggled, and he pouted. He assumed an expression of extreme vacancy, and then began pulling faces at his reflection in the broken glass window of the summerhouse. At one point he took out a penknife from his pocket and started stabbing it repeatedly into the wooden bench beside him. I felt my irritation rise, and discovered that I had a violent longing to slap him quite hard.

'Shall we end our lesson there?' I said at last. 'By tomorrow, I should like you to have learned by heart the first twenty-six lines of the poem—up to *And justify the ways of God to men.* Can you do that?'

He jumped up, looking enormously relieved, although I suspect no more than I.

'I suppose so,' he said. He gave me an unexpectedly sweet smile. 'You're awfully pretty, aren't you?'

Before I could think of a suitably severe reply, he had picked up the wooden sword and swooped out and away across the lawn, making wild lunges with the sword as he went. I rescued *Paradise Lost* from where Lionel had dropped it and made my way back to Dimbola. We had not got off to a promising start, but it was, after all, very early in my career as a governess. Things would no doubt improve.

# 27

The next day, Lionel was late, and I began to worry that he would not appear at all. Eventually he came running in, breathless and beaming.

'Mary,' he said, 'do you know anything about astronomy?'

'Not a great deal,' I said cautiously, 'why? What has that to do with *Paradise Lost*?'

'Oh, I don't care for that old stuff,' he said carelessly, 'I think I should learn about astronomy instead. Papa likes to watch the stars. If I knew about their names and so forth he would certainly approve, wouldn't he?'

'Well—I suppose—' I didn't in fact know anything at all about astronomy, but I felt sure there must be books on the subject at Dimbola, and any subject that elicited enthusiasm in my wayward pupil stood a far better chance of being rewarding to teach than Milton.

'Papa's built a platform on the roof of the house,' Lionel went on, 'just so he can watch the night skies!'

'Has he?'

'Why don't we go up there when it gets dark, Mary? Then I can learn about the stars and the planets and—and everything!' He was dancing about now, eyes glowing.

'Are you allowed up there, Lionel?'

'Not exactly,' he admitted, 'but if we were to go up the back stair, and then climb out of the window, we could easily get there without being seen. Just think how much I would learn!'

I should have said no, of course, but I had to admit that the idea of getting onto the roof at Farringford to look at the stars sounded like a rather delightful adventure, and certainly more appealing than trying to convey the wonders of seventeenth-century poetry to a reluctant twelve-year-old. Thus it was that later that evening, as night was falling, I was once more in the grounds of Farringford and flitting across the lawns like a shadow. At the back of the house the heavy wooden door stood on the latch, and Lionel was waiting just inside.

'This way, Mary!' He was breathless with excitement. The door led directly to a narrow spiral staircase, and I followed him to where, at the top, another stout door was just ajar, letting a gleam of light through. He pushed it open very cautiously. As we stepped through, I caught my breath. We were in a book-lined room with a great oak desk and a high-backed chair set in a window embrasure. There was a strong smell of tobacco.

'Lionel!' I whispered, now somewhat alarmed. 'This must be your father's study! What if he catches us?'

'He won't,' said Lionel confidently. 'Mr Allingham is visiting, and they are sitting round the dining table drinking port. Come on, Mary!'

We left the study by its other door, went down a few stairs, along a narrow passage and up another short flight of steps, and came to a tall sash window. Lionel raised it as quietly as he could, and began to clamber through. After a nervous glance over my shoulder, I followed him, wriggling rather awkwardly through the gap, encumbered by my skirt and petticoats. I found myself standing in a narrow gully between two steeply pitched roofs. Lionel was edging along the gully ahead of me to where, a few yards along, there was a vertical metal ladder. He swung himself up, and I gathered my skirts under one arm and began to climb. It was a brilliantly clear night, and rather cold; I was shivering when I finally hoisted myself onto the platform, but once there I gasped in wonder. The moon was a delicate crescent, and the stars were fierce points of light, spread above us in a glittering web across the dark sky. They seemed close enough to touch.

'Well?' said Lionel gleefully. 'Isn't that a sight, Mary?'

'It is! Oh, what an extraordinary thing to be up here!' I turned slowly, gazing up in wonder, and then looking down to where the gardens below were bathed in moonlight, every flower and leaf, every blade of grass etched in silver. It was a while before I recollected the avowed purpose of this exercise.

'Now, Lionel,' I said, fishing out the book I had found on Mr Cameron's shelves, 'we may perhaps be able to identify Orion—' but of course even in the moonlight it was too dark to read anything at all. 'Well, we will observe,' I said, 'and then we will study the book closely tomorrow. That is the Great Bear, you see, and—'

Lionel clutched my arm. A sound had come from below: the sound of a window sash being abruptly lifted. I looked down from the platform to the gully along which we had come. Through the window the rough unruly head of Mr Tennyson was emerging, followed by his shoulders.

'So you see, my dear Allingham,' said a resonant voice, 'I think it quite absurd to describe a tree in that manner ...'

'My father!' hissed Lionel. 'Oh, Mary, what shall we do? He quite forbade me to attempt to climb up here—'

We looked at one another in dismay.

'Quick,' I whispered. 'Look, we can get underneath. They won't see us there.' I looked back towards where Mr Tennyson, followed by a second figure, was now approaching with what seemed alarming speed. He glanced up, and for a terrible moment I thought he had actually seen me. With a courage born of desperation, I lay down at the edge of the wooden structure and managed to slither over until I was hanging by my hands, then let go and landed with a bump on the tiled ridge below. Lionel followed, and we managed to scramble back underneath the broad wooden structure, into the space between the platform and the sloping roof, where we crouched, hardly daring to breathe, clinging to the ridge tiles so as not to slide down. We heard steps, and the metal ladder rattling, and then two sets of feet tramping above us, sounding alarmingly close.

'Orion is very distinct tonight.' That was Mr Tennyson.

'You said we might see Orion, Mary!' whispered Lionel. 'I wonder which star that is?'

'Shush,' I hissed in his ear. 'We must keep perfectly quiet. And anyway,' I added, 'Orion is a constellation, not a star.' He gave a small, petulant sigh.

'Remarkable,' said another, faintly Irish voice—Mr Allingham, I supposed. 'What a magnificent place from which to view the stars, Tennyson!'

There was the sound of a striking match, and a faint waft of smoke drifted down to us. The two men talked on. At one point a flake of burning tobacco fell between the boards and onto my arm and I had to smother a squeak of pain. I heard the melancholy call of an owl, and Mr Tennyson saying 'Ah! *Birds in the high hall garden, when twilight was falling—*'

Oh, no, I thought. Please, please don't quote the whole of *Maud*, or we shall be here until daybreak. Mercifully, however, he contented himself with just a few stanzas, accepted Mr Allingham's compliments on his genius, and then we heard him begin to climb down the ladder and edge back along the roof, his companion following close behind him. At last they disappeared through the window, and Lionel and I crawled out onto the roof and hauled ourselves, gasping with relief, back onto the platform.

'That was a near thing,' said Lionel. He sounded rather chastened. We stayed up on the roof for another ten minutes or so, to make sure that our escape route was clear.

'Lionel,' I whispered, as we crept at last down the ladder and back along the gully, 'perhaps we should abandon the idea of my giving you lessons. I don't really think I am cut out to be a governess.'

'Oh, I think you are a lovely governess,' he said. 'Although perhaps we had better give up astronomy for now. But I could study something else—not poetry—something interesting—wild animals, perhaps, or railway engines—'

'We'll see,' I said. I didn't feel like arguing. Somehow we managed to get back into the house without being seen, Lionel ran off to his bedroom, and I went cautiously back the way we had come, only to find that of course now Mr Tennyson was in his study, holding forth to Mr Allingham again. I heard his voice, fortunately, before I opened the door, and there was nothing for it but to try to find another way out. By pure luck there was no one about, and I tiptoed down the main staircase and out through the front door, then ran like a hare through the moonlit garden and the wood and back to Dimbola Lodge.

I met Lionel again the next day in the summerhouse, as we had arranged, but it was only to tell him that I had definitely decided not to become a governess.

'I should never have agreed to go up onto the roof,' I said. 'That is not the sort of thing real governesses do.'

'We weren't caught, though,' he argued. 'And it was fun, Mary.'

'If we had been caught,' I said crossly, 'you would have had nothing worse than a telling-off, but I should have been dismissed.'

'Maybe,' he said carelessly. 'Still, I think it a great pity, when we could have more adventures.'

'Governesses don't have adventures,' I said. 'That's the point, Lionel. They teach sensible subjects, and keep their charges in order, and insist on rules being obeyed.'

He was not really too disappointed, I guessed. I, on the other hand, was left feeling distinctly gloomy about my future. I had enough self-knowledge at least to realise that even if I found a place such as my imagination had conjured, I had neither the patience nor the skills to become a good teacher. Lionel was soon sent off to another school, but it seemed that I would have to go on being a parlourmaid for the foreseeable future. It was back to dusting and sweeping, fetching and carrying, knowing my place.

The morning after the stargazing adventure I found my work more than usually irksome, and I was sulkily trying to do as little as possible. I had to clean the parlour that morning, a job I did not usually mind too much since I did it alone and there were always books lying about that I could snatch a few moments to dip into, but that morning even the books seemed dull. I cleared the ashes from the fire and straightened a few cushions, then began reluctantly to polish the tall mirror that hung above the fireplace. On the mantelpiece stood, as usual, a collection of notes, *cartes de visite,* and invitations to dine or lunch. I rubbed the duster in a perfunctory way along the front of the mantel shelf. Today one card, bigger than the rest, had been placed in the centre. It was impossible to miss: a stiff white rectangle with gilt edges and flowing script. It was a wedding invitation from the Jacksons, Julia's sister and brother-in-law, inviting Mr and Mrs Cameron to the marriage of their daughter to a Mr Duckworth. I picked up the card and read it several times, then replaced it carefully. I had no idea who Mr Duckworth might be, but I felt absurdly pleased. Well. Whoever he might be, I thought, good luck to him.

# 28

Billy went on walking out with Elsie for a while, and when she faded from view there was a succession of replacements, always a pretty girl or two hanging around, waiting for him at the back gate or gazing at him in church. The succession of young men who hung around for me, I disregarded. Hillier seemed happy enough with Tom Gilbert, and Kellaway and Louisa had admirers too, but I could not summon enthusiasm for any of the Freshwater lads. It was not that I thought myself too good for them—who did I think I was, in any case? They simply did not make my heart beat faster. That was all. Billy and I had stayed friends, sort of—cautiously on my part, awkwardly on his—but he and I couldn't go back to how we had been.

'Men and women can't be friends. Not ever.' This was the view of Louisa. 'Men is quite different from us, see? They can be husbands, or sweethearts, but not friends, Mary. Even the good ones. They's just too different.'

Perhaps she was right. We were in the kitchen, up to our arms in flour while we discussed this interesting topic. Mrs Lyle had taken to her bed with a head cold, it was Kellaway's afternoon off, Hillier was in the fowl-house being an angel, and Julia wanted scones for tea and apple tart for dinner. When a loud knock sounded on the front door, we looked at each other in exasperation.

'Hilda might get it,' said Louisa, without much hope.

'She's upstairs sorting laundry,' I said. 'Anyway, she never answers the door unless she thinks it's going to be someone grand.'

'It's Billy's job to answer the door, by rights.'

'Huh,' I said. 'I'll go.'

Before I could dust the flour from my arms, however, we heard Julia's voice from the hall. She must have come from her studio to retrieve some forgotten garment or accessory and found the visitor on the doorstep. Shrieks and shouting ensued, but that was perfectly normal whenever a visitor appeared, whether it were a famous man of letters, an eminent painter, or the man who brought the coal.

'Some poor soul's going to be photographed now, whether they will or no,' said Louisa, rolling out the pastry with some vigour. When the bell rang from the front parlour she offered to go ('But watch them scones, Mary, or they'll be hard as a rock again.'). It's true, I wasn't the best at baking. I didn't have the knack. Or the inclination. Within a few minutes, though, Louisa was back, looking puzzled.

'Mistress says you'm to go straight to the parlour, Mary.'

I sighed, but in fact I was glad at the prospect of getting away from the oven and the heat of the kitchen. I began to take off my cooking apron.

'What is it now? Do they want tea already?'

'I can't say. 'Tis a gentleman with her, but I don't know who he may be.'

I tied a fresh apron around my waist and went off to find out what was required, hoping I wasn't going to have to dress up as something absurd. I wasn't feeling in the mood to be a romantic heroine. Poor Hillier was presumably still stuck in the fowl-house dressed in a nightgown and crowned with lilies.

As I went into the room, the sun was dazzling straight through the bay window, and for a moment it was in my eyes so that I could only make out a tall figure silhouetted against the light. Julia bounced up from her seat and came bustling towards me.

'Mary! Here is someone who wishes to see you—'

Julia did not sound quite her normal self. There was something in her voice—not disapproval, exactly, but a note of being slightly put out. Julia loved surprises but only if she was creating them for other people. When I saw who the visitor was, however, I had no space in my thoughts to care for what Julia did or did not think at that particular moment. It was Henry Cotton.


'Mr Cotton has something to ask you, Mary.'

Henry stepped forward, hesitantly. He was looking at me with what seemed to be a mixture of joy and terror. I became, suddenly, acutely aware of my floury arms, my flushed face, my drab servant's dress.

'Go on, out into the garden, both of you,' said Julia, flapping her shawl at us both as though we were chickens she was shooing out of doors. We obeyed, as people tended to obey Julia, and went out into the hall and through the front door into the sunshine. There we stood on the doorstep, looking at each other, until Henry gestured that we might walk around the side of the house and into the garden. Once there, we stopped again. Henry still had not uttered a word.

I was slightly dazed. It seemed unreal to see Henry Cotton here. He belonged in the elegant setting of Colnaghi's gallery, or the exotic enchanted world of Little Holland House, not here; and I—how must I seem to him, the girl in the blue silk gown he had presumably expected to see now wearing her maid's uniform, standing in a none-too-neat garden in Freshwater, with a clothes-line flapping behind her and her hair scraped into a cotton cap? Cinderella, stripped of her ballgown and her golden coach, now back in rags among the pumpkins.

'M-mary.' He cleared his throat and began again. 'M-miss Ryan—you received my letter, I hope?'

'Yes. Yes, I did.'

'B-but you did not r-reply—'

His stammer, always worse when he was anxious, seemed more pronounced than I had remembered.

'The letter did not seem to require a response.' And truly, it had not crossed my mind that I might reply to that brief and obscure note.

'But you thought, I trust, that my c-course of action was correct?'

'To pass your examinations and then go to India? Well, yes, of course—'

'India—the thought d-does not alarm you?'

'Alarm me? Why should it alarm me?'

'Oh, M-mary!' He began, unexpectedly, to laugh. 'You really are the most wonderful girl—I believe you are as b-brave as a whole pride of lions!'

I was not following this at all.

'Mr Cotton—'

'Henry. Please. P-please call me Henry.'

'Henry—I was not sure why you wrote to me at all. I'm glad you are decided on your future, of course, but my approval or disapproval of your actions must surely be quite immaterial—'

The laughter stopped, and he looked first incredulous, and then dismayed.

'But surely—M-mary, surely you understood what I was s-saying, what I was asking?'

'No,' I said. 'What? What were you saying, Henry?'

'That I w-want you to come to India with me. You m-must, surely, have understood that. You could not think anything else, after—after the time we—when we w-were at the Prinseps' and you—that is, when we said goodbye—what else could I have m-meant?'

I took a step away from him. I had a memory of having heard Mr Cameron refer to women who sailed out to India and Ceylon to, as he put it, comfort our troops. And now, presumably, Henry Cotton was suggesting that I might travel to the subcontinent with him as his—his *doxy*! Had our kisses and embraces made Henry think I might be such a woman?

*And aren't you such a woman, Mary Ryan?* asked Mammy's voice in my ear. *You gave yourself to Billy Hemmings readily enough, my girl, and it's only by the grace of God you weren't ruined by it.*

Henry was still gazing at me anxiously, searching my face as though he hoped to read his future there. I found myself taking another step away from him, hardly able to think, feeling my face grow hot, and a plunge of sickness inside.

'M-mary, I am an idiot,' said Henry suddenly. 'Of course this is m-much too sudden a question. But please—only say that you will think it over—that you will not say n-no before you have had time to consider—'

I could not speak. I gave what must have been an ungracious nod and then I turned and walked away from him as steadily as I could, going not towards the front door through which we had left the house but to the garden door used by the servants. Know your place, Mary Ryan.

'Well?' said Louisa, expectantly, as I went back into the kitchen. She was just taking the scones from the oven, and her face was scarlet from the heat. I hoped she would put my own heightened colour down to the same cause. 'What did she want?'

'Oh—it was nothing—'

'You been a mighty long time over nothing, Mary.' Louisa looked at me shrewdly. 'And you come in from the garden door, too. What's going on, then?'

'It was—a misunderstanding. She had lost a shawl and thought I'd taken it to mend, but when I looked for it of course she had left it in the fowl-house all the time.'

It was a feeble enough story—why would Julia suddenly demand her shawl in the middle of a social visit?—but then, Julia constantly surprised all of us.

'And the visitor? Who might he be, then?'

'He is a gentleman from London.'

'Another of her poets or painters or what have you, then?'

'No,' I said. 'That is—I hardly know.'

'Well, then split these scones and butter 'em for me, Mary, and take the tray up, will you, while I do finish the apple tart? She's rung for tea a moment ago.'

I swallowed. 'Would you take the tray up, Louisa? I'll do the tart.'

She eyed me doubtfully.

'Very well. But mind you crimp the pastry just so, not like last time, eh?'

I nodded obediently. I was not going to walk into the parlour with a tea tray to face Henry after what had just passed. Henry and Julia, sitting together, cosily chatting—Julia, who had said *Mr Cotton has something to ask you,* and then sent us out together into the garden to be alone. He had confided in her, I supposed, said—what? *oh, Mrs Cameron, I've come to ask your parlour-maid if she'd like to come out to India with me as my mistress,* and she had presumably replied *oh yes, Mr Cotton, of course, I'll ring for her now* ...

*How could you?* I said fiercely under my breath, although whether I was addressing Henry, Julia, or myself, I hardly knew.

As soon as I had done the apple tart I suddenly remembered something, and when Louisa returned I fled to the fowl-house. As I had surmised, poor Hillier was still there, sitting patiently on an old kitchen chair, swathed in muslin and clutching a stem of lilies. Both she and the flowers were visibly drooping.

'Has she forgotten me?' she asked wearily.

'Yes, she has. You can get changed. I don't think she'll be photographing you any more today.'


I was summoned into Julia's presence again later. Henry had gone by then, shown to the door by Louisa, who came back to report that now she had got a good look at the visitor she could tell us (Hillier and Kellaway being by now gathered into the kitchen to hear the news) that he was an extremely handsome young gentleman.

'And he do have the most beautiful curls, like a—like a prince in a fairy tale.'

'Get away with you,' said Kellaway. 'You been at the gin, Louisa? A prince, indeed!'

'Well, I'm right, ain't I, Mary Ryan?' said Louisa, appealing to me as the only other of us who had seen this vision.

'I didn't notice,' I said, trying to sound nonchalant. My friends went off into peals of laughter at this, and I did my best to join in

223

as though it were all a game, just the sort of teasing and chatter we always indulged in when we discussed the stream of people who passed through Dimbola. We were used to them, the glamorous and the eccentric and the strange, the writers and artists and thinkers, the distinguished men and women of the age, the cooks and porters and shopkeepers dragged in because they had interesting faces and might model for a photograph. We indulged in much pleasurable speculation, generally, about the Camerons' guests; surmising who might be courting whom, admiring or criticising the women's clothes, pretending to swoon at a handsome face or relating how we had evaded the attentions of some predatory toff. Just now, though, I found it hard to behave as I would normally have behaved, and it took all my resolve even to smile.

'I daresay he'll be off back to London soon, in any case,' I said.

'Ooh, I do hope not,' said Hillier. 'Not afore I have taken a good look at him, if he be as handsome as you do say.'

'As long as it's just a look you take, Mary Hillier,' said Louisa, poking her in the ribs, and causing more laughter still.

The summons from Julia came almost as a relief.

'Well, Mary,' she said, sounding half excited, half astonished, 'here is a turn-up for you, my girl! Did you have any notion that Henry Cotton would pursue you to Freshwater after all this time?'

'None at all.' That at least was true.

'I had no idea that you had more than a few minutes' conversation with him at Little Holland House.' She gave me a sharp look. 'I assume you must have had rather more than that, in the circumstances?'

'Hardly,' I said. 'Believe me, I am quite as surprised as you that Mr Cotton should arrive here with such a—with such a purpose.'

224

'Well. It is indeed an extraordinary thing for him to do. But then young men can be very impulsive, and to do him credit, he tells me that he waited until his future was assured, with a post in India, before he dared to approach you. That speaks well of him, does it not?'

'I suppose so,' I said woodenly.

'But he says he understands that this must all seem rather sudden. He has gone off now to take a room at Plumley's, for he says he will stay in Freshwater until he has your answer.'

'Oh—'

So he would be here, calling on Julia, dining with the family, while he waited for me to decide on just how high a price I put on myself.

'I must say, Mary,' went on Julia briskly, 'I am surprised you did not say yes immediately, for it is not an offer you are likely to get again. But you must do as you see fit, I suppose. You have always known your own mind, I will say that.'


Know my own mind? If only I did, I thought, as I lay in my hard narrow bed late that night, unable to sleep, unable to think of anything else but of what Henry had asked me. I tried to think calmly and rationally about the situation, but my attempts at rationality were constantly undermined by my feelings: of outrage, that Henry should ask me so calmly to become a kept woman; of disgust that Julia should connive so blithely at his sordid proposal, as though she were nothing more than the Madam of a brothel; of shame that I had evidently encouraged him, by my own behaviour, to see me in that light.

*So high-minded you've become, Mary Ryan!* It was Mammy again, of course. *You weren't too grand to lie down for Billy Hemmings, were you, and for God's sake, Mary, when are you going to get another chance like this? Travel, frocks and jewels no doubt, and he's not a bad man, you can tell that, even when he tires of you he'll probably set you up in a little house somewhere, which is more than I ever got, and more than you can hope for if you stay as a servant all your life. Even if you marry some dull respectable man from your own station, it'll just be hired lodgings or a tied cottage, no security, whereas you say yes to Henry Cotton and you might get a bit to put by for the future, you won't have to fear the workhouse at least ...*

And yet, Mammy—and yet. I knew, somehow, even in the maelstrom of these thoughts, that I would say no. It was not that I was too virtuous or too prudish to accept his offer. I was realistic enough to see what an opportunity it was, and I did want all those things very badly; freedom, adventure, money, the possibility of safety. Also, I acknowledged to myself, I wanted Henry. The set of his shoulders, the smell of his skin, the light in his eyes when he looked at me, the way he said my name. I wanted his kisses, his touch, the feel of his arms about me. I wanted to go to bed with him. But I would say no to him because I did not want him to have the power over me that he would have if I said yes. I did not want to be beholden to him, or to anyone. Not to Billy, who would have reluctantly made an honest woman of me if he had absolutely had to; and not to Henry, who would be my protector and benefactor until such time as he wearied of me or took a wife. *The need to be grateful all the time.* No. If I were to spend my life with a man, it would be as an equal. Not as a beggar.

# 29

I hardly slept at all that night, and the face that looked back at me from the tiny clouded cracked mirror that was all Louisa and I had in our room was pale and drawn. I went about my tasks mechanically, almost grateful for the demands which at least gave me little time to brood on the extraordinary events of yesterday. We were busier than usual that morning because Julia was giving a luncheon party and what with extra hands being needed in the kitchen (Mrs Lyle was going all out—asparagus soup and chaudfroid of chicken and lobster cutlets) and then Julia's sudden decision to have the parlour cleared of furniture so that she might inflict some sort of amateur dramatic event on her guests after the meal, I was weary and dishevelled as well as miserable by the time the first guests started to arrive. Julia had invited the Tennysons, with Mr Lear who was currently staying with them at Farringford, and the Allinghams and the Liddells—and, I supposed, gloomily, Mr Cotton. I was going to have to give him his answer, and the sooner the better, for then surely he would leave Freshwater for good and that would be the last I need ever see or hear of him again. I felt a painful tightness in my throat at this thought, and all I really wanted to do was to fling myself on my bed and cry for a week and then forswear men for ever. But servants cannot give in to such desires just as they please, and I was obliged to take the first course into the dining room and place the dishes on the table and offer glasses of hock with every appearance of civility and servility even though I felt very much like pouring the wine over the heads of all the guests and then throwing the lobster cutlets in their smug well-bred faces. Picturing this gave me a few moments of bad-tempered satisfaction. I might except Mr Tennyson from this treatment, I decided, for in fact no one could call his face well bred at all—he generally looked more like a great rough shaggy bear—and of course darling Mr Cameron, who had wandered in accidentally and found himself at a party he had had no idea was even planned—but the rest of them could drown in the asparagus soup for all I cared, including Henry Cotton and Julia. Especially Henry Cotton and Julia.

I didn't meet Henry's eyes while I circled the table, although I could feel his gaze constantly burning into me. I kept my head averted, and when I had to pour him some wine I just stared straight ahead. Getting out of the room and back to the kitchen was such a relief that I felt tears finally springing to my eyes, but I dashed them away and busied myself with adding some final touches to the chicken. Louisa and Hillier took in the next course, so I was left alone with Mrs Lyle. She gave a groan and sank into her favourite chair, fanning herself with a cabbage leaf.

"Tis just the pudding now, Mary, and the cherry compote and strawberry creams are all ready. Why don't you come and sit for a while? You look done in, my girl.'

This unaccustomed concern weakened me still further. I left the sink and sat opposite her at the kitchen table.

'Thank you, Mrs Lyle,' I said.

'What is it, then?' she asked, abrupt but not unkindly. 'You've been looking like you've lost a shilling and found a penny ever since yesterday.'

For a moment I thought of telling her everything. What would she have said? Respectability was important to Mrs Lyle. If I told her of Henry's offer she was quite likely to march into the dining room and hit him over the head with her best frying pan. Attractive as this idea was, discretion got the better of me.

'Oh, it's just—you know. Men,' I said.

She snorted. 'If it's that Billy Hemmings making you upset, pet, I'll be giving him a piece of my mind the moment I see him as'll make him rue the day he was born.'

'No,' I assured her, 'no, it's not Billy. Not now. It's—someone you don't know, Mrs Lyle. I'll be right, soon enough.'

'If it's some toff who's taken liberties with you, just you tell me and I'll sort him out.'

I shook my head.

'I—' I spoke slowly, wanting to tell her the truth, even if were a fragment of the whole. 'I met someone who—was not quite what I believed him to be. The thing is, I hadn't realised how I felt until now—until I understood that I could never be with him—not on his terms, at least—'

It was an incoherent account, but Mrs Lyle seemed to grasp something of the situation readily enough. She nodded with gloomy satisfaction.

'I expect he wants what he can get without the bother of putting a ring on your finger?'

'I suppose that's it.'

'And you think yourself too good for what he's offering?'

'Yes. Yes, I do, actually. I think myself much too good.'

I waited for her to tell me that I was only a servant, that I had once been a beggar, and that having ideas so far above my station was ridiculous. She didn't, though.

'So do I, Mary. You are. Much too good for some idle man who should know better to treat you so. So are we all, pet. But that's the way of the world.' She heaved herself to her feet. 'Come on, now, let's get the puddings taken in, and then we'll have a nice cup of tea and the world will seem a better place.'

I decided to take the coward's way out. I would stay out of the way until the guests had all gone, and then I would write a letter to Henry and have it taken to Plumley's Hotel. He would read it, he would realise I was not something to be bought and sold, and he would go. I would never have to see him again.

The luncheon party seemed to go on for hours and then the amateur dramatics took over. I volunteered, rather I think to everyone's surprise, to wash all the silver and the dishes and scour the pans, and then I dried everything too and polished up the glasses and put it all away. This was partly to show Mrs Lyle that I was grateful for her rough sympathy, but mostly to ensure that I was away from the company and the right side of the green baize door. The right side for me, that is, the servants' side. Know your place, Mary Ryan.

At last the guests seemed, with agonising slowness, one by one, to be leaving. I heard the front door opening and closing, Julia's goodbyes ringing out, Mr Tennyson's gruff tones, Mr Lear's nervous bleat, muffled thank-yous and farewells from the others. It was growing late by the time the house finally grew quiet.

'Now, go outside and get a bit of fresh air into you, lass,' said Mrs Lyle. 'Go on. And put that man, whoever he may be, out of your pretty head. Plenty of respectable men out there would be glad to have the chance to treat you right, I dare say. The new gardener up at Farringford, now—'

I didn't stay to hear about the solid qualities of the Farringford gardener, whom I already knew to be a rather gormless fellow with a round face and no chin. I heaved a sigh of relief and untied my apron and made for the door. I would walk up to the downs, perhaps, feel the sea winds blow through my hair and cool my face, sit on the smooth turf up by the beacon, watch the falcons and the gulls swoop and call. I would be alone. I stepped outside and took a long deep breath of evening air, raised my face to the sky from which the light had nearly gone, and closed my eyes.

'M-mary.'

I gasped and opened my eyes. It was Henry, who seemed to have been sitting on the garden bench under the apple tree. He rose and came towards me. I could not help a tiny lift of the heart when I saw him, even as dismay rapidly descended.

'Mary, I have been w-waiting for you.' Well, of course he had. Why had I not realised that he would? 'I hope—that is, I suppose it is too soon for you to have c-considered your answer, but I had to see you.'

'You saw me in the dining room,' I said rudely, 'didn't you notice? I was serving the food.'

'Of course I saw you, I c-could see no one else, but how could we talk then? It's ridiculous that you should be waiting on me. I hate it. It should be the other way round. I should be your servant, Mary, in fact I am your servant, and I always will be—'

'Really?' I said bitterly. 'Pretty words, Mr Cotton, but you know that I would always be the servant in any relationship we might have. I am a parlourmaid, and worse than that, I was a beggar child. Did you know that? Oh, yes, of course, I was forgetting. Julia made sure you knew long ago, didn't she? She acquired me, practically bought me, when I was ten years old. But I'm not a child now, I'm a woman, and I'm not for sale.'

'For sale? Of course you are not for sale—'

And then suddenly, with no warning, he dropped to his knees on the grass in front of me.

231

'I promised I would give you as much time as you needed,' he said urgently. 'But I can't help myself. I asked you yesterday, I am asking you today, and I will ask you every day of my life until you say yes.' He took a deep breath. 'M-miss Ryan. Mary. Marry me. Please. Say you will marry me, and come to India with me as my wife. I am begging you, darling Mary, begging for your hand in marriage.'

I did not say anything for a while. My thoughts whirled and fought and settled. Henry stayed kneeling at my feet, kneeling on the muddy lawn, careless of his expensive clothes and of how absurd he appeared. I looked down at him, at his bright tangled curls and his handsome face lifted to mine, his eyes beseeching and bright with unshed tears. Then I reached out and took both his hands and pulled him to his feet.

'Henry,' I said. 'There is no need to beg.'

# 30

And just like that, in the space of ten minutes, in the garden at Dimbola Lodge on a spring day, my life changed. Henry and I stood looking at each other in silence for a moment, and then he gave a great shout of joy and lifted me off my feet and spun me around until I was helpless with laughter and we were both dizzy.

'Come on,' he said, putting me down at last and taking my hand firmly in his, 'let's go inside and tell Mrs Cameron.'

'She will be astonished,' I said, wondering in some alarm what Julia would say, how she would react. Screams, certainly, but of delight or dismay?

'Oh, not she. I asked her permission to address you as soon as I arrived yesterday, and she gave it quite readily. That's why she sent us into the garden.'

'Her *permission*—? To ask me to marry you?'

'She is sort of a mother to you, isn't she? Whom else should I have asked?'

'But did you need anyone's permission, apart from mine?'

'I want to do everything properly, Mary,' he said earnestly. 'Everything.'

We walked sedately back into the house and found Julia alone in the parlour. She didn't seem surprised.

'Well?' she said, as soon as she saw us. 'Well, Mary, Mr Cotton, what is the answer to be?'

Of course as Henry was still holding my hand it was probably clear what the answer was to be. He beamed at her.

'Mrs Cameron,' he said, with not a trace of a stammer, 'Mary has done me the very great honour of consenting to become my wife.'

Julia did not shriek or scream, after all. She looked at me, a long look, and then at Henry.

'It is a fairy tale, indeed,' she said, almost to herself. 'Well, Mary—my dear girl—' She swam towards me and enfolded me in a warm enveloping embrace of sandalwood and photographic chemicals and fusty shawls. 'You will be very happy, I feel sure, and,'—releasing me and turning to Henry—'Mr Cotton, you have a treasure here. Beauty! I said, the moment I saw her, all those years ago, and I was right, was I not?'

'You were absolutely right, Mrs Cameron,' said Henry, looking at me as though he could never tire of doing so, 'she is the most beautiful girl in the world.'

Julia nodded as though this observation was nothing new to her. She was already eyeing Henry in an appraising manner.

'And you, Mr Cotton!' she exclaimed, 'you have your own share of beauty! Oh, I shall be making some excellent photo-graphs of the two of you—that hair, now—you have the locks of Sir Lancelot—'

Even the prospect of dressing as Sir Lancelot did not appear to dampen Henry's spirits. He grinned and gave a slight bow.

'Of course, if you wish, Mrs Cameron—'

'I most certainly do wish—that fine face and manly look—oh, yes, I see it now, a series of the most artistic sort—or, now let me see, perhaps you are a Sir Galahad, rather—'

'My *strength is as the strength of ten, because my heart is pure*,' he murmured, and I started to laugh.

'Exactly!' said Julia, evidently not seeing the funny side of this, 'dear Alfred will be delighted—you will be a perfect illustration to his Idylls, Mr Cotton—we might begin tomorrow, I think, don't you? I imagine you will be staying in Freshwater now?'

'Certainly,' said Henry, 'Freshwater is now the dearest place in the world to me.'

Julia looked from Henry's face to mine, and back again.

'Well, this is the prettiest romance,' she said, 'and I shall take all the credit for it.'

I imagined then that she was joking.


Henry took his leave of Julia and I said I would show him out. When we got to the front door I opened it for him (force of habit) but he suddenly seized my hand and pulled me outside into the dusk and along to the side of the house, away from where anyone could see us, and took me into his arms and began to kiss me, long kisses full of sweetness and tenderness and passion, with the scent of the first roses around us and the moon rising over the sea. He certainly had proved an apt pupil. When he finally left me, reluctantly and with many whispered farewells and murmurings of just-one-last-kiss, to walk across the fields back to his hotel, I stayed there in the darkness for a while, while my heart slowed back to normal. Then I heard a footstep.

'Who was that?'

It was Billy, standing by the house wall, arms folded. In the darkness I couldn't really see his face, just a glint from his eyes.

'That was Mr Cotton. He is someone Mrs Cameron knows from London.'

'He knows you too, Mary Ryan.'

I realised Billy must have seen us.

'Yes, he does.'

'He was kissing you.'

There was something in his voice I hadn't heard before, an abruptness, a roughness.

'Yes,' I said, raising my chin, and trying to stare at Billy directly. 'he was. He has asked me to marry him.'

'*What?*'

'He has asked for my hand in marriage.' This sounded prissy, even to my own ears.

'*Marriage?*' He sounded stupefied. 'But he's a toff, ain't he?'

'Yes, he is, I suppose, if you must put it like that. Nevertheless, he wants to marry me, Billy.'

'You can't!' He was almost shouting now.

'Why not?' I shouted back. 'Because I'm a servant, Billy, is that why not? Because I was once a beggar? Because I have ideas above my station?'

'Yes, Mary Ryan, all of that! How can you stand to be part of that world? They'll destroy you, so they will, with their rules and their regulations and their stupid stuck-up ways. You're a free spirit, Mary, not a society lady, you'll hate it: drawing rooms and endless visits and wearing white gloves. There won't be any roaming free on the downs for you, you'll be imprisoned.'

'Not me,' I said. 'No one's going to imprison me. It's poverty that imprisons people, servitude, being looked down on. If I want to roam free then I shall.'

He shot out his hand and grasped my arm and pulled me roughly towards him.

'You don't belong with him, Mary. You belong with me.'

'I belong where I choose to belong. Now let me go. You're hurting me.'

He didn't let me go. He gripped my arm tighter and with his other hand he forced my face towards his.

'Come on, Mary, come with me now, we'll leave this place, we'll get to America and we'll be free. Men can be free, there, it doesn't matter where you come from, you can get rich and people don't look down on you then.'

'And how are you to get rich, Billy Hemmings? By finding gold in California?'

'By—yes, well, maybe I will! Or I'll find work on the railways; there's money to be made that way, I've heard—'

Perhaps that was what made a hard shutter come down in my heart. I put my hand against his chest and with every bit of strength I possessed I pushed him away from me and stepped out of his reach.

'Like my father, Billy? He came to England to get rich when we had to leave Ireland, but he didn't. He worked on the railways too, he worked hard enough, but he never got rich, that's for sure. He was a good man, he loved me, he taught me to read books; but he was paid hardly enough to keep his family and then he began to drink and so did my mother and they quarrelled every night and at last he went. He walked out and he left us and he never came back. If you want that life you can have it, but it's not for me. I want something better.'

He was standing very still now. He didn't reach out again.

'And another thing,' I said, determined to get it out even though my voice was shaking. 'You say that men can be free in America, but men are free everywhere, Billy. Women aren't. You'll always have more choices than I will. So off you go, go to America, make your fortune, and good luck to you. I'm going to find mine in the only way I know.'

He didn't say anything after that, just turned and walked back towards the stable.

I stayed there in the shadows for a while, half-expecting him to come out again, take me in his arms, kiss away the tears that were now streaming unchecked down my face. He didn't, though. I stood, irresolute, for a while, and then I dried my face with the edge of my shawl and walked slowly around the edge of the lawn and back to the safety of the house.

I awoke very early the next morning. Louisa was still deeply asleep. The events of the previous day rushed back at me and for a moment I wondered if it had all been a dream—a ridiculous cliché of a dream, that Henry had galloped towards me on a white horse, swept me up and carried me far away. I heard a faint distant sound from outside, and I got quietly out of bed and tiptoed to the window. The dawn was just beginning to soften the darkness, and in the half-light I made out a figure walking fast along the lane carrying some sort of bag slung over one shoulder. He was whistling a tune I knew. *The girl I left behind me.* I knew then that it hadn't been a dream.

# 31

'You'm a dark horse, then, Mary Ryan.'

This was Hillier. That morning, over breakfast, I had taken one deep breath and announced to my assembled fellow servants that I had become engaged to be married to a man I had met in London.

'I suppose I am,' I said, laughing.

'Was he working at that big house you stayed in? Is that how you met him?'

'Oh—no, he is—well, he's not a servant. He's a—' I was almost embarrassed to say the word. 'He's a gentleman, I suppose.'

'A gentleman?' They all looked rather shocked. 'A real gentleman, with an eddycation and a house and money?'

'Yes. Yes, I suppose so. But he's very—ordinary, really, in a nice way, I mean—'

'Well. Well, I never. Marrying a gentleman! Will we all have to curtsey to you now?'

'Curtsey to me? Of course not! What a horrible idea. I shan't change, you know, I shall still be me.'

Louisa was looking at me very hard.

'Mary Ryan! It ain't that handsome gentleman with the curls you be going to marry? The one I said looked like a prince?'

'Yes. It is. That very one.'

A general hubbub of astonishment rose, everyone talking and laughing and asking questions at once. Mary Hillier jumped up and put her arms around me and held me very tight.

'I shall give you this hug now, Mary Ryan, in case you get too grand to be hugged by the likes of me.'

'Too grand? Well, hardly,' I said, hugging her back. But—was I imagining it?—there was already a slight hesitancy as the others too offered their congratulations and embraces. There was already a shift, a tiny distance between us now. I did not want it, but it was there.


Henry kept his room in Plumley's Hotel. He was to stay in Freshwater for three months, while preparations for the wedding were made. We would be married in August, and then we would set sail for India.

My position in the household at Dimbola became, unsurprisingly, distinctly strange from that time on. Julia decided that I should carry on in my position—I had nowhere else to live, after all, and I could hardly do nothing while continuing to share my attic room with Louisa when she was slaving as hard as ever—but that I should have three afternoons a week free to meet Henry and make plans for my wedding. At my request Julia deducted this time from my wages; I did not want my friends to perceive any unfairness in our relative situations. None more than I could help, in any case, but the strangeness of the situation was manifesting itself in new ways on a daily basis.

To begin with, I had enough savings to buy, oh, a hat, perhaps, or a petticoat; but I would, I supposed, be expected to have a wedding dress, a veil, shoes, a going-away costume, a trousseau. And then, the event itself—the church, the wedding breakfast, the flowers—how was this to happen? The bride's father pays, that is the convention. In the absence of a father, an uncle or a brother might step in. But for a beggar girl, whose mother was a vagrant, whose father was probably lying in a pauper's grave somewhere—what happens then? Henry had delicately indicated that I must let him know if I needed new clothes, that he would buy anything I wanted, but I had said firmly that although when he was my husband he might buy me anything he pleased, until that day I would not ask him for anything. I would marry him in my old brown dress and clumping black boots if I had too, I decided gloomily.

Then Henry went away to see his family who lived near Bristol to tell them of our engagement, which was another source of alarm. He had made occasional references to his father who had retired from his work as a civil servant in India, and a grandfather with a country estate in Devonshire. I could not imagine that the news that he was to marry someone of my sort would be met with unalloyed joy by these rather alarming-sounding people.

I was clearing the breakfast table on the morning after Henry's departure when Mr Cameron wandered in, wearing his nightshirt with one of Julia's shawls round his shoulders.

'Can I get you some fresh tea, sir?' I asked. 'This has gone cold.'

'Oh, tea, yes—' He looked vaguely round as though expecting some to manifest itself from the air. 'In a minute, Mary. But I gather from Julia that you may be leaving us. I was not sure I had understood her correctly. Thought I'd find you and ask you myself.' He sat down and patted the chair next to him. I took it.

'I'm getting married,' I said. 'To Mr Cotton.' He looked blank. 'He was here at luncheon a few days ago,' I reminded him, 'a tall young man with curly hair.'

'Ah—yes, I do recall someone of that description ... but what I want to know is, are you happy, Mary?'

241

'Very happy. We are going to live in India. We will go to Calcutta first, and then to a posting in Midnapore. Mr Cotton has secured a position out there.'

Mr Cameron brightened. 'Has he, now? You will like that, Mary. Beloved India. The most beautiful place in the world, the east.' Then he sighed. 'We will miss you, though, Mary. You've been part of the household for a long time.'

'I will miss you too, sir,' I said, suddenly realising that this was true.

'So. There's to be a wedding, eh?'

'Yes. On the first of August.'

'Well, Mary, I wish you every blessing.' He stood, and I assumed the interview was over.

'Thank you, sir. Shall I get you that tea?'

'Tea, yes, that was it—and, Mary, about your wedding. We will take care of that, you know. No need to worry about anything. Julia wants to, I know, but she might have forgotten to mention it, I dare say. So anything you need—a dress, and so forth—and all the trimmings—bit of a party—better have some champagne, too, can't have a wedding without a few bottles of something decent to drink—' and he wandered out of the room, still tea-less and murmuring to himself. I heard him shuffle along the corridor, and the odd word floated back to me. 'Hock, and a claret too—not port, not at a wedding—better stick to the champagne, perhaps—' The footsteps stopped and turned and he reappeared. 'Mary. I could give you away, if you like. In church, I mean. In place of your father. Just a thought.'


Julia threw herself heart and soul into arranging the wedding. My dress was the first thing on my mind, and on hers too, it turned out.

'I have just the thing, Mary. A length of stuff from Ceylon. I did use it once or twice in a tableau but it has hardly a mark on it. Now, where can it be, I wonder—'

It was found eventually, crumpled in the bottom of a dressing-up box, yards and yards of figured ivory silk. Julia had no idea about dresses, but I had. I made sketches and notes and on my next free afternoon went to see the dressmaker in the village. She didn't usually do much beyond plain sewing, but she had made the grey Sunday dress which I had always liked, and she became very excited indeed by the prospect of making my wedding dress. She studied my drawings, made a tentative suggestion about the sleeves, and got out some cambric for a toile. I showed her Julia's gift, and as I unwrapped the parcel and drew out the silk the rich fabric glowed in the dingy cramped shop, folds upon folds gleaming softly, falling through our hands. When she draped it about me and turned me to face the mirror, light came into her face and she beamed.

'You will look a picture, Miss, so you will.'

Oh, I did hope so.

She must have recklessly cast aside all her other clients in favour of my dress, for after a further couple of fittings it was only a matter of days before it arrived at Dimbola, lying in sheets of tissue paper in a wide flat box. It was exactly as I had imagined: cut to sweep the floor, fine lace around the low neckline, a broad sash to emphasise my waist. Julia said that I must try it on in her dressing room—she insisted, in fact, saying that I must see myself in the full-length mirror there, and I was grateful because it would have seemed so odd to be stepping into a silk gown in the attic bedroom, where Louisa might have come in and seen me. The drawback was that Julia herself, having (to my relief) sent Hilda away, was throwing herself into the moment with gusto, bringing out endless frumpy shawls I might want lest I should get a chill going to church and various bits of yellowing lace in case I should like to decorate the dress further. I managed to decline these kind offers, but then she gave one of her excited shrieks.

'But we must not forget—what is it people say—something new?' she cried, 'something borrowed ... no, something old—'

'Something old, something new, something borrowed, something blue,' I supplied. 'Well, my dress is new, and I have borrowed a handkerchief from Louisa. But that's just a saying, isn't it?'

'Bad luck will follow if you don't have all those,' she said. 'Now, let me think—yes, here is something old, Mary—' She rummaged in one of her many boxes and drew out a silver bangle. 'There! Old as the hills, that one, it came from India. So we just need something blue. Well, we will find a nice blue ribbon to tie in your hair, shall we?' More rummaging, and a none-too-clean and rather frayed blue ribbon was produced. 'There you are!' she said triumphantly. 'All done! Well, you will be the loveliest bride there has ever been, I do declare.'

I had already decided about my hair. I would wear it loose, with a wreath of white roses from the garden. Hillier, who was clever with that sort of thing, had sweetly said she would make the wreath for me on the morning of the wedding, and Louisa was to curl my hair. Blue ribbons did not feature in this plan at all. However, I thanked Julia, and I took the blue ribbon away when I had changed back out of my precious dress, for I did not want to seem ungrateful when there was so much to be grateful for. I thought I might tie it round my stocking top, where it could not be seen. Luckily, however, as it turned out, the ribbon was not needed. Henry returned from his visit to his family that evening, and he had brought me a gift.

We were walking along the beach, and when we neared the great arched rock at the end of the bay Henry drew out a little leather box and presented it to me.

'My wedding gift to my beautiful bride,' he said. He watched me rather anxiously as I opened it. Inside, on a bed of white satin, lay a pair of earrings, their colour the deepest and most intense of blues. 'Sapphires, from Ceylon,' he said. 'I thought they would suit you, Mary. When I dined at the Prinseps you were wearing a dress the colour of sapphires. You were the most beautiful girl I had ever seen.' He lowered his voice, not that there was anyone to overhear us. 'The first time we kissed—do you remember?'

The blue jewels glittered in their little box. Oh, those earrings. Tear-shaped drops, surrounded by diamonds. Gorgeous. Perfect. My something blue.

'Of course I remember,' I said, smiling up at him, suddenly wanting him to kiss me again. He drew me into the shade of the cliff and put his arms around me.


Henry's visit to Somerset had not been a happy one. To his surprise—although not to mine—his parents disapproved strongly of his engagement to a parlourmaid. He tried to tell me this politely when I asked how it had gone, but it was evident that the news of his intended marriage had not been well received.

'Perhaps when they are actually at the wedding, and meet the Camerons, they will feel differently,' I said hopefully. 'They will see that I have respectable friends, at least.'

'Mmm. Although—the thing is, Mary, they won't be there. They are refusing to come.'

'Oh.' I was mortified. My vague idea that Henry's family, once I had met them, would be warm and welcoming and embrace me as a daughter, shrivelled and died. 'Oh, Henry, I am sorry.'

'Sorry? Why should you be sorry? It is I who should apologise for their ungraciousness.'

Actually, I quite agreed with that sentiment, and when Julia heard she was furious, although not in Henry's hearing.

'And who do they think they are, these Cottons?' she demanded. 'What absurd snobbery! Ha! We will do very well without them. The guests at your wedding, Mary, will be people for whom no one need blush.'

'The guests. Yes. Mrs Cameron, I should write a guest list, I suppose. I don't have very many friends to invite, and no family at all—'

'But I have been blessed with a whole galaxy of friends, Mary,' she declared grandly, 'many of whom will wish to be at your wedding, I am sure. Let me see, now—Alfred and Emily, of course, and their boys, dear Philip, naturally, Il Signor, the Liddells—perhaps Sara and Thoby will come down from town— the Allinghams, certainly—would Robert Browning be free, I wonder—'

On she went, blithely listing her famous friends. Would they really wish to attend the wedding of Mary Ryan, parlourmaid? I supposed that if Julia made her mind up, they would have very little choice.

'And of course anyone else you particularly wish to invite, Mary,' she added, almost as an afterthought.

I conferred with Henry, who had written down some names himself: some friends he had known from school, two or three from university, a man he been climbing with in the Alps. His list was scarcely longer than mine, so we both resigned ourselves to being heavily outnumbered by the Camerons' circle at our own wedding.

'They are being astonishingly generous,' I told him, 'arranging the whole thing, paying for everything. And it's true that I do at least know all the people Julia is planning to invite, in one way or another.'

'If you wish them to be there, Mary, then so do I. Now, show me your list?'

He read the names. Louisa, Hillier, Kellaway. Mrs Lyle. Hilda. (Yes, even Hilda. She could sit a long way below the salt.)

'These are—the, er, the people with whom you work?'

'They are my friends. I wish them to be at my wedding.'

He swallowed.

'Darling, might our guests not feel just a little—well—uncomfortable, if they find themselves sitting next to those they are not really accustomed to meeting socially? It might be awkward for everyone.'

'If they do find things awkward then it will be helpful for them in the future, Henry. New experiences are always an opportunity to learn, I find.'

'Oh, do you—?' He sounded slightly alarmed at this idea. 'But, yes, I suppose you may be right—'

'Think of what Mr Tennyson wrote in *Ulysses*.'

'Er—remind me?'

'*Yet all experience is an arch wherethro'*
*Gleams that untravell'd world whose margin fades*
*For ever and forever when I move*,' I quoted. 'Isn't that marvellous?'

'Oh—it is, yes, and I see what you mean—I think—'

It will do them all good, I thought to myself. God knows I had had to experience that sort of thing often enough. If Adolphus Liddell has to make conversation with Hilda then let him exert himself and do so, and vice versa, frankly. And the sooner Henry grasps that idea the better it will be for both of us.

# 32

I decided that I did not want bridesmaids. There were two reasons for this. The first was that I felt I could hardly ask just one of my close friends and not the others, and if I were to ask all three, Louisa and Hillier and Kellaway, to be bridesmaids then I would seriously deplete the number of my own guests. The second was that I feared it would underline the difference that was now appearing between us. Bridesmaids are by definition inferior to the bride. I did not want my friends to have to follow me into church, wait on me, fuss over me. I wanted them there to enjoy the day as my equals.

'You should have someone to hold your flowers, though, Mary.' This was Julia's opinion. 'And help you into the church—hold up the train of your dress, that sort of thing.'

'I'm sure I shall manage,' I said. In fact, I felt that I would have quite liked to have someone to do that, but I could not think of anyone else. As it turned out, though, I found a perfectly splendid wedding attendant in a quite unexpected quarter.

It was a fine July afternoon and I was walking with Mr Tennyson on the high down. I was sorry to think that there would not be many more walks with him, both of us striding out into the wind, across the cropped grass, and I think perhaps he was sorry too. He had got used to me, I think, and rather liked to have someone to recite to, someone to listen thoughtfully to a new line of verse, or to be gently lectured on the art of writing poetry. He had of course heard the news of my engagement from Julia practically within hours of her having heard it herself, for she had decided, after the first few moments of surprise or even shock when Henry had arrived so unexpectedly at her door determined to persuade her parlourmaid to marry him, to claim our union as a triumph of her own brilliance at matchmaking.

'You see,' she told everyone—and I mean everyone: the Tennysons, her family, the servants, Dear Philip, the butcher's boy, Il Signor, the Rector, the man who sold the fish—'this sprung entirely, but entirely, out of that Prospero and Miranda picture I made! I have, by my art, cemented the welfare and wellbeing of this real King Cophetua. Oh, the dear boy,'—(*the dear boy* was how she now always referred to Henry)—'his eighteen months of constancy, his romantic soul—yes! It is one of the prettiest idylls of real life that could ever be conceived, and I shall always, always congratulate myself on this happiest of outcomes!'

And so on. I found this mildly irksome, for a while, but it was so very—well, so very Julia, that I was able to smile indulgently. It did not cloud my happiness; not, that is, until around the tenth time I heard her refer to Henry as King Cophetua, when I thought I would remind myself of exactly who this Cophetua was. His name sounded faintly familiar, but I leafed through books of Greek myths and Roman poetry without finding any mention of him. I could have asked Julia to tell me, but it seemed too late for that, in the same way that one feels unable to ask for someone's name after one has met them more than once and failed to catch or to recall it. So when I was with Mr Tennyson that afternoon, it came to me that he would certainly know the reference, for he seemed to me to live in a world of legends and stories, knights and heroes, goddesses and mermen.

'Ah, Cophetua,' he said instantly, 'of course. You must have read my own verse on the story, Mary?'

I hadn't, that I could recall. But really, he had written a prodigious amount, and I must have read very nearly everything else.

'Forgive me,' I said, 'it's stupid of me, I know, but my mind has gone blank. Would you remind me?'

He never minded reciting his own poems, and he struck up immediately as we went down the slope that leads from the beacon westwards towards the Needles.

*'Her arms across her breast she laid;*
*She was more fair than words can say:*
*Bare-footed came the beggar maid*
*Before the king Cophetua ...'*

Mr Tennyson went on reciting. The girl had a lovesome mien, apparently, dark hair, and superb ankles. He ended, with a flourish:

*'Cophetua swore a royal oath:*
*This beggar maid shall be my queen!'*

A king who marries a beggar-maid. Well, how entirely appropriate. So Julia was busy telling everyone that this was the story of my marriage. I would never, it seemed, be allowed to forget my birth, my past, my parentage; she would remind me and the world of it, even as I had begun to think that I might leave it behind me for ever.

I walked on at Mr Tennyson's side, lost in a mixture of shame and fury and resentment, until I became aware that he was addressing me.

'We would be pleased if you would use our carriage, Mary, for your wedding; to and from the church, of course, and perhaps to take you to Yarmouth for the steamer when you leave—'

I was jolted back to the present.

'That is so kind, sir. We would be very happy to. Thank you.'
Goodness, I thought, my wedding is growing more impressive
by the minute: famous guests, a silk wedding gown, now a
carriage …

'And I have another thought. I think Lionel should be your
page.'

'My page? Oh—I had not thought of a page—forgive me, sir,
but did you say *Lionel*?'

'Certainly. Lionel seems to have formed an attachment to you,
Mary. He even suggested to me that I might employ you as his
governess.'

'Did he?' I said nervously. 'What an extraordinary thing to ask!'

'I thought so, too,' he said. 'But I gather you did have the
kindness to begin some instruction in the science of astronomy.'

I shot an alarmed glance at his profile. Impossible to read what
was happening behind that massive head and dark beard. Had
Lionel confessed to our night-time adventure?

'Ah, well,' I began uncertainly, 'I did—that is, he seemed
interested—'

'I saw you, Mary,' he said, and I thought there was more than
a hint of laughter in that deep sonorous voice. 'You and Lionel,
hiding on the roof when I was up there with Allingham. I tackled
my son about it a few days later, and he confessed. He did have
the grace to say that it had been his idea, and you had only meant
to help with his studies.'

I said a silent thank you to the absent Lionel for his loyalty.

'I am very sorry, sir,' I said, in as contrite a voice as I could
muster. 'I should never have gone along with the scheme.'

'Well, well. No harm done, after all. But I felt Lionel should
make amends to you for leading you into such an escapade. So
I asked him what he would do to show his remorse, and he said
he would be a page at your wedding.'

'That would certainly be a very graceful gesture,' I said, now also beginning to laugh. 'Will he—will he mind very much doing that, do you think?'

'Whether he minds or not, I shall insist that he carries out his duties most conscientiously. Make him carry your gloves, Mary, or whatever pages do.'

*They carry things and wear nice clothes*, I had said to Billy Hemmings once long ago. I suspected that Lionel would rather enjoy wearing a velvet coat and being admired and having his photograph taken.

'Then I should be delighted to have Lionel as my page, sir,' I said. 'Thank you.'

I tucked my hand into his arm and we walked on.


Henry did not generally dine at Dimbola Lodge during his stay in Freshwater. It would, we both agreed, have been very odd for him to be waited on at the table by me in my servant's dress, and odder still for me to have dined with the family while my friends waited on me. Not that Julia suggested that I might do so, in any case. In the evenings, however, he sometimes walked to the house after he had dined—at Plumley's, or a village inn— and I would change into my blue dress and we would sit in the parlour, a little apart, usually, from the Camerons, and talk of our life in India.

We were to travel directly after the wedding celebrations to London, and thence by train to Paris, where we would stay for a few days to visit the Great Exhibition. On we would go to Marseilles, where we would pick up the steamer through the Mediterranean to Egypt; take a further train from Alexandria to Cairo, where we were to stay in the Shepheard's Hotel; and then go on from Cairo to Suez. From Suez the Peninsula & Orient steamer would take us to Aden and then to Calcutta, stopping en route—to the delight of the Camerons—at Pont de Galle in Ceylon.

As Henry and I made these plans, I wondered, quite frequently, whether this could truly be happening. We pored over maps and timetables, read brochures advertising hotels, speculated happily about dining by the Seine and walking through bazaars and seeing the Pyramids.

'We can shop in London and in Paris for anything you may need for the journey,' Henry assured me, 'and by then, of course, you will be my wife and it will be perfectly proper for me to buy you clothes and hats and so on. How does that sound?'

That sounded utterly delightful. I had my grey dress as a going-away costume, and several sets of pretty underwear purchased from my friendly dressmaker, but I was not confident that I would be looking elegant enough for my new life in any garments bought here. I thought of Miss Jackson and her cast-offs. *Rather dowdy, but I don't imagine that will matter in Freshwater ...* Well, I thought, I shall never wear anyone's cast-offs again, and I shall never, ever, be dowdy. Shopping in London and Paris for linen frocks and silk evening gowns and delicious hats and kid gloves and pretty shoes should ensure that.

I packed up the few possessions from my old life. I gave the blue silk dress to Louisa, who was about the same size as me.

'You sure you don't want it, Mary? It is the loveliest dress I ever seen.' She was already stroking it lovingly, her eyes round with desire.

'I would like you to have it, Lou,' I said. 'And I'll give my best shawl to Hillier and my Sunday bonnet to Kellaway.' I wished I had more to give my friends; but I would, I had already decided, send them all presents back from Paris which would astonish and delight them.

Once my clothes were disposed of, there was hardly anything else. When Louisa had gone downstairs, I drew out the wooden box from under my bed and opened the lid. Inside lay my life's treasures: the letter Henry had written me; a doll, its face cracked, one arm missing; a white pebble; a scrap of faded velvet; two nursery books, their covers rubbed and worn, their spines broken, their pages marked and crumpled; a red hair-ribbon, neatly coiled. And two little pieces of blue sea glass wrapped in tarnished wire. I picked out the glass drops and held them either side of my face. For a moment I thought of taking them with me. I stood and looked at myself in the little blotched mirror. I would have liked Billy Hemmings to have been at my wedding, I thought. I would like him to have seen me dressed in white silk and lace, with roses in my hair and sapphires and diamonds in my ears, riding in the Tennysons' carriage, entering the church on the arm of Mr Cameron, attended by Lionel in a velvet coat. I weighed the blue glass earrings in the palm of my hand for a moment; and then I dropped them back into the wooden box and closed its lid. Then I shoved the box back under the bed. There was nothing there I needed now.

# 33

A wedding is, naturally, an occasion for photographs. Julia announced that of course she would photograph me in my wedding gown on the morning of the day itself; but before that, she planned to take a special picture to mark this romantic idyll. We—Henry and I—were to be photographed on the very eve of our marriage, and the tableau was to be a surprise. We would be so delighted, so thrilled, at the perfection of her idea, that she intended to keep it a secret until the moment when we entered the studio. My heart sank, rather, for I feared another dressing-up session, but I supposed it would be the last I would ever have to do, so I resigned myself to going along with it with as good a grace as I could muster; while Henry was, as always, politely enthusiastic. Straight after breakfast she was off to the studio to prepare, and then she sent for Henry, who was to go in first, with instructions that I should follow in a quarter of an hour.

Henry was dressed in a velvet robe, and wearing a ridiculous cap with a feather in it. He gave me a boyish grin as I entered the fowl-house. He did look completely absurd, but of course still handsome.

'Here, Mary, into this white robe,' said Julia, who was clearly brimming with excitement. It was the usual white wool monstrosity. I pulled it over my head; it was like a tent, covering the dress I was already wearing. This was clearly not going to be the most flattering photograph ever taken of me. It would be the last time, though, surely, that I would ever be obliged to go through these charades. 'And loosen your hair—yes—just let it flow down your back—there! Now,'—this was her moment of triumph, she clearly thought—'Henry, you see—does he not look magnificent? He is to be King Cophetua!'

I froze. I looked at Julia in disbelief.

'*King Cophetua?*'

'Yes, yes, don't you see, Mary, it is perfect, it is your own story—oh! so romantic, my very own creation of an idyll—'

She really did not see it. She really did not see me, Mary Ryan, a person, with feelings and dreams and hopes and rages and passions. She saw only the blank page on which she, Julia, had written a fantasy.

I turned to Henry, standing there in his velvet cap, looking now a little sheepish.

'We are to pose as King Cophetua and—?'

I'm not going to say it. He can say it. Go on, Henry, say the word. *Say it.* But he didn't. He swallowed hard. I think the situation might have only just dawned on him.

For a moment I considered turning and walking away. Leaving; running. Getting away, away from Julia, from Henry, from Dimbola Lodge, from Freshwater, from the Isle of Wight, from England. Going to America, perhaps, like Billy, being free at last, free of my chains, my history, my place. And before I walked away, I thought, I would go up to the stupid camera and I would just push it over, hear the satisfying crash of the glass plates, watch Julia's face, and then I could say what I am really thinking.

*The Beggar Maid, Julia? That is how you see me? Still?*

And to Henry: *you didn't think, somehow, that this might be slightly awkward?*

But I didn't. Why not? Good manners? The survival instinct? Practice? I took a deep breath.

'Forgive me, Mrs Cameron,' I said, as lightly as I could, 'but you know how fond of Shakespeare I am. I had hoped you might photograph us as Romeo and Juliet.'

There was a moment when I thought she was going to insist, but Henry, who presumably had come to his senses at last, echoed my request, and it didn't take long to bring her round. In fact within minutes she was claiming the idea as her own. Luckily the costumes were perfectly interchangeable, Julia's ideas of romantic medieval dress being fairly vague. I stepped forward and allowed Henry to embrace me, although I couldn't relax. He held me in his arms, just a little too hard, squashing my face against his chest. I stayed there, rigid, while Julia huffed and flapped and ordered us to look up! look down! *look* at her, Henry! look *happy*, Mary!

Unsurprisingly, it was a dreadful picture. I loathed it and still do. All the gloomy rage and resentment I was feeling is in my face. And it makes me look as though I have the beginnings of a double chin.

As soon as it was done, she had yet another idea.

'Dear, dear Mr Browning! Last time I saw him he reproached me for never making a photograph for one of his poems, don't you remember, Mary? I must put this right for him. What shall we do? Which shall we choose?'

I was waiting for her to say *My Last Duchess*. Another victim, another helpless hapless woman. Not the most appropriate subject for a bride on the eve of her wedding, you might have thought, but if Julia could imagine that making me pose as King Cophetua's beggar maid was a good idea then I didn't imagine casting me as a wife whose indiscriminate smiles led to her murder by her husband would give her a moment's pause.

'*Sordello*,' I said quickly.

She looked slightly put out that I had made yet another suggestion of my own.

'Not *My Last Duchess*?'

'No,' I said. '*Sordello*. The moment when Palma gives him the scarf.' I reminded her of the story: it's long and complicated, but I was thinking of the part when a poet wins the prize of a scarf from his true love for his skill in versifying.

Perhaps Julia saw something in my face that she hadn't seen before, because this time she agreed; but of course she immediately started ordering us about once more.

'Now, Henry, stay in the dark velvet, I think, and the jewelled cap—then if you stand here—and you, Mary, the white gown, of course, is perfect, but perhaps we can fix a clasp in your hair—and here's a length of silk for the scarf—now kneel at his feet—'

'I can't very well bestow a scarf on him if I am kneeling at his feet,' I said.

'True,' said Julia, a little reluctantly, but conceding the point. 'Then sit, here, on the chair, and Henry, stand before her—'

I sat on the chair. Henry smiled down at me. Julia started bustling about with the camera, moving the lens to and fro, shouting instructions. I looked up at Henry.

'Kneel at my feet, Henry,' I said. 'Palma is a lady. You should kneel before her.'

Henry sank gracefully to the floor. I took the scarf and put it round his neck, pulling him towards me.

'Take the hat off,' I said. He did.

'Lower your head.' He lowered his head. I pulled him a little closer and I heard him catch his breath.

'And close your eyes.' He closed his eyes.

Julia had, for once, fallen silent. She had emerged from the black cloth and was looking at us. Over the top of Henry's bright tangle of curls, I met her gaze. We stared at each other for a long moment, while Henry stayed obediently still, his head bent, his eyes closed. His chest was pressed against my knee, and I could feel his heart thumping. Something passed between Julia and me, then; recognition, perhaps.

I smiled, and bent my head downwards towards Henry's, holding the scarf in my hands, letting it rest lightly on his shoulders. We stayed quite still while Julia fussed and fiddled and finally took the photograph.

It's still my favourite picture, that one, for all sorts of reasons. It shows Henry's handsome looks, his bright curls, his glow, his gentleness. I am half-smiling, so for once I don't look tragic or droopy. I'm not swooning or dying; I'm not abasing myself; I don't look like a victim, or a servant, or a beggar. I just look like me. But most of all, I like that photograph for what it doesn't show: Julia Margaret Cameron, looking through her camera, and seeing me, Mary Ryan, for what was perhaps the very first time.

# Epilogue

Mary Ryan and Henry John Stedman Cotton were married at the parish church in Freshwater, Isle of Wight, on the 1st August 1867. She was 18; he was 21. The bride was given away by Charles Cameron; Lionel Tennyson was her page; Alfred and Emily Tennyson lent their carriage to the happy couple; and the witnesses were Charles and Julia Margaret Cameron.

The couple lived in India for seven years, and had three sons and one daughter. When her children reached school age, Mary—evidently resisting the usual practice of sending children to English boarding schools while their parents remained in India—came back to London and lived with them in what Henry described in his memoirs of 1911 as *'a charming and quiet pied-à-terre in St John's Wood, which was always my children's home, and where we still live.'* The Cottons seem to have enjoyed a sociable life there, mixing with the group of artists known as the St John's Wood Clique which included Val Prinsep. One distinguished member, Philip Calderon RA, painted Mary and her children in 1879 when she would have been 30. In the picture she is wearing an extremely glamorous dress and hat, and child-bearing does not appear to have affected her graceful figure. She looks the epitome of beauty and elegance.

Henry Cotton had a long and distinguished career. He supported Indian Home Rule, served as President of the Indian National Congress (one of the few non-Indians to do so), and vigorously opposed Curzon's invasion of Tibet and the partition of Bengal. He also served as a Liberal Party Member of Parliament for Nottingham East, and remained a writer and activist on behalf of Indian rights until the end of his life. He was appointed a Knight Commander of the Order of the Star of India in 1902, and Mary thus became Lady Cotton.

Henry Cotton described Mary in his memoirs as '*my devoted companion and helpmate for better and for worse through many years of vicissitudes and successes, sorrows and aspirations, clouds and sunshine. A halo of tender affection hangs in my memory over Dimbola Lodge in Freshwater Bay and the quiet village church where we were married, over Little Holland House, and every link and association of all the hours of happiness which must always be inseparable in my mind from the names of Cameron and Prinsep.*'

Mary died in 1914 and Henry a year later.

Julia Margaret Cameron always claimed the credit for their marriage. In her account of her photographic career, *The Annals of My Glass House*, she wrote: '*...entirely out of the Prospero and Miranda picture sprung a marriage which has, I hope, cemented the welfare and well-being of a real King Cophetua who, in the Miranda, saw the prize which has proved a jewel in that monarch's crown. The sight of the picture caused the resolve to be uttered which, after 18 months of constancy, was matured by personal knowledge, then fulfilled, producing one of the prettiest idylls of real life that can be conceived, and, what is of far more importance, a marriage of bliss with children worthy of being photographed, as their mother had been, for their beauty; but it* *must also be observed that the father was eminently handsome, with a head of the Greek type and fair ruddy Saxon complexion.'*

Mary Hillier married Thomas Gilbert, and lived in Freshwater until she died aged 88. She is buried in the churchyard at Freshwater, close to the Tennyson family grave (although the Great Poet himself, of course, lies in Westminster Abbey).

Billy—William Hemmings—never got to America. He went back to London, where he married Isabel Newson in 1873 (six years after Mary's marriage to Henry Cotton), and had three daughters and at least one son.

Alfred Tennyson was created Baron Tennyson in 1884. His house in Freshwater, Farringford, has been splendidly restored to its Tennysonian state and is now open to the public.

Julia Margaret Cameron's niece, Julia Jackson, married Herbert Duckworth, a solicitor, in 1867, and had three children. After his untimely death she remarried. Her second marriage, to Leslie Stephen, resulted in four children, Vanessa (Bell), Thoby, Virginia (Woolf), and Adrian. Virginia Woolf wrote a short comic play, *Freshwater*, about her great-aunt's household at Dimbola Lodge.

The Camerons eventually left Freshwater and returned to Ceylon, taking their coffins with them, and both are buried there. Julia's last word was 'Beautiful'.

Julia Margaret Cameron is now acknowledged as an important pioneer of photography, and her pictures are in collections in museums in England, Ireland, and America, including the V&A and the Getty Museum.

Dimbola Lodge in Freshwater is now a museum and gallery. It still retains the glorious spirit of Julia Margaret Cameron and her circle of famous men and fair women, and—I like to think—also of the little Irish girl whose vivacity and charm still shine from so many of those magnificent photographs.